BEFORE NOW

HOPE E. DAVIS

ISBN: 9781701656666

*For my sisters,
Alike, but unique*

ACKNOWLEDGMENTS

Cover by Victoria Cooper

Edited by Jaclyn Seelagy and Kaye Hardy

I N THE TWENTY-FIRST century, twins are a common sight in society. This wasn't always the case. All over the world, throughout history, twins have been received with mixed emotions. The Igbo society in Nigeria, Africa, thought twins to be a bad omen sent from the gods. In contrast, the Yoruba tribe praised them as a gift. Because of the opposing views of society and religion, twins were often killed, or left to die by their parents.

There are many sorts of twins. The most common, especially in Western society, due to modern fertility treatments, is the fraternal twin. This occurs when two different eggs are fertilized in the womb by two separate sperm at the same time. Both twins then have their own amniotic sac and placenta during the course of their development. Fraternal twins can be two boys, two girls, or one of each sex. Regardless of the sex, these children may look alike, or look completely different and have their own set of genes.

Perhaps more commonly known is the identical twin, which occurs when a woman releases a single egg, which is then fertilized by a single sperm, and splits into two embryos in the week following conception. These twins are almost always either both males or both females, and if for some reason there is one of each, there is usually a chromosomal defect present. The twins can either each have their own amniotic sac and placenta or share them, depending on how early the egg splits. Identical twins make up only about thirty percent of all twins worldwide. Contrary to common belief, a tendency toward identical twins is not genetic, and does not run in families. To this day, doctors aren't sure why a fertilized egg decides to split.

Sometimes, when a fertilized egg splits, the split is incomplete, too late, or the two parts of the split egg develop too close together. When this occurs, conjoined twins are formed. Conjoined twins have many different classifications, but the main definition is two twins who develop in the same placenta and, as a result, share one or more major body parts. This is very dangerous, and often, depending on the body part shared and the difficulty needed to separate them, conjoined twins die shortly after birth or during infancy. Those that survive face a whole different set of challenges as they grow.

One type of identical twin is perhaps the most interesting and rare of all. When a woman's egg splits after the seven-day range considered "normal" for identical twins to form, but not so late that conjoined twins form, the result is something incredibly unique. Late splitting twins often form asymmetric identical features. These can range from something as small as a mole appearing on the opposite side of each twin's face, to something as large as one twin being left-handed and the other right-handed. In extreme cases, some sets of these twins are reported to have organs on the opposite sides of the body. When this occurs, these twins are known as mirror image twins.

PART
ONE

NOW

R EMI CRACKS OPEN her left eye, sleep still muddling her brain. She was dreaming of her glory days on the swim team, until the dream became a nightmare and she was pulled from the water and strapped to a back board, unable to move. Dreaming is not abnormal for Remi, but this was definitely one of the weirder ones.

Rolling over, she notices her bed does not feel nearly as soft as it usually does. In fact, she realizes, she's lying on the ground. As her sense of smell awakens, her nostrils fill with the scent of dirt.

Just where the hell did I pass out last night? Remi wonders. This isn't like her at all.

She opens her other eye, and the room comes into focus. It's dark, and she can't see the outline of the door. That's not right, she almost always leaves her apartment hall light on at night in case she needs to go to the bathroom. Although sometimes Daisy, Remi's roommate, shuts it off.

Remi begins to feel around with her hands, only to realize she's not on her bedroom floor. Her bedroom floor is hardwood, she's definitely lying on some sort of cold concrete.

The night before starts to flood back to Remi. She went to a party with her twin sister, and they had a few drinks. She ended up sharing an Uber home to her sister's place. She's been to her house a few times, but doesn't think she's ever been in this room before. Is this the basement?

"Rayna?" She tries to call out loudly, but it comes out the volume of normal speaking voice. She clears her throat and tries again. "Rayna?" Once again, it doesn't come out as loud as she wants, but she doesn't think she could speak any louder without some water.

The room is pitch black, and her eyes won't, or can't, adjust. Remi begins crawling around on her hands and knees.

The room is empty. There's no furniture, no clothes, nothing. She finds the outline of the door on one of the walls. The door itself feels off. And there's no knob on this side. She touches her hands lightly to the walls nearby. The entire room, including the door, feel like cement.

Just where in the hell am I? she wonders.

And where is Rayna?

Remi sits back on her heels and takes a deep breath. She runs a hand down the front of her body to feel what clothing she is wearing. It's the same hoodie over a tank top and a pair of jeans that she left the house in the night before. The outfit she remembers wearing to the party. At least that's one good thing. Her shoes are gone, and she vaguely remembers that she was, at one point, wearing sandals.

How much did she have to drink last night? Remi can't remember. She doesn't have a hangover, and no headache, so it couldn't have been that much. Could it?

She moves to sit with her back against the wall, and pulls her knees up to her chest. *Think, Remi, think!* She wracks her brain for details of the night before. Nothing solidifies, beyond planning to go to the party, then ending up in an Uber with Rayna.

So just how did she end up here?

"Hello?" she calls out. "Anyone out there? I think something happened…" Her voice again is not near loud enough and simply echos off the concrete walls.

What she really needs is some *water*. She crawls around the room once again, looking for something, anything, to quench her thirst.

There's nothing.

Remi lies down in the corner, curling her knees to her chest. She can feel the tears starting to gather and quickly looks up to force them back. Crying will not help the dehydration situation, and she knows it. She pinches her eyes shut and takes deep breaths to calm herself. *I can figure this out*, she tells herself. *After all, I've always been the smart twin.*

BEFORE

S HE SQUINTS AT the numbers on the paper in front of her, willing them to make sense. Math has always been her strong point, but every now and then these debt sheets get the best of her. She reaches for her calculator and zeroes it out, time to start from the beginning.

"Heeeeeeyyyy."

Remi sees her sister Rayna peering around the doorframe and spins her plush swivel chair to face her fully.

"What do you want?"

Her sister steps fully into view. Besides the clothes, it's like looking in a mirror. They're identical twins, and were one hundred percent identical as toddlers. People kept saying as they grew, they would develop differences. But for whatever reason it never happened.

Both women now have thin but athletic frames, dark hair, and dark features. Their skin is the same color, and neither of them visits tanning beds. They're both health conscious, and always slather on the sunscreen when they go outside. They even wear the exact same clothing and shoe sizes. Both are cursed with thick, unruly curly hair, which most of the time does its own thing regardless of how each of them tries to style it differently. To make it even more difficult to identify them, both girls grew out their bangs sometime in middle school, and liked it so much they both maintained the trendy style over the years.

"What do you say to going to a party with me?" Rayna wiggles her perfectly plucked eyebrows. Remi rolls her eyes. She should've known this would be a party invite by her twin's purple mini skirt and white tube top.

"I can't," Remi says, motioning to the pile of papers on the mahogany desk in front of her. "I've got work to do."

Rayna inspects her glittery manicured nails, pretty much the only way to tell them apart. Rayna's are always done in bright colors and sparkles, and Remi's are only painted with a home-done French tip, if they're done at all.

Rayna rolls her eyes. "Aren't you supposed to do work, at you know, work." She emphasizes the last word.

"You know, sometimes my work comes home with me. Especially during tax season."

Remi is a CPA for a large firm downtown. And while her hours are mostly nine to five, for the first four months of the year she almost always brings work home with her. She doesn't usually mind, though. Her compensation is generous and the overtime even more so.

"Ugh, always such a goody two shoes," Rayna says as she turns to leave the room. Now it's Remi's turn to roll her eyes.

As kids, Rayna and Remi were joined at the hip. Born only six minutes apart, their parents liked to joke they didn't know who came first because they always did everything together. But that was a lie, Rayna was the firstborn.

As they grew up, although their looks stayed the same, their personalities diverged completely. Remi loved books, numbers, and tennis, while her sister enjoyed the swim team, soccer, and, to their parents' dismay, boys. Now that they're in their mid-twenties, Remi has caught up in the boys department, and they both have boyfriends. But they're still as different as night and day.

Remi attended college for finance, finding a well-paying job right off the bat as a CPA. Her sister, on the other hand, is still trying to find her way in life. College wasn't for her, even though she initially attended on a swimming scholarship. Her current passion of the week is fashion design, but that somehow translates into a job serving at a local restaurant, a job which she only works the bare minimum needed to pay the bills.

The girls live in an apartment together, but Remi has a feeling Rayna will soon be moving out. Her relationship with her boyfriend Zeki is quickly becoming serious. They've been together for almost two years, and Remi senses a proposal on the horizon. Rayna jokes that she "isn't that into him," but two years is longer than Rayna has spent with anyone else, so Remi figures she must have some sort of feelings for him.

Personally, Remi isn't a huge fan of Zeki. Sure, he's nice, tall, attractive, and, well, rich, but she's always sensed something off about him. Rayna complains that she's just being a nit, that everyone can't be as perfect as her, but Remi feels that her intuitions are not misplaced when it comes to Zeki.

She sets down her pen after coming up with an answer that doesn't make sense for a third time. Some money is missing, and Remi can't figure out why.

Leaning over, she opens one of her expanding file folders to pull out another bundle of papers. The answer has to be there somewhere.

"So, you coming?"

Rayna is back, leaning against her doorframe. She has since applied a generous amount of makeup and slid large hoop earrings into her ears. She looks great.

"I already told you, I can't. Just go with Zeki," Remi suggests, putting her nose back into her ever-growing pile of work.

"He's no fun at parties," Rayna whines.

"And I am?" She doesn't look up from the page she's reviewing.

"You're hilarious when you're drunk."

Remi groans. "That was one time, I've only gotten drunk with you one time!" She's never been a drinker but she's known to occasionally indulge in a drink or two. Or five, at their mutual friend's recent birthday celebration.

Rayna laughs. "It was a fun one time." Remi can practically hear her smirk as she once again turns and heads back to her room.

The girls currently share a two-bedroom apartment in the heart of downtown. Remi can afford the place herself—she could afford a house by herself—but Rayna can't with her current income. And they both like the amenities of being centrally located.

Neither of them owns a car, finding driving to be just too difficult in a busy city. Both girls choose to ride the metro to and from work, and Uber when necessary.

She hears Rayna's keys and jewelry jingle as she walks back by the doorway on her way out.

"Last chance!" she calls out over her shoulder.

"Bye!" Remi shouts back. Rayna huffs, and the front door slams shortly after.

Remi smiles and turns her attention back to the numbers in front of her.

Her Apple laptop lies on the corner of her desk. She has it opened to

Excel, which has found the same errors she has. Although most financial things are done electronically these days, sometimes the only way to find the origin of errors is to go back through and verify there isn't a data entry error. And in this case, there isn't. She'd been on these same accounts for months now. And no matter what she does, the numbers just don't work the way they should.

Her phone buzzes from the corner of the desk, the screen lighting up with a text. It's her boyfriend, John.

"Dinner?" the text asks.

She texts back a quick "of course" and turns back to her work.

John and Remi met in college and quickly became friends. Their relationship morphed into romance shortly after they graduated. They've been dating for just over a year now, and Remi can tell he's interested in living together, but they both have leases they can't break for awhile. Remi has nine months left on hers, he has seven left on his. John works as a beer sales representative, which is great for him because he makes a decent wage while getting to try all sorts of new beers. Doesn't matter to Remi much, because she doesn't like beer.

She's halfway through the audit of the receipts when there's a knock at the door. Remi figures it must be John with the food. She quickly closes her work and slides it into her work messenger bag. Although most people can't understand the numbers covering the pages, she's still under a strict confidentiality agreement.

Remi opens the door and embraces John in a giant bear hug that almost makes him fall backwards.

"Woah, I see someone missed me."

"More like you're bringing me food," she jokes, grabbing the bags of take out from his hands while placing a small peck on his lips.

Remi quickly goes to the kitchen to get plates to eat off of while John switches on the TV. A year in and they have this routine down.

They're both busy professionals and often find it hard to make time for each other on weeknights, and it has been especially difficult with her work lately. Dinner while chilling on the couch is easier than dressing up for a date.

Remi walks back into the living room, curious to see what movie he's selected. John stands in the middle of the living room, scrolling through the channels. She smiles at the sight of her best-friend-turned-boyfriend.

John is taller than Remi. Not by much, but she is also fairly tall for a woman. He's slender, with dark hair and light skin. And Remi is pretty sure that, besides their parents, he's the only one on this earth who can tell the twins apart. When she asked him about it back during their college years, he simply smiled and said, "you two talk differently," and left it at that.

After a few more minutes of scrolling, he selects a channel playing a movie. Remi isn't big on TV, so she doesn't care much what he picks, as they usually just end up talking through it anyway.

"So how was your day?" he asks as he takes a bite of a chicken wing.

Remi shrugs. "Not too bad, I suppose." She wants to tell him about the errors she keeps encountering in the accounts, but decides it's probably against her confidentiality contract. "How was yours?"

"I landed a new weekly order, which is nice. Always an accomplishment." He sets down the chicken wing to take a bite of the salad. "Where's the usual vermin? I brought enough for her, too."

"She's my sister you know." Remi scolds him at the use of the word 'vermin' but the smile never leaves her face. John and Rayna have never gotten along. And she has never been able to pinpoint why.

"I know, that's why I brought her food." He motions to the box on the coffee table overflowing with wings.

They both chuckle. John turns to the TV for a moment to get caught up on what's playing. She opens her mouth, intending to ask John about his weekend plans, when suddenly, her phone rings from the kitchen counter.

John's eyes meet Remi's.

"No one ever calls you."

"I know, strange," she replies as she gets up and walks over to the phone. The screen reads "private number," so she decides not to answer, sending it to voicemail instead. If it's truly important, the person will leave a message or call back later. Remi doesn't really have many friends, and Rayna and her parents never use a private number, so it likely isn't important.

Remi returns to the couch, leaning back into John with her food in her lap. Buffalo wings are one of her favorites. The two lovebirds begin talking about his day at work. Most days are fairly uneventful, but some days, like today, he has interesting stories to tell about things he observes while visiting restaurants.

Listening quietly, Remi enjoys her food, glancing every now and then at the clock. She needs to head to bed soon if she's going to wake up early tomorrow and be well rested for work.

Remi hates cutting their chat time short, but she needs her beauty sleep. After finishing her dinner, she stands up, taking her empty plate and John's to the sink. She sets them in gently, planning to clean them in the morning. John yawns loudly from his spot on the couch.

"You staying tonight?"

"Of course," he responds with a smile, heading to Remi's bedroom.

She follows shortly after, the phone call completely forgotten.

NOW

S HE MUST HAVE dozed off again, because before she knows it, she jolts awake, panting. She had the strangest dream about being locked in a…

Remi glances around at the darkness surrounding her, brushing a hand over the cement floor. There are cracks every so often, but they're small, as if the floor has been re-cemented recently.

It wasn't a dream.

Now she's starting to panic. Seriously, what is this place? And if she's here alone, where is Rayna? Last she remembers they were together.

Breath in. Breath out. Deep breaths. Freaking out isn't going to help the situation any, she lectures herself.

Once her breathing returns to normal, or as normal as it can be considering the circumstances, Remi stands up and begins to feel her way across the room once more. As she heads in the direction where she thinks the door might be, her foot collides with something. It makes an odd sound as it falls.

Kneeling down, she runs her hand over the floor until it connects with something cool and cylindrical.

Water! Remi immediately picks up the plastic bottle and begins drinking. The water tastes funny, but her throat is so dry she doesn't care. Halfway through the bottle, she realizes she should probably save some, who knows when she'll get water again.

There's condensation on the outside of the bottle. And Remi realizes this means it was obviously placed there recently, but by whom?

"Hello?" she calls out again, her voice stronger this time. "If this is a joke this isn't funny!" She carries the bottle with her as she shuffles towards the door. It's still closed tight. She tries pushing on it just like before. It doesn't give. Remi feels around the edges again, only to realize there's no hinge. Maybe it isn't a door after all.

Her eyelids start to feel heavy, which is odd because all she's done is sleep all day. If it is even still daytime. There must be drugs in the water.

"How dare you drug me!" she slurs out in what might be a yell, but comes out garbled. "Good luck getting in with me sitting here," Remi threatens, sounding drunk and sliding down to sit leaning against what she's been calling the door.

She's asleep the moment she hits the ground.

NOW

THE LIGHT FILTERS through the navy blue curtains and the woman groans as it brings her back to the world of the living. She groans again and rolls over. Her head is pounding. This hangover is going to be a bitch.

She reaches her hand out to her boyfriend Zeki's side of the bed, only to find it cold and empty. Her eyes immediately snap open in panic before she remembers he's on a business trip and won't be back for a few days.

Rayna looks down and realizes she's still wearing her clothes from the night before. Even her shoes. She sits up to slip off her sandals, scrunching her eyes when she realizes they're not her sandals. *Why am I wearing Remi's sandals?* she wonders. *Ugh, no matter, we must've switched them when we were coming home last night.*

While she's sitting up, Rayna decides to also slip off her cutoff jeans before burrowing back under the covers. Now she's much more comfortable.

She closes her eyes, intending to go back to sleep, but her mind starts to go wild as it always does when she lies down. That's one thing Remi and Rayna have in common besides their looks: both are plagued with active minds that never sleep. Most nights they're plagued with nightmares and strange dreams.

Honestly, that's probably one of the few things that have kept the two girls together over the years, even as their paths have diverged. In college, they chose to live together to keep costs down, and oftentimes they would both be up in the night and unable to fall back asleep. When that would happen, they would both end up on the couch, either reading or watching late night sitcoms—depending on who got there first.

Rayna smiles. Sometimes she misses the days when she and Remi lived together. They had different lifestyles, which of course led to bickering, but they were sisters and best friends through and through. In fact, Rayna is secretly happy Remi came home with her last night. Remi rarely takes her up on the invitation to use one of her guest rooms.

Zeki and Rayna recently purchased a three bedroom, two and a half bathroom house just outside the downtown area. It wasn't her first choice location, but most of the money was Zeki's, and Rayna didn't really have a say. Not that she cared to argue about it anyways. Zeki is her dream man, according to her list, and she has convinced herself she would do anything for him. A house is a house to her, it's just tough because she doesn't have a car.

When they first moved here about a year ago, Rayna continued to Uber to her job waiting tables until she got fed up with the surge pricing and difficulty getting a ride during rush hour. She brought up the issue to Zeki, who was quick to convince his girlfriend to quit her job and try to find another that didn't have commuting during rush hour.

It's a weird feeling not having a job, and Rayna isn't exactly sure it was the right decision. After all, she's now fully reliant on Zeki to pay all the bills. It's easy for him, though, as his bank job easily makes four times what Rayna did.

Despite how low Remi thinks her to be, Rayna really does miss working. Granted, she doesn't enjoy the type of work her twin does, but she likes to keep busy. Not working for the past three months is secretly killing her.

That's another thing: not seeing people every day is tough, especially with the frequent business trips Zeki takes. Rayna really misses being in the city. The suburbs are lonely.

At first she tried to make friends with the neighbors, but none them want to be friends with a twenty five year old. They're all older, or in their thirties with kids, and definitely don't give off a vibe of the type of people Rayna would like to hang out with. Then after what happened two months ago, no one dares to talk to her. Rayna pinches the bridge of her nose at the embarrassing memory.

They would love Remi, though.

She pushes the thought away angrily. Sometimes she can't believe Remi is her sister, much less her twin. They're completely opposite personalities.

Except last night. Rayna giggles. She got her sister successfully drunk for the second time in her life. And man, it was a laugh.

At first, Zeki tried his best to help Rayna fit in, suggesting yoga classes and local groups some of the neighbors belong to. Zeki is a smooth talker and somehow seems to know everything going on in the neighborhood. Even as some of his plans to have her attend local events like barbecues failed, he would still send or leave her random messages telling her how beautiful she was. Then she messed it all up.

She feels herself drifting off into dreamland, reminiscing about the last night Zeki took her out to a nice sushi spot. She's almost asleep when she hears something that sounds like someone pounding on the front door.

Rayna puts her pillow over her head, willing the person to go away and the pounding in her brain to stop. But it continues.

"Grr," she growls as she gets out of bed and stomps across the room. She grabs her purple silk robe from where it hangs on the back of the door and slides it over her shoulders, knotting it at the waist. "This better be good," she huffs to herself.

She stomps down the hallway, trying to be quiet as she passes the closed guest bedroom door. Remi is sure to have just as bad of a hangover, if not worse.

She walks through her mess of a living room, thinking about how she needs to tidy it up, and soon.

She arrives at the front door and tears it open, coming face to face with Remi's boyfriend, John. "What do you want," Rayna growls. She and John are not friends. Especially not after what happened last night.

"I just want to talk to her. Please." His eyes look a little sad. She almost believes him for a moment. Almost.

"Not gonna happen," she responds as she slams the door in his face.

"Fine, then I'm gonna sit out here all day!" he yells through the door.

"It's a free country!" Rayna shouts back before she turns on her heel and heads for the bedroom. When she reaches the bottom of the stairs, she realizes she's close to the kitchen. And therefore, close to the Tylenol.

She heads into her wreck of a kitchen and digs through the medicine cabinet with one hand, the other one pressing on her temples. Zeki has offered to hire a maid service to clean, but Rayna feels if she didn't have any cleaning to do, she would feel even more useless than she already does. After digging through the cabinet for what feels like forever, finally her hand finds the Tylenol.

She picks up the bottle, noticing the pills expired last month, but shrugs and dry-swallows four. Expired Tylenol can't be that bad, could it?

Heading back for the stairs, she makes a pit stop at the fridge, grabbing a large bottle of V8 and swallowing a couple gulps. Dry swallowing the pills while on a hangover was not a good idea.

Rayna feels her way back up the stairs, keeping her eyes closed. She figures she'll feel better after some sleep.

Without another thought, she throws herself on the bed, falling asleep, her robe still knotted tightly at her waist.

RAYNA
BEFORE

Rayna sits on the floor, slowly packing her shoes and trinkets into the cardboard box in front of her. She's never been good at packing. In fact, she's pretty sure shoes and trinkets aren't supposed to go in the same box together, but she's too tired to go ask Remi how to pack.

Today's the day that Rayna moves out of the apartment she and her sister have shared since college. It's extremely bittersweet, but Rayna knows that it's time.

It will be different living with Zeki. And she'll no longer have someone to sit up with in the middle of the night when her nightmares get bad. But Zeki didn't give her a choice.

A few weeks ago, on Saturday night, Rayna was sitting in her room reading the latest Vogue when she heard a commotion in the living room. When she went out to investigate, she was not prepared for what she saw.

A drunk Zeki was trying to embrace Remi, his hands under her shirt. Remi tried to push him away. "Zeki get off of me!" she said harshly.

Zeki drunkenly mumbled something that resembled, "oh, baby, don't be like that." But Rayna didn't give him a chance to finish.

"What the hell is going on here?!" she yelled angrily, her voice much louder than that of her younger sister.

Remi finally managed to escape Zeki's grasp and moved across the room. "I was leaving to go meet John for dinner and I opened the door to find him passed out on our step. I tried to help him in and he thought I was you and started making a pass at me!" The anger and hurt was evident in the tone of her voice.

Rayne raised her eyebrow at Zeki, who was obviously too drunk to defend himself. He stumbled, unable to stand on his own now that Remi had moved across the room. Rayna rolled her eyes and helped him hobble to her bedroom, flashing her sister an "I'm sorry" look over his shoulder. Remi nodded in understanding.

Zeki remained too drunk to discuss anything for the rest of the evening. And Rayna wasted her Saturday night waiting for him to sober up. Taking care of a drunk person while completely sober is the worst.

The next morning, Zeki apologized to Rayna, but he also told her angrily that if she didn't still live with her twin this wouldn't be a problem. And as much as she hated to admit it, he was sort of right. After all, practically no one can tell them apart.

Their relationship has been great ever since. They're headed back to where they were before, but the honeymoon stage is definitely dissipating. Rayna felt the only way to fix it was to cave to his demands and move in with him, to which he quickly agreed.

"You almost done?" Her sister's brokenhearted voice interrupts her thoughts.

"No," Rayna sniffles, blinking back tears. She usually isn't this emotional, but she can't help it.

Remi senses her distress and comes to sit on the floor, embracing her. "It's not like you're moving states away. I can still come visit on weekends. And you know you're welcome here, anytime."

Rayna nods. "I know." It isn't just that she's going to miss her twin, she also worries about how Remi will afford this place on her own.

As always, Remi knows exactly what she's thinking. "I put an ad on Craiglist. I'll find a roommate quick, I'm sure. This is a great location."

She's right. "I want to vet anyone you even think about allowing to live here. I don't want you meeting people on your own either."

Remi holds up her hand. "Scout's honor. I'll have either you or John meet every person with me and I'll make sure it's in a public place."

"You're not even a boy scout," Rayna says sarcastically, her sorrow replaced by her usual sassy attitude.

"Maybe I signed up." Remi wiggles her eyebrows with just as much attitude.

Rayna looks at her sister, pushing her shoulder playfully. "When? You barely have time for your twin, much less a scout troop. Do they even allow girls anyways?"

Remi nods. "They do now, but honestly, probably not twenty five year olds." Both girls collapse in a fit of laughter.

"When does the moving truck come?" Remi's back to her somber mood in a blink.

Rayna glances at the clock on her phone. "Thirty minutes." She surveys the room and the mess which still occupies every surface. She should have started packing earlier, but she's a procrastinator. And she always pays the price.

Remi looks at the box of random items sitting in front of her twin and raises her eyebrow. "Want help?"

"I thought you'd never ask."

Remi smiles, then quickly crosses the room and begins slipping her sister's outdated CD collection into a box. "Why do you even still keep these? Everything is digital these days."

She shrugs. "I guess I keep hoping they'll come back into style like record players did."

"I don't think record players ever truly came back into style."

And just like that, they're bickering as they almost always do.

With Remi's help, they pack a large portion of the items very quickly. Rayna has to admit, although her nitty sister often drives her nuts, she does everything well that she puts her mind to, and with uncanny speed. Remi even manages to strip the bed and stand up the mattress before the movers arrive.

The movers are two young gentlemen, one of whom is very attractive. Rayna can't help but think that if she were single—she quickly smacks that thought out of her head. She's moving in with her boyfriend today.

The men load everything quickly, and honestly there isn't much. Rayna is only taking the furniture and items in her bedroom and bathroom, leaving all the kitchen and living room furniture for Remi. Zeki's place is already furnished, and she couldn't stand to deprive her sister of any of her kitchen wares.

The moving truck pulls out, heading across town to Zeki's place, where he'll be waiting to meet and unload. He's probably the most excited about this out of anyone.

Rayna turns back to the apartment to head inside and say goodbye one last time, only to find her twin standing silently behind her. They embrace without a word. Remi has tears running down her face. The girls don't need words, everything has already been said. They continue their hug for another moment, then Rayna pulls away to call an Uber.

Both girls sit silently on the curb, waiting for the Uber to arrive.

When it does, they don't say anything more.

Rayna steps into the car, watching out the window as Remi's form on the curb fades into the distance. She knows this isn't the end, but something tells her this won't be the fresh start she wants, either.

NOW

S HE DOESN'T KNOW anymore if she's awake or asleep. The room is too dark to tell. She isn't sure what day it is, or how long she's been in here.

Remi has yet to see or hear anyone enter or leave the room. At some point she acquired another water bottle, probably filled with the same spiked water. She knows she'll have to drink it at some point, but she's trying to hold off, to keep her bearings. It's tough, and she's starting to get really thirsty. Her stomach rumbles, reminding her it's also been awhile since she ate.

She stands up and reaches above her, trying to feel for a ceiling. She isn't short, but even with her arms outstretched she can't feel the ceiling—so this probably isn't her sister's cellar like she originally thought.

Trying to keep her thoughts off her hunger and thirst, Remi walks around the outside of the room, placing her feet heel to toe as measurement. The room is twenty-four of her feet on the long sides, fourteen on the short sides. She's basically in a large rectangular closet. She crawls along the floor, noticing the occasional small cracks she noticed before, across the room and back. She looks for anything, a nail, slivers of glass, something she can use to defend herself when whoever put her here comes back. She finds nothing.

She sits back down by the door, wondering what to do. She's already run out of ideas. There seems to be no way out, although she knows one must exist for the water bottles to be placed inside.

Speaking of which... She opens the half filled bottle from earlier and takes a long drink. She knows it will put her back to sleep, but she's resisted as long as she could. The water, although it tastes funny, helps ease the tension gathering in her muscles. Definitely a roofie or sleeping pills.

Although she can't gauge time, she knows some has passed, and she hopes someone's noticed she's missing by now. Her initial thought is John, but then she winces as she remembers the horrid fight they had the night before. He probably doesn't care where she is now. The thought makes Remi sad, but she pushes it away. She can worry about him later.

She thinks about her sister, whom she was with the night before. Rayna has to know she's missing, right? Remi pictures her carefree other half and shakes her head. Rayna wouldn't notice if her own hand went missing.

Well. Guess that leaves Daisy, her roommate, who will notice when the rent and power bill don't get paid. Which is at least a month away...meaning Remi is screwed.

She lies down on her back on the hard cement, waiting for sleep to overtake her. Before she drifts off into oblivion, a thought peeks around the corner of her mind. But before she can grasp the idea, it's gone as quickly as it arrived.

BEFORE

"Yes, meet me on the Starbucks off of Corporate and 5TH." Remi scribbles notes as the woman on the other end confirms the meeting. "Alright, see you then." She hangs up the phone, setting it on the desk next to her notepad. She sighs and leans her forehead on her hands.

This will be the fifth person she's interviewed as a potential roommate. The other four have been absolute duds. The first one didn't have a consistent job, the second had a kid, the third didn't even show up for the interview. And the fourth, well, she looked like a slob with no idea what personal hygiene meant, and Remi eliminated her based on personal preference.

Maybe she's being too picky. Anyone she finds won't be as close to her as Rayna was.

Remi picks her phone back up and opens the text conversation. Four messages sit there, unanswered by her twin. It isn't like Rayna not to answer texts.

She glances at the clock on her phone, wondering if she has time to go visit Rayna's new place tonight. With a sigh, she realizes it's already almost nine and she has at least another hour of work to finish before bed.

It's Thursday, at least she can head to Rayna's after work tomorrow and check on her then.

Remi debates texting Zeki to make sure nothing happened to her sister, but she hasn't spoken to him since the day he mistook her for Rayna and tried to grope her. Things have been awkward ever since.

Who is she kidding, Remi has never gotten along with Zeki. He's always given her a major "sleeze" vibe. He seems like the kind of guy who only does things because they're easy or benefit him, never just to do something nice.

Her stomach rumbles, reminding Remi she missed dinner in her rush to find a roommate. She could afford the place on her own, but having a rommate is more cost effective. And Remi likes to save for a rainy day.

At least this Daisy seems like a good bet. They've spoken on the phone for about half an hour, and seem to have similar likes and dislikes. Like Remi, she's a self confessed workaholic. She admits to spending more hours at work than anywhere else. Daisy also claims she's clean, in her early thirties, and has no children. She seems perfect, and Remi hopes they'll get along just as well in person tomorrow.

She sends a quick text to John, letting him know to meet her at the Starbucks tomorrow to help vet the new possible roommate. Remi originally wanted her sister there, but the first text Rayna didn't answer had to do with the new roommate. And she hasn't answered any since.

Screw it! Remi thinks, putting her pen down and grabbing her phone and keys. It's Thursday, Rayna is probably still at work at the restaurant. Remi will go and visit her there. She can't stand not knowing why her texts are going unanswered, especially when she knows how glued her twin is to her phone.

It takes Remi twenty minutes to get to the restaurant via the metro. An Uber would be faster, but she isn't as trusting of the app as her sister is. She's felt uncomfortable with many Uber drivers in the past.

Not that the metro is any safer. It's probably all in her head.

Remi checks her phone as she pushes open the door to the restaurant. It's almost ten, but the sign on the door says they're open until eleven o'clock. She looks around the white tablecloth steakhouse. She's been here before, but she's never seen it so empty. The host stand is abandoned, the host probably already headed home. There are three occupied tables throughout the restaurant, none with more than two people, and one only has one man in a suit. There are no servers in sight.

She takes a seat at the bench inside the door, intending to wait until she sees a server to ask about Rayna.

She doesn't have to wait long before she sees her sister exiting the double swinging doors from the kitchen, a plate held in her hand with a towel. Remi stands up, intending to call out to her, but pauses, deciding she'll wait until her sister drops off the plate she's carrying. She's doing her job.

Rayna sets the plate in front of the lone man, a smile on her face. Remi smiles, happy her sister is okay, but her smile quickly fades as her sister touches the man's arm. She watches as Rayna leans over, obviously flirting. With a man who isn't Zeki.

She stands, open mouthed, for what seems like forever but is probably only a few moments before her twin glances up and notices her. Rayna quickly straightens up and excuses herself from the patron, making a bee-line for Remi.

"What are you doing here?" she exclaims, grabbing Remi's biceps and turning her away from the scene she just witnessed.

"What am I doing? Who is that man?" Remi shout-whispers back.

"I'm serving him his steak, obviously." Rayna rolls her eyes, but doesn't loosen the grip she has on her sister's arms.

"Rayna, you know you can't lie to me. You were flirting with him!" Remi scolds. She tries to wriggle out of her sister's grasp to no avail. Rayna has always been stronger than her.

"I was not flirting! Now leave." Rayna's face contorts in anger as she releases Remi's arms.

"You haven't answered my texts in weeks! Are you okay?" Remi crosses her arms, not intending to leave until she has some answers.

Rayna glances back over her shoulder, Remi follows her gaze to see the solo male patron looking their way. Rayna groans in obvious disdain.

"I'm fine. But you need to leave. Now," she emphasizes.

Remi's torn. Obviously something is going on here, but this is Rayna's work place, and they're creating a scene.

"Okay, but text me back from now on, okay?"

Rayna nods. "I will. Don't worry." With another hurried glance over her shoulder, she rushes back to the man.

Remi turns to leave, but something tells her to stay a moment more. She glances back in time to see Rayna place something small and white in the man's hand. Just what has her twin gotten herself mixed up in?

Shaking her head, Remi knows there's nothing she can do about it at this moment, and she turns and pushes open the door, heading back into the night.

NOW

S HE JOLTS AWAKE to the sound of something thumping on the wall.
"Remi, you okay?" she calls out, stepping out of bed into her slippers. She stops by her vanity mirror as she heads toward her bedroom door, cringing at her reflection. She needs to shower, and bad.

As she heads down the hallway, the thumping sounds grow in intensity, with varying amounts of time between them. What is she doing in there? "Remi?" Rayna calls through the closed door.

Seconds later, the door is ripped open. But instead of seeing the face of her twin, she comes face to face with a crazed looking Zeki.

"What the fuck did you do with my shit?" he screams.

Rayna takes a step back, covering her ears with the palms of her hands. "Well hello to you to," she retorts.

Zeki seeths. "I asked you a question. Now answer it."

Most women would crumple under the firey gaze of an enraged Zeki, but Rayna's used to it. His moods are unpredictable, and they no longer scare her. Usually she's able to calm him down within a couple minutes after helping him solve the source of his frustration.

"Now babe, what are you looking for, then maybe I can tell you?"

"You. Know. What," he replies through gritted teeth.

Rayna peeks over Zeki's shoulder, noticing the destroyed guest room behind him. "No, I don't, and why are you destroying the guest room?"

There's no sign of Remi in the wreckage. She must've gone home this morning while Rayna was nursing her hangover. Hopefully she went home alone and not with John.

"I don't know what you're looking for, but let's start picking this room up and I'm sure we will find whatever it is." Rayna moves to step past her boyfriend.

"Don't pretend you don't know."

Rayna leans down and begins picking up the books he tossed on the floor. She doesn't personally care about them, she bought them to add to the décor of the room. "I really don't know Zeki, why don't you fill me in?" She stands up, placing the books back on the shelf.

"My stash, where is my stash?" Zeki crosses his arms, staring his girlfriend down.

Stash? Rayna has no idea what he's talking about. What would her boyfriend possibly have a stash of— "Are you doing drugs?" Rayna's voice breaks at the thought.

Zeki rolls his eyes. "God, you really are dumb. I'm not doing them, just selling them."

She stands there in shock. How has she lived with this man for a year and not known he's selling drugs?

He scoffs at her expression. "How did you think I afforded this house, huh?"

"But...but you're a banker..." Rayna whispers in disbelief, more to herself than to anyone else.

Zeki snorts. "I'm a bank teller. Bank tellers don't make shit. Why do you think I went on all those business trips?"

Rayna feels the color leave her face as she realizes she's been a fool. Bank tellers don't take business trips.

"And now, you better tell me what happened to my brick before I lose a big sale."

"B-Brick?"

"Of cocaine," Zeki elaborates, obviously annoyed at his girlfriend taking so long to figure everything out.

"You were keeping cocaine in the same house we live in?" Rayna nearly screams, her cool demeanor vanishing. "I could've been arrested!" She feels like she's falling.

"Well obviously I hid it good," Zeki replies, pointing to the bookshelf. He pulls out one of the shelves, turning it around so Rayna can see the hollowed out inside. "Now I know you're the one who found it, so tell me what you did with it before I hurt you."

Rayna feels truly scared for the first time in her life. She's never seen Zeki like this before. "I swear. I didn't find it. You have to believe me," she begs as he steps toward her.

"Then who was in this room? It was a mess when I got home!" he seeths, stepping closer.

Rayna unconsciously steps back, surveying the room. She can't be sure, but she thinks if it was this trashed last night, Remi would have said something. And it isn't like Remi to trash a room...

Zeki growls, obviously not liking how long she's taking to answer.

"Remi was over! No one else, I swear!" Rayna shouts, her legs trembling in fear.

"I knew that bitch was trouble. Now go get my stash back from her, before she does something dumb like call the cops!"

Rayna squeezes her eyes shut, trying to picture Remi ransacking a room to find a cocaine stash, but try as she might, she can't picture it. But she needs to get away from Zeki before he hurts her. "Yeah, I'll go r-right now and get it back. I'll be right back!" Rayna quickly edges her way around the still angry Zeki, heading down the hall to leave, before realizing she's still in her bathrobe. She probably can't get an Uber looking like this.

She turns and heads to her room, grabbing the cut-offs from the floor and slipping them on. She tosses on the first shirt her hand touches, not bothering with her hair or makeup. She can do all that at Remi's.

Rayna runs down the stairs, grabbing her shoes on her way out the door, planning to slip them on outside. She still needs to call an Uber, but she wants to get out of what she's starting to consider the danger zone.

When she reaches the end of the block, she collapses in a fit of sobs.

How could she miss that the man she's dating has been dealing drugs? How has she not noticed? How could she be so dumb not to question where all his money comes from?

And now that she thinks about it, what else has she missed?

Maybe Zeki isn't the guy she thought he was...

BEFORE

RAYNA GROANS AS she checks her bank account balance on her phone. God, when did she spend so much money?

Granted, she's never been good about saving, nor has she really *wanted* to save for a rainy day. She's always assumed that Remi would have her back.

And Remi is great at saving money, her subconscious reminds her.

They've been living separately for two months now, and it has been really hard to adjust. For her, anyway. Remi doesn't seem to have a problem at all. In fact, she recently found a new roommate who plans to move in later this week. The woman's name is Daisy.

Rayna isn't sure how she feels about her sister's new potential roommate, but she also knows she doesn't have the right to say anything. She blew her sister off for weeks while she interviewed potential roommates, and she didn't even have a good reason. She was just too lazy to go.

Too lazy or too depressed? her mind nags.

"Both," she whispers to herself.

It's been hard adjusting to not seeing her sister every day. She thought it would be easy shifting to live with Zeki. It's not.

Their relationship has vastly improved since her move, which is great, but also makes her feel like an even worse person when she needs to ask Zeki for money to buy groceries or other essential items. Not to mention, she hasn't gotten her nails done in weeks.

Work has been slow lately, which is to be expected, as it's the down season, but with her expensive Uber ride to and from work, Rayna isn't even breaking even.

Her phone buzzes in her hand, a banner coming across the top of the screen to let her know she has an incoming message.

DARYL: Hey it's Daryl. I came in and ate dinner the other night and you gave me your number. You still interested in that business venture we discussed?

Rayna reads the text twice. Sure, she's been expecting it, but it doesn't make what she's about to do any easier.

Well, desperate times call for desperate measures.

RAYNA: Yes. When do I start?

She grimaces as she presses send. Can she really do this? She taps her phone lightly on her chin and she waits for the response. It finally comes.

DARYL: Tomorrow. Meet me at the Hilton Hotel downtown.

RAYNA: Okay. See you then.

She doesn't think she's ever typed in such full sentences before, but she's also never gotten a new job through text before.

You've also never had this sort of job before, her mind reminds her.

Come to think of it, her subconscious sounds extremely similar to Remi. She and her sister have similar voices, but the one in her head is definitely not her own.

Speaking of her twin, Rayna promised she would text her, and that was days ago. More broken promises Rayna just can't face.

Either way, she opens up the texting screen on her phone and sends a quick "I'm sorry" text to Remi, apologizing while also saying she's been very busy lately. The second part isn't necessarily true, but it sounds better than, "sorry I didn't get back to you, I was too busy lying in bed regretting my life decisions."

She's just pushed send when Zeki walks through the door.

"Hey babe," he greets her with his signature smile.

Rayna jumps up, trying to act somewhat excited to see him. "Hey," she replies as she kisses him on the lips.

"Did you have a good day?" he asks as he slides his backpack off his shoulders. Rayna has always wondered why he doesn't carry a briefcase like most bankers, but she has never dared to ask.

"Yep, how was the bank?"

He smiles widely. "Great. You working tonight?" He gives her a once-over, probably taking in the fact that she hasn't even dressed yet for the day.

Rayna shakes her head.

"Well, go put some clothes on and I'll take you out to that Italian place you like." Zeki pushes her toward the stairs, giving her a suggestive pat on the bottom.

Rayna smiles and heads upstairs. She doesn't really feel like going out tonight at all. She'd honestly rather sit on the couch a binge watch TV if it was up to her. But Zeki likes to go out, and he especially likes to show off Rayna.

He hasn't mentioned any friends coming to dinner tonight, but she's noticed lately that he wants to go out whenever they were off, and wherever they go, there's always another couple to dine with them. Sure, a few have been from the neighborhood (Zeki trying to help her make friends, again), but some have been from his work, and others still have been his friends from high school. The parade of people never seems to end.

As she slides into a short cocktail dress, Rayna finds herself wondering if this is how Remi feels all the time. Rayna has always been a party girl, while Remi wanted to stay home. Maybe she's finally maturing?

The thought makes her laugh and grin sheepishly in the mirror. She isn't maturing. This is a phase. Only a phase.

She quickly touches up her makeup and heads back down the stairs, already planning what she'll order when they get to the restaurant.

NOW

REMI WAKES ONCE more to find nothing has changed. She's still sitting in a pitch black environment, a plastic water bottle by her head. The water is no longer forming condensation down the sides, so she has to have been asleep for awhile.

She tries counting to pass the time, then reciting all the things she was required to learn back in Bible school when she was little. She no longer believes in God, but at least the Bible verses help pass the time. After she runs out of Bible verses, she begins to sing songs. She's never been much of a singer, especially not a cappella, and soon she cringes at the sound of her raspy voice.

Remi knows it's time to face the facts. She wants to believe that an accident happened or some sort of mistake has occurred. But the truth is, she's prisoner here. Someone isn't letting her leave.

Although she's never been into TV, Remi has read a lot of detective books over the years, and begins to imagine what the police will do first when they find her missing.

First, they'll ask her friends and family if she has any enemies. Remi wracks her brain. Does she? She doesn't think so. Her circle of friends is actually quite small. She and Zeki definitely don't get along, but it's more of a relationship of avoidance than one of malice.

She and John got into a fight last night. Or two nights ago, however long it's been. And it wasn't a small fight, more like one of those relationship ending fights.

Remi sighs. John is mad, but he would never do this to her. The fight was on both ends. They were both wrong.

She winces as it comes back to the front of her mind.

BEFORE

S HE PRESSES "10" in the hotel elevator, feeling her nerves accelerate as the elevator ascends.

Rayna has never done anything like this before, but she's stuck in a hard corner and doesn't know what else to do. She knows she could ask Zeki for money, but honestly she doesn't want him to think she's unable to pay for her own things. She also could probably ask Remi for money, but that would be even more embarrassing.

She comes to the door marked "1004" and knocks.

Daryl, the man from her table at the restaurant, pulls it open a crack. Seeing it's her, he opens it all the way to allow her to step inside.

The room is some sort of suite. The first room she steps into is a living room, with a kitchen to her left. There's a closed door on her right, as well as an open door straight ahead where she can see the end of a white bed.

As she observes the room, a scantily dressed woman appears from the closed door on her right. She's wearing a sort of lingerie outfit that leaves nothing to the imagination.

"Kiki." The woman sticks out her hand to shake. Rayna takes it.

"Rayna," she replies.

"You need to come up with a fake name for your protection," Daryl says from where he stands in the kitchen. He's putting together some sort of camera tripod.

A man in nothing but boxers walks in from the bedroom, heading straight for the fridge and grabbing a bottle of water. He must have overheard the conversation, because he's quick to pipe in, "she looks like a Leila."

Daryl looks at Rayna. "That work?"

Rayna really doesn't have a preference, so she shrugs and says, "sure."

Kiki tosses a lace teddy similar to her own at Rayna. "Put this on, then come to the bedroom."

Rayna bites her lip and nods, heading for the bathroom.

Rayna has never been shy, but this ordeal gives a whole new meaning to the word. Hopefully, no one will recognize her from whatever site this ends up on. She put on extra makeup this morning, hoping to at least somewhat hide her identity.

She slides on the teddy and adjusts her curls in the mirror. *Here goes nothing,* she thinks.

Rayna exits the bathroom just as Daryl sets the tripod up in the living room facing the couch. He begins to fiddle with the video camera.

The man who hasn't introduced himself sits on the couch, seemingly without a care in the world. Kiki checks her makeup in the mirror.

"Ready, Leila?" Daryl asks.

Rayna nods and heads toward the couch.

Two hours later Rayna, sore and re-clothed, stands as Daryl counts money into her hand. He counts twenty hundred-dollar bills.

Two thousand dollars. Rayna stares in disbelief as she realizes she made a thousand dollars an hour for the past two hours.

But was it worth it? her inner voice asks. She pushes the thought away. As soon as the money is in her hand, she shoves it in her purse and heads for the door. She doesn't even say goodbye to Daryl or Kiki. Turns out, the other man's stage name is Franco.

Rayna suppresses tears as she rides the train. Though the train only goes two thirds of the way to her home in the suburbs, she doesn't care. For once she wants to walk.

When she pushes open the door, she hesitantly calls out for her boyfriend. "Zeki?" There's no response. He must still be at work.

She heads up the stairs to the bedroom, pulling the wad of cash out of her wallet. Two thousand is what she usually makes in two weeks at the restaurant. And she just made that amount in two hours. Unbelievable.

She grimaces at what she's done. She definitely isn't proud of it, but she also doesn't feel ashamed as she should. She knows she should tell Zeki, but just thinking of how angry he would be, she changes her mind.

What Zeki doesn't know won't hurt him.

BEFORE

Remi knocks on her boss's door, all her work of the past three weeks tucked under her arm.

"Come in," he replies.

She pushes open the door and steps into Jonathon's office. Remi is the only female CPA for the company, and she and the two male CPAs all report to Jonathon. Before today, Remi hasn't been in his office since her interview. Usually, if he needs something, he comes directly to her desk.

"Remi!" he says excitedly as he sees her walk through the door.

There's no hiding it, everyone in the office knows Remi is his favorite. And not because she's a woman—mostly because she outworks both her coworkers on a daily basis. Jonathon says it's because she's the smartest, but Remi also senses it has something to do with her work ethic. She spends more time at her desk and less time at the water cooler flirting with girls. Go figure.

"What can I do for you today?" Jonathon asks, turning away from his computer and clearing a spot on the desk for her to set her files. She takes a deep breath as she slides into the seat on the other side of the desk. This does not escape Jonathon's notice. "What's wrong?" he asks.

Remi doesn't say anything at first, she simply begins to open files and turn them to face her boss. She's taken the liberty of highlighting all the suspicious deductions and non-matching amounts she's come up with over the last five weeks.

Jonathon raises his eyebrows. "What's this?" he asks.

"Someone is stealing from the company," Remi says somewhat quietly. Saying it out loud sounds even more accusatory than it does in her head.

Jonathon's quiet as he looks at the numbers. She can see him calculating in his head just how much money is missing. "Wow." He lets out a breath.

Remi continues, "I'm not sure exactly who. But I think I've narrowed it down."

Jonathon nods. "To who?"

"Well, these files are all saved online where I can see who accessed them and when. And the only three people who have accessed these over the past two months are myself, Jared, and Lyle." She winces as she says her two male coworkers' names. "Now, they may not have physically taken the money, though it's highly probable, but one of the two of them at least knows who did, and is helping them cover it up."

Jonathon nods again, his eyes still glued on the papers on his desk. "Wow," he repeats.

"You said that already."

"I know," Jonathon replies. "I just don't know what else to say. They've both been with the company so long, I didn't ever expect anything like this from either of them." As if realizing Remi is still there, he stops short in his ramblings. "Thank you for bringing this to my attention, Remi. I will have our auditor sent these documents immediately. Are these my copies?" He motions to the papers still spread on his desk.

"Yes. I printed out three. This one is for you. I have one in my desk if you need a second one. I have a third one in a secure location. Just in case either of them gets wind of this and the online file is damaged or mysteriously deleted." Remi's covered all of her bases.

Jonathon raises an eyebrow, clearly impressed. "You really did think of everything."

"It's what you pay me for," she says as she stands up and prepares to leave the room.

He nods. "Of course. And Remi, don't mention this to anyone else just yet. I wouldn't want either of our guys to end up in the wind with so much company money."

She agrees and leaves the room, heading back for her desk. She turns the corner to see Jared's lean frame leaning against her desk. He taps his foot impatiently, as if he's been waiting for her.

"Yes, Jared?" she asks as she slides into her seat and logs back into her computer.

"What was that about?" He tilts his head toward Jonathon's office. "You never go in there."

"Well, you don't ever go in there either." She tries to get him off topic.

It doesn't work. "I know, none of us do. So why did you go in there?"

Remi sighs, trying to make up a lie quickly. "I just needed help with a project." She doesn't make eye contact with Jared, and begins working on an Excel document, hoping he'll take the hint and leave.

"Why didn't you ask us? That's what we are here for." Jared motions to Lyle, who has stopped working and lifted his head to see what they're talking about. Remi really wishes they had actual cubicles rather than desks facing each other in an "open" floor plan.

"It was nothing, okay? I was just asking a couple questions, and then I was going to come to you guys for help okay?" Remi knows it sounds angry, but she's never been good at coming up with a lie on the fly.

Jared can tell he's breaking her down. "What questions? Maybe I can answer them."

Remi shakes her head. "No need, they were dumb, okay? Now just drop it."

Jared lifts his hands in surrender. Remi knows she sounds crazy. He turns and heads back to his desk. Lyle puts his head back down.

She can see the rift between the three of them growing right before her eyes. They've never been friends, like she hoped when she first got this job, but she definitely doesn't want them to be her enemies, either. They're supposed to be a team.

But if one of them is stealing from the company, it doesn't really matter, because they won't be here for much longer anyway.

Remi glances up from her computer screen to see Lyle observing her quietly. The minute her eyes meet his, he quickly glances back down at his work. Lyle has always been kind to her, and Remi senses he only follows Jared because Jared has been here the longest, almost ten years. Lyle has been here for eight, and it had been the two of them against the world for six years until Remi was hired two years ago. The way she figures, they originally saw her as a threat until they realized neither of them was going anywhere.

Or maybe they see her as a threat now, because they're both stealing from the company. Remi shakes her head, all these thoughts of accusations making her brain hurt. She stands up and collects all her folders, sliding them into her shoulder bag.

This doesn't escape Jared's notice. "Leaving early? It's only three."

"I have a headache. Plus, I always take my work home anyways and finish it there, so I don't think it matters if I leave two hours early." Honestly, Remi doesn't know if it matters or not. This is her first time doing it. But she isn't lying about finishing her work at home.

Jared shrugs. "If you say so." He turns back to his work, but Remi doesn't miss the glare he gives her from the corner of his eye.

Lyle doesn't even look up from his computer.

As Remi heads for the door, she begins to think that it has to be Jared who stole the money. Why else would he be so suspicious of her? She makes a mental note to report his behavior to Jonathon tomorrow, by email, so Jared won't ask why she was in his office again.

With a sigh, Remi pinches the bridge of her nose as she waits for the train. She really wishes she could tell someone about this. Maybe Rayna, or John. But she can't, this is her dragon to slay.

Not that they would understand, anyway.

NOW

AFTER CRYING FOR what probably appears to passersby a suspicious amount of time, Rayna finally comes to her senses, using her wrist to wipe away the rest of her tears.

She needs to get to Remi's, she'll know what to do.

Pulling her cell phone out of her pocket, she realizes it's almost dead—probably because she didn't bother to plug it in during her drunken stupor.

"Great. Just flipping great," she mutters under her breath as she begins the long walk to the train station. There's no way one percent of battery power is enough to order herself an Uber.

Rayna can't believe this is happening to her. She's always kept her life together, and now it's falling apart before her eyes.

She can't solely blame Zeki. After her stint making money as a porn actress, things have never been the same, even though she constantly lied to herself and said things were.

Rayna pulls out her phone, trying to check the amount of money left on her transit card, and it powers down completely. The battery is officially dead.

Luckily, when she walks into the train station a few minutes later and swipes her card, the machine accepts it with a beep. At least she's smart enough to have foresight and leave money on her transit card.

The train ride seems to take forever as the suburbs pass one by one. Why did she let Zeki talk her into moving out here, anyway? She's always been a city girl. She and Remi have that in common.

After getting off at her stop, she begins the quick walk back to her sister's place. It's odd seeing her old neighborhood again. Nothing's changed, but it still feels different.

Because you've changed, her subconscious reminds her. Rayna has grown up quite a bit in the last few months, which is probably why she pushed Remi to party really hard last night. She needed something to remind her of the old days.

Arriving at Remi's door, Rayna pulls out her key ring to unlock the deadbolt, but quickly reconsiders and raises her hand to knock.

John opens the door. "What do you want?" he seethes.

Rayna's surprised to see her sister made up with her boyfriend so quickly. In fact, she wasn't expecting to see John at all. "Um... Can I talk to Remi?" she asks in a hesitant voice that doesn't sound like her at all.

"Well, duh," John rolls his eyes. "That's why she's at your place."

Rayna feels her eyes go wide. "Uh...Remi isn't at my place."

John's eyes widen as well. "But she's not here. I was waiting for her to come home."

They stare at each other in stunned silence for a moment. Then John steps aside. "I think you better come in."

Rayna nods mutely and steps past him, making a beeline for her sister's room.

"I told you, she's not in there!" he calls after her.

"I know, idiot," she shouts back as she flips her sister's light switch and walks to her bedside table. She picks up Remi's iPhone cord, plugging in her phone. "I need to charge my phone."

John's followed her and stands in the doorway. "You haven't even tried calling her?"

God, John pisses her off so much sometimes. "No," she retorts, "because my phone is dead, obviously. Have you tried calling her?" she snaps back.

He shakes his head. "No, because I assumed she was with you." As if a light bulb suddenly went off in his head, he pulls out his phone and dials.

He waits a moment before he begins speaking. "Hey Remi, babe, I know you're mad at me, but please, your sister and I are worried, call us back." He hangs up and looks at Rayna. "It went straight to voicemail."

Not that Rayna doesn't trust him, but the minute her phone powers up, she dials her sister's number while her phone's still attached to the cord. She, too, gets her sister's voicemail right away. She doesn't leave a message and instead hangs up. "That's weird," she mumbles, more to herself than anyone else. "Remi never turns her phone off."

Hearing those words must strike a nerve, because before her mind registers what's happening, John crosses the room and begins madly tearing up Remi's desk. He pulls out every paper, tossing various stacks over his shoulder.

Rayna grimaces. Her OCD sister is definitely gonna be mad when she sees this mess.

"Stop!" Rayna calls out. "What are you doing?"

John pauses and shakes his head. "Her work number has to be here somewhere."

She cocks an eyebrow. "It's Saturday. I'm pretty sure her office is closed on Saturdays."

"Is it?" John questions her certainty.

Rayna realizes she actually doesn't know. "Uh, let me Google the company." She picks back up her tethered phone, opens Safari, and realizes she has no idea what company her sister works for.

John realizes her dilemma. "Really? You don't know?"

Rayna rolls her eyes and gives him a "do I look like I know" look.

John quickly answers, "Johnson Finance."

She types it in and clicks on the number that comes up. She puts the phone to her ear. It rings once, then comes up with a menu of options. She puts the phone on speaker.

John moves closer and they both listen to the menu options quietly. When the menu finishes, he pipes up, "press 3, the one for accounting, I think that's her."

Now it's Rayna's turn to say, "really, you don't know?"

John shrugs. "She really is private about her work life."

She nods silently as the phone line transfers and begins to ring. It rings for awhile before an automated answering service answers, letting them know that business hours are Monday through Friday, from seven in the morning until six in the evening. Rayna hangs up.

"So she's not at work."

John motions to the desk. "Her shoulder bag is here, anyway. I've never seen her go to work without it."

Suddenly, a thought strikes Rayna. "How did you get in here, anyways?" she asks in an accusatory manner. Remi's mentioned that John doesn't have a key.

"Daisy," John answered with a shrug, naming Remi's roommate, whom Rayna has, embarrassingly enough, not yet met.

"Is she still here?" Rayna raises an eyebrow.

He stands up and heads for the door. "Not sure, but let's find out."

Rayna sets down her phone and follows him. They head down the hall a few steps, to the closed door of the room that once belonged to Rayna.

John knocks, calling out, "Daisy?"

There's no reply.

He tries again. "Daisy?"

Nothing.

Slowly, John twists the knob and pushes open the door to Daisy's room. It's too dark to see anything. John flips on the light.

The room is barren. There's a queen bed against one wall, covered by a plain white duvet. The shelves where Rayna kept her CDs stand bare. There's a three-drawer dresser at the end of the bed. Otherwise the room is empty, except for a small nightstand by the bed.

Rayna pushes past John. She isn't normally one to snoop, but she's curious.

She slides open the closet door to find a total of about ten shirts hanging. On the floor of the closet is an empty white laundry basket, the type one would buy at Target for five dollars.

John comes up behind her.

"Doesn't seem like her roommate has much stuff," Rayna comments as she turns to face him.

He shrugs again. "I've only met her a few times, she works a lot."

Rayna slides the closet door closed and heads back for the door of the room. She doesn't want to get caught snooping. It's just so weird how few personal effects are in the room. Don't most people have at least some sort of trinkets or decorations? And what woman only has ten shirts hanging in her closet?

The two of them return to the living room, silently sitting on opposite sides of the couch. They both appear deep in thought.

Finally, John breaks the silence. "I think we should call the police."

Rayna nods, standing to retrieve her phone from her sister's room. John shakes his head and holds out his hand. "I got it," he says as he pulls out his cell from his pocket and begins to dial.

Rayna hears the faint sound of someone picking up on the other end.

"Yes," John says, his voice all business. "I think my girlfriend might be missing."

NOW

As THE HOURS draw on, Remi finds herself reverting back to her religious ways.

First, she prays to God, apologizing and telling Him if He just gets her out of here, she'll start going to church again. Then she realizes that maybe it isn't even the correct religion. She decides she should also pray to Buddha, just in case.

When that doesn't work, she begins to up the ante.

"Please, God," she mumbles, her throat parched once more. "If you get me out of here, I swear I'll become a nun, I swear it."

Her voice sounds foreign even to her. She lifts each of the two water bottles to her mouth in turn, hoping to coax out a drop of water. No luck. She sets the bottles back down, defeated. What is she going to do if she never gets out of here? What will her parents think?

Suddenly, the room is awash with light. Remi winces and squeezes her eyes shut. After the pitch black, the brightness hurts. She peers through her fingers.

She's slightly too delirious to tell for sure, but she thinks maybe the light is coming from the ceiling.

There's a sound.

And then she's plunged once again into dark.

If the brightness wasn't painful enough, the return to the pitch black hurts even more.

Once her brain recovers, Remi blindly crawls over to where the sound came from.

Her hand encounters a cold plastic container. Another bottle of water.

Remi raises it to her mouth and drinks like she's just spent the past three days wandering the desert. She can't be sure, but she thinks this water tastes normal—not drugged like the others.

She forces herself to stop drinking as the bottle nears half empty. She doesn't know when she'll get water again.

Remi feels exposed out in the middle of the room, and crawls forward to the wall, turning to lean her back against it.

She ponders what she just saw. A light coming from the ceiling, a bottle of non-drugged water materializing.

Maybe God is real, after all.

BEFORE

"A NYTHING I CAN do to help?" Remi asks as she peeks around the doorframe into her new roommate's bedroom. It's been a month since their first meeting, they hit it off very quickly, and today is finally move-in day.

"Nah," Daisy responds from where she stands by the closet. "I really don't have much." She brushes a strand of her long blonde hair behind her ear.

Remi always dreamed of having long golden locks as a child. As she grew up, she learned to be happy as a brunette, but she's still slightly envious. Daisy is thin, not unlike Remi, and although she wears glasses, she has high cheekbones and a thin face that give her a very delicate look. Remi self-consciously touches the baby fat that's always existed in her cheeks. No matter what she does, or how she diets, it never goes away.

When they met at the Starbucks a week ago, Remi confirmed that they had similar work ethics and cleaning habits. Daisy seems a little less stressed than Remi, but she figures that's probably a good thing.

Daisy finishes hanging what appear to be only ten shirts, then walks back over to the single box in the center of the room. She bends her tall frame to open the box. Remi has never been short, but Daisy towers over her at a height of almost six feet.

"Is that it?" Remi asks, motioning to the single box she just finished opening.

"Yeah." The tone in her voice is almost sad as she opens the box to reveal a mix of jeans and shorts. She slides them slowly into the drawers of the dresser that are not even near full.

"Um. Really?" Remi asks incredulously. Maybe it's just because she has a twin obsessed with clothes, but ten shirts and a handful of bottoms do not seem like any woman's wardrobe.

"Yep." Daisy begins to break down the box. She only came with two.

The room fills with silence.

"Well," Remi finally speaks up, "want to order a pizza to celebrate becoming roommates?"

"Sure," Daisy replies. "Let me just take these out to recycling." She picks up the empty, collapsed boxes and heads for the front door.

One pizza and two bottles of red wine later, the women lie in a giggling heap on the floor as they watch the movie 'How to Be Single.'

"Ooo, here comes my favorite part!" Remi laughs as the screen fills with a scene of the two main characters at the spa.

"Oh my God, how have I not seen this move before?" Daisy asks as she pops open their third bottle of wine. She reaches over to drunkenly fill Remi's glass to the brim.

The sound of Remi's phone ringing makes them both jump and causes wine to slosh over the side of Remi's glass.

"Oh shit!" Daisy begins using one of the brown pizza napkins to scrub furiously as the floor. "I'm so sorry!"

Remi stands to get her phone, a smile on her face. "No worries, I've got baking soda in the kitchen. We can get the stain out later." She walks over to where her phone sits on the end table. She picks it up to see that it says 'Private Caller.' That's weird.

She answers. "Hello?"

There's no reply.

"Hello?" she tries again.

She thinks maybe she can hear breathing on the other end of the line.

"Is someone there?" She makes eye contact with Daisy, who has her eyes furrowed in confusion.

Remi shrugs and hangs up. It was probably a butt dial.

"Oh, well, if it's important they'll call back." She takes her spot back, on the floor next to Daisy, leaning her back up against the couch.

Daisy finishes filling her glass and takes a long, silent sip.

"Everything okay?" Remi asks, startled by the sudden one-eighty in her roommate's behavior.

"Crank calls make me nervous," Daisy replies, shifting her eyes from one side of the room to another.

Remi raises her eyebrows. "We don't know it was a crank call. It could've just been a butt dial from someone who likes to keep their number private."

"If you say so," she responds, turning back to the TV just in time for the lead character to deliver a great one-liner. Daisy bursts out laughing, her happy mood returning in full swing.

Remi also turns back to the TV, a little confused at her roommate's sudden passage through the emotions. Ah, well, everyone has their quirks, she supposes.

As the credits run, the girls finish off the third bottle of wine. Remi is actually quite surprised, she isn't much of a wine drinker.

They sit in silence on opposite ends of the couch, wine glasses cradled in their hands as their feet meet in the middle.

This time, it's Daisy who breaks the silence. "Remi?" she asks timidly.

"Hm?"

"Can you do me a favor?"

Remi giggles, the wine obviously going to her brain. "You just moved in today and you already need favors?"

She means it as a joke, but Daisy doesn't laugh. In fact, her expression becomes more firm. "I'm serious."

"Uh..." Remi tries to recover from her social faux pass. "What is it?"

"Can you not tell anyone I'm living here?"

"Um..." Remi does a mental count. "My boyfriend John knows because he met you, obviously, and I told my twin sister in a text..." She isn't sure what else to say.

"That's okay. But can you not tell anyone else? Please?" A pleading look occupies her face.

"Uh, sure, why?" Remi's curious now.

Daisy doesn't seem to have an answer prepared. "Uh...I'm just a private person, and well, you know, I don't want any...visitors." She says the last word in a hushed tone, as if visitors are something extremely unsavory.

"No...visitors?" She's a little shocked, to say the least. Not that she's a party person by any means, but who doesn't want their friends knowing where they live? "Uh...sure, I won't mention it," she adds hesitantly.

Daisy's face breaks into a smile. "Thanks so much, I really appreciate it." She moves in to give Remi a hug.

Granted, it's an awkward hug, with Remi still holding her glass of wine in one hand. But it's also somewhat reassuring. Despite the weird 'no visitors' thing, she thinks she and her new roommate will get along just fine.

BEFORE

D ARYL: C AN U come thurs?
Rayna finishes reading the text on her phone, quickly setting it back down and turning her attention back to the TV. Her phone buzzes again.

DARYL: 4k. easy scene.

She groans and sets her phone down again. She hasn't responded to Daryl in three weeks, not since having the first job for him, why is he still texting her?

DARYL: ok fine. U force my hand. 6k. they love you and want to see more.

Rayna closes her eyes and pinches the bridge of her nose. Six thousand dollars? After her last experience in the pornography industry she swore that would be the end. But can she really say no to six grand?

Zeki walks through the living room on his way up the stairs, pausing when he sees her sprawled out on the couch under a blanket.

"Hey, babe."

"Hi," she says back sweetly, putting the TV on mute.

He smiles at her. "I'm leaving town again tomorrow, but I'll be back in a couple days."

She's used to these business trips by now. "Neat, where to this time?" she asks, glancing at the TV out of the corner of her eye hoping she isn't missing any of the action.

He shrugs. "Somewhere in Colombia, maybe Bogota?" His eyes shift as he says this, and something doesn't seem right to Rayna, but she really doesn't feel like fighting so she brushes it off. Well, for the most part, any-way.

"Bankers meeting in Colombia?"

"Er, yes, we bankers meet all over the place," Zeki quickly catches himself. Without allowing her to ask any more questions, he announces, "I'm headed upstairs to pack," and turns and leaves the room.

Rayna pushes the mute button once more to turn the volume back up, but she finds her heart is no longer in the show she's watching. She glances back down at the unanswered text on her phone. Can she really do this again?

She quickly pulls up her bank app and checks her account balance. She grimaces. Since quitting her restaurant gig two weeks ago, she's been doing nothing but spending money.

She could ask Zeki for money.

Lifting her phone to eye level, she types her response.

RAYNA: Ok fine. But this is the last time.

She takes a deep breath as she presses the send button. She knows she shouldn't be doing this, but she also can't face the humiliation of asking her boyfriend for spending money.

DARYL: Great c u then.

Rayna doesn't bother to type out a response. She'll text him the night before to verify the location.

With a sigh, she falls back on the couch just as Zeki comes back in the room. Her phone buzzes from where she tossed it on the couch. Rayna doesn't bother reaching for it.

It doesn't escape Zeki's notice, though. "Who are you texting these days?" he asks, a note of suspicion in his voice.

Rayna shrugs. "You know Remi, she's a bit clingy." She doesn't like lying to him, but she also can't bear the thought of explaining Daryl to him.

"I haven't seen her in awhile, how is she?" he asks politely. But Rayna can see he really doesn't care one bit.

"Fine."

"Well, want to watch a movie or something?" He changes the subject, motioning to the TV.

Rayna instantly perks up, it's been a while since they did something as simple as watch TV together.

"Sure! I've been really wanting to see that new movie Adrift." She smiles.

Zeki doesn't smile back. "I've already seen it."

"Oh." Rayna isn't quite sure how to respond to that. Is he saying he doesn't want to see it again? Or is that just him being informative? Either way, there's another movie she's wanted to see. "I know it's sorta childish, but I've also been wanting to see Wreck-It Ralph Two." She looks at him, her eyes hopeful.

He shrugs. "Seen it."

She almost growls in frustration. "Fine, what do you want to see?"

Zeki picks up the remote from its spot on the couch. "I'll find something."

So that's what this is. Zeki doesn't actually want to watch a movie with her. He just wants to turn something on, then fool around.

Rayna huffs and picks up her phone, scooting over so there's room for him to sit on the couch. He doesn't even seem to notice his girlfriend's obvious annoyance at his behavior.

And to think, she almost felt bad about agreeing to do another porn video.

At least Daryl is paying her.

On Thursday, Rayna arrives at the same hotel as last time, but heads up to a twelfth floor suite as she's been instructed. She knocks on the door and has a sense of déjà vu as Daryl opens it, just the same as before.

"Leila!" He hugs her in a friendly manner, greeting her by her stage name as she walks in. "Glad you could make it," he adds cordially, as if this is some sort of dinner party.

The room is set up just as before, which makes sense, as it's the same hotel. A man she recognizes from the last shoot sits on the couch.

"Franco, if you don't remember," he says.

Rayna nods. "I remember."

Just then, there's a knock at the door. Daryl goes to answer it as Rayna heads to the bathroom.

She closes the door behind her, but is unsure why since they're about to see everything anyway. There's a white lace bra and underwear set laid out on the counter. She slips it on, surprised that they fit her decently well.

When she exits the bathroom she runs into someone's chest. She looks up to find an unfamiliar face looking back down at her. "Mondo," the man says. He holds out a hand and Rayna hesitantly takes it. He's muscular, but not in a way that says he overdoes it with steroids. But he definitely stands out next to Franco, who, although somewhat attractive, is very thin in comparison.

She takes a moment to glance around, noting that Daryl is setting up his tripod just as before.

She looks between Mondo and Franco. Are they waiting on anyone else?

Daryl takes a look through the camera as Mondo changes in the bathroom from which Rayna just emerged.

Before she knows it, Daryl turns to Rayna. "You ready?" He adjusts the camera a tiny bit and motions to where the guys are sitting on the couch.

Rayna realizes nervously that no one besides Franco, Mondo, and herself seem to be here. "I...err..."

Daryl seems to realize exactly what she's thinking. "That's why it pays six thousand."

NOW

THE APARTMENT IS filled with police officers as they poke around, trying to figure out what happened to Remi. They were quick to separate John and Rayna. She's currently sitting on the couch in the living room, while John is with a male officer in Remi's bedroom.

"So, how long has your sister been missing?" The female officer has her cell phone sitting on the coffee table, recording everything they discuss.

Rayna tries to calculate in her head. "Uh, well, the last time I saw her was around one in the morning, and now it's ten in the evening, so I guess twenty one hours."

The officer raises one eyebrow. "So we are under the twenty-four hour mark where we typically start to investigate. But on the phone the gentleman—" she checks her notes on the iPad she carries, "—John, said the two of you suspect foul play?"

"You don't know my sister," Rayna tries to explain. "She never goes anywhere besides this apartment and work. Her and John don't even go out to dinner, they always order in, or he picks up takeout."

"And John is?"

"Remi's boyfriend," Rayna clarifies.

"Where does Remi work?" the officer asks, obviously trying to get the basic questions out of the way.

"Johnson Finance," she answers, glad she figured out the answer an hour before.

"And does she like her job?"

"Very much so. My sister is a math geek." In fact, Rayna has never heard her sister say anything bad about her job at all. "John and I tried calling her work earlier, to make sure she wasn't there, but the office is closed."

The officer nods. "I'll have one of my officers double check. Just in case she had a key or something and went in to do extra work."

That doesn't sound right to Rayna. "I don't think my sister has a key."

"Why not?" The officer peers at her.

"Remi's really junior in her firm. She only started about three years ago, straight out of college. I doubt they trust her that much."

"Are you saying your sister isn't trustworthy?"

"Wait—No! That's not what I'm saying at all," Rayna feels her frustration flare. This cop is twisting her words around. "Remi is the most trustworthy person I know, it's just that she's the most junior person in the finance department. I highly doubt she'd be the one the get a key. It's a large firm."

The officer writes down a few notes and is silent for a minute.

"Do you have a picture of her?" The officer looks around the apartment.

Rayna notices for the first time that her sister *doesn't* have any pictures of herself anywhere. In fact, all the decorations are very neutral pictures of black and white scenery.

Ah well, not an issue. "She looks just like me. Remi and I are identical twins." She motions to her face. "And yes, people have issues telling us apart."

The officer sets down her iPad. "Tell me about when you last saw your sister."

"Last night." Rayna shakes her head in shame. "She didn't want to go out, but she'd had a bad night so I insisted." She glances at the ceiling as she pictures herself the night before. "I told her she had to meet me at this stupid nightclub by my house. I live in the suburbs, so all the clubs out there are stupid, but I wanted her to forget."

The officer continues making notes in her iPad, not saying anything.

Rayna crosses her legs nervously, but continues. "So she got there probably at about eleven and then I started stuffing her full of booze." Realizing how bad that sounds, she quickly elaborates. "Remi doesn't drink much, or ever really, so it doesn't take much to get her drunk. I bought her a drink or two and then we did a couple rounds of shots. She was pretty drunk by twelve thirty.

"She wanted to leave, which was fine by me, I don't really like to party anymore anyways. And at one we got an Uber and headed back to my house, which was maybe a ten minute drive. We got to my place and I tucked her into my guest room and—" Rayna takes a deep breath as the implications of her words strike her, "—that's the last time I saw her."

"And you didn't worry about her until now?" the officer asks, observing Rayna with suspicion in her eyes.

"No, I was, uh...just as drunk as my sister and didn't wake up until ten am. When I did wake up, the door was closed to the guest room so I assumed she was still sleeping." She pinches her eyes closed, trying to remember what she did in her hungover stupor that morning. "I went downstairs because someone was banging at the door—"

"Who was banging at the door?"

"Uh, John. John was banging at the door. Then I headed back upstairs and fell back asleep."

The cop sets down her iPad, obviously becoming more interested in the story. "Why was he banging on the door?"

"He and Remi had a fight last night and he wanted to talk to her. That's why we went out in the first place."

"A fight about what?"

Rayna grimaces at the mental image of her sister sobbing as she told her the story over the phone. She doesn't realize it, but she subconsciously shakes her head.

"That bad?" the officer asks, waiting for a response.

Rayna's head jerks up, she forgot the cop was there for a second. "Yeah," she replies. "My sister found out that her boyfriend John is currently married."

NOW

T IME DRAWS ON. At first, thinking of escape is enough to keep her
mind busy, but soon, it isn't enough. Her thoughts begin to drift to
all her recent mistakes and the events that led to her going out with Rayna
in the first place.

She begins to rock back and forth and sob as the memories from last
night flash through her mind.

John texted her and asked if she wanted to pick up dinner for them.
She asked for her favorite order from a local Mexican joint. He said he
would be right over.

Remi closes her eyes, picturing vividly the final straw in her life that's
fallen apart over the course of the last month.

*She was sitting on the floor in front of the TV, deciding to lay work to rest
for the remainder of the weekend. It was Friday night, after all.*

*There was a knock at the door and Remi jumped up to answer it, ready
to stuff her face with tacos.*

*When she threw open the door, she found a young blonde woman on her
doorstep, definitely not John.*

"Can I help you?" she asked the woman.

*The woman glanced around nervously. "I'm uh...Patrice..." She stuck out
her hand for a handshake.*

*Remi didn't take it. "Okay, and how can I help you, Patrice?" She was
confused as to why this woman was here and what she wanted.*

"I'm looking for John..." She tried to peer around Remi.

"Um, why?" Remi noticed what the woman was doing and stepped out onto the doorstep, closing the door behind her.

Patrice raised her eyebrows. "Because he's my husband."

With those four words, Remi felt her world crashing around her. It took everything she had not to sink to the floor in a pile of tears. But she held it together, just barely.

"John isn't married. He's my boyfriend." Remi didn't know why she said it, but it just came out automatically.

Patrice shook her head. "John and I have been married since we were eighteen."

Remi couldn't hold it together any longer. "I, uh, I have to go," she stuttered, before she opened the door to her apartment, stepped inside, and closed the door behind her.

She collapsed in front of the door sobbing, and that's where John found her ten minutes later.

"What's wrong, babe?" he asked sweetly, helping her stand and walk over to the couch. Remi found her legs were so shaky that the minute he stepped away to go grab the food, she collapsed once again into a heap.

"There was some woman...at the door...before you..." she huffed out between sobs, "she said...that you and her...married...at eighteen."

John didn't immediately say anything. He just sat down next to her on the couch.

"Tell me...she...was lying..." Remi forced out.

John shook his head. "I can't."

"So you're MARRIED??" Remi screeched in a voice she had never heard before.

John nodded. "Babe, let me explain."

"EXPLAIN WHAT?" she yelled, hoping that Daisy was still at work and not overhearing this exchange.

"Listen," he said, reaching to brush her hair out of her face. Remi swatted his hand away. He placed it awkwardly back down at his side. "We were, or are, married but we've been separated for years."

Remi felt her eyes go wide. "And that's supposed to make me feel better how!?"

He looked at her sadly. "Trust me Remi, I love you, we were going to make the divorce final, we just hadn't gotten around to it yet."

She had heard enough. "Get. Out."

John didn't move.

"Get out now! I don't ever want to see your face again you FUCKING LIAR!" she screamed and pointed to the door.

After looking at her for another moment, he slowly got up and walked to the door. So slowly, it was as if he wanted to say something more.

But he didn't. He quietly closed the door behind him and that's the last time she saw him.

Remi just can't believe she's wasted two years of her life on some guy she thought was perfect for her, when really he's been betraying her trust the entire time. And he's the one who pushed for them to be in a relationship.

She continued to cry for a while after that, until finally, she calmed down enough to call the only person she wanted to talk to, Rayna.

Not that it matters now. Remi is starting to think she's going to die in this room. Her stomach is growling at unreal volume levels, letting her know she hasn't eaten since lunch Friday, however many hours ago that was.

The water is sure to run out again soon, and she doesn't know when, or if, she'll get more.

Subconsciously, she knows she should be trying harder to find a way out of here, but her heart is too distracted by the scene from Friday night playing itself over and over, in an everlasting loop.

All Remi knows is that, for once, she wishes she was her sister. Rayna would never let someone walk all over her like that. Rayna probably would have punched Patrice, and John, and a wall.

She giggles at the thought. Rayna definitely would have done some damage. If only she didn't move out all those months ago.

BEFORE

IT'S A DREARY day, and Remi barely felt like coming to work this morning. But she did. And now she's wishing she called in sick.

Lyle and Jared have barely spoken to her since she was in Jonathon's office last week. Although she doesn't think anything has been mentioned to them, she's sure they suspect something.

Remi's surprised she hasn't heard anything back from Jonathon yet. She thought for sure he would want to put a stop to the theft as soon as possible. Maybe it's more complicated than she thought.

She's looking down, typing on her computer, when she hears Lyle clear his throat. She looks up in time to see him motion something to Jared. Great, now they're communicating using a secret language. Maybe they really are in on the theft together.

Glancing at the clock, she notices it's almost noon and heads for the break room to eat the lunch she packed. John brought over steaks last night, and Remi wasn't able to finish hers, so she brought the rest for lunch.

She opens the communal fridge and reaches for her box of food on the middle shelf. When she picks it up, it feels lighter than she remembers it being. She closes the fridge and flips open the lid to the box.

Her steak is missing.

So maybe that's what Lyle and Jared were snickering about.

Rather than let them see a reaction from her, which is exactly what they probably want, Remi transfers the mixed veggies and half of a baked potato to a paper plate and sticks it in the microwave. Ah well, she can stand to lose a couple pounds anyway.

She eats her lunch in silence while surfing her phone. She isn't much for social media, but no one else is in the break room to chat with.

After she finishes, Remi heads back toward her desk, but is intercepted by Jonathon. He motions for her to follow him.

He leads her back to his office, closing the door behind him.

"How are you today, Remi?" he asks politely as they each take a seat on opposite sides of the desk.

"Good, and yourself?"

"Good, good," he responds. "So, I've been looking into this theft."

Remi scoots to the edge of her chair. "And?"

He shrugs. "I can't quite narrow down who it is, because you all access the same database for receipts, etc. I have one of our tech guys trying to narrow it down, and to find where the money is going, but it's going to take more time."

This is not the answer she was hoping for.

"In the mean time, I'm having the tech guy come in later tonight and install desktop spyware to monitor activity on each computer. Yours included."

"Okay?" Remi isn't sure where he's going with this.

"Have you noticed any suspicious activity since our last talk?"

She shakes her head. "Nope. Jared and Lyle are suspicious of me, but I think that's always been a thing."

"I meant in the database and spreadsheets."

"Oh, no, but I haven't really been looking."

"Okay, well I just wanted to let you know I'm working on this. Didn't want you to think I forgot—it's just a slow process." Jonathon stands and holds the door open for her. "Let me know if you notice anything odd, okay?"

"No problem," Remi replies. She exits and heads back to her desk.

Luckily, it looks as if Lyle and Jared have taken their lunch, or the liberty of visiting the water cooler. Either way, their desks are delightfully vacant.

Remi is a little confused as to why Jonathon hasn't approached Jared or Lyle yet. Wouldn't employee questioning be one of the first orders of business?

Maybe she's wrong, maybe the sneak attack that Jonathon is orchestrating will catch whoever stole the money red handed. She will just have to wait and see.

Her thoughts are interrupted when Jared slides into his desk, making eye contact with her. "Well, if it isn't the teachers pet," he scoffs.

So they did see her go into his office. Remi rolls her eyes, not offended in the slightest. "What is this," she asks, "high school?"

Jared makes a face at her but doesn't respond. Lyle chooses that moment to reappear as well. He doesn't say anything, he just raises his eyebrows at Remi in a silent accusation.

"So, want to update us on what Mr. Jonathon had to say?"

God, their lack of English skills is appalling. "First off," she corrects, "Jonathon is his first name. So it would be Mr. Tidwell. And secondly, what goes on between myself and Jonathon is none of your business."

"You know office romances aren't allowed here," Lyle pipes in.

"You guys never let that stop your water cooler flirt fests," Remi fires back.

"That's different," Jared sneers. "That's just flirting. No one is doing anyone else any *favors*." He winks at Lyle as he says the last word.

"How do you know I'm not just flirting with Jonathon?" she asks.

"Flirting with the door closed...hm?" Jared raises his eyebrows.

Remi's over this juvenile dialogue. "Whatever. I'm getting paid to work, so if you need me that's what I'm going to be doing." She turns her attention back to her computer with gusto.

"I think I need one of your favors," Jared says in a voice that Remi knows is meant to annoy her. She chooses to ignore him.

Lyle snickers from his desk. Obviously he's enjoying the show.

The rest of the afternoon passes fairly uneventfully. Remi actually manages to finish the majority of her work, even with Jared making snide comments and mocking her every few minutes. Really, what do they think she is, twelve?

Finally, as the clock strikes five, she grabs her stuff and heads straight for the door. She's in such a hurry and so annoyed at her coworkers she's forgotten to investigate what happened to her steak. Oh well, it isn't that big of a deal.

Remi steps on her train to commute back to her apartment, happy to see there's a seat available for her today. She sits down and pulls out some of her notes on a client's account, intending to work through the twenty minute ride home.

She's about halfway there when her phone vibrates in her pocket. She picks it up to see "private caller" on the screen.

She considers ignoring it, but then realizes it could be the IT guys at work. Maybe they need the password for her computer to install the spyware.

"Hello?"

There's no sound on the other end.

"Hello?" she tries a second time.

She thinks perhaps she hears heavy breathing. A sense of déjà vu hits her as she remembers the call from a week ago, when Daisy moved in. Maybe someone's crank calling her.

"Can you please stop calling this number? Thanks," she halfheartedly demands as she hangs up the phone. She wishes there were a way to block this private caller without blocking them all. But then, she supposes that would defeat the purpose of being a private caller.

Remi slides the phone back in her pocket, her mind drifting away from the documents in front of her. She's never received crank calls before this, and she wonders what the person on the other end of the phone wants. Is it just to annoy her? Or is there something more sinister?

As she steps off the train, she hopes today's calls will be the last of the strange empty line crank calls. But she knows she's probably not that lucky.

RAYNA

BEFORE

S HE STUFFS THE six thousand dollars in cash into her purse and hurriedly leaves the hotel room without saying goodbye to Franco or Mondo. She hopes she never sees either of them again.

Rayna knows this has already gone too far, she shouldn't have come back here today. But as Daryl counted out the six thousand dollars into her hand, she couldn't help but feel powerful. But then, she keeps coming back to what Zeki would think if he knew what was going on. And Rayna knows it wouldn't be good.

She takes an Uber to her bank and deposits all but two hundred dollars. This will last her quite awhile, that's for sure. Then she walks to the nearby coffee shop and purchases a hot tea to calm her nerves.

While sitting at the table, she picks up her phone multiple times, daring herself to message Remi and tell her what's going on. Her twin has always had her head screwed on straight, and she would know what Rayna should do.

But she never quite gets up the nerve.

She finishes her tea, leaving the cute mug on the table for the employees to clean up, then she uses her phone to get another Uber home.

As the car pulls up to the curb, Rayna looks up toward the big house. The lights are all off, giving it an empty vibe.

She doesn't know why, but suddenly this house doesn't seem like the one she helped pick out a few months ago.

Rayna unlocks the door and heads inside. She stops by the kitchen to pop a bag of microwave popcorn, then heads for the couch. She absentmindedly picks out a movie and pushes play.

Her phone buzzes from where she left it on the coffee table.

ZEKI: Can you pick up groceries before I come home tomorrow?

Rayna reads the text and thinks for a moment before responding. Zeki

71

sure seems to be getting demanding lately, and Rayna isn't too ready to part with the money she worked hard to earn this afternoon just yet. She decides to try something.

RAYNA: Sure, can you send me $$?

She turns back to the movie, awaiting her boyfriend's response. She doesn't have to wait long.

ZEKI: What? You don't have any?

She feels her anger bubble up, and all the shame she feels about her activities earlier today fades away. All this time, she's been telling herself she should not go through with it, that she should just ask Zeki for money. And look what happens.

Rayna doesn't even bother texting him back. She's so annoyed that she let herself feel embarrassed this entire time, when really she shouldn't have been. Zeki's the one who told her to quit her restaurant gig, now he gets annoyed when she asks for money.

She picks up her phone again, ignoring the text from Zeki and opening a new conversation.

RAYNA: Let me know when you need me again. Interested in more scenes.

She feels no regret as she pushes send. He's quick to reply.

DARYL: no problem. Tues? Not as high as today, but 2k again.

RAYNA: Perfect.

She tosses her phone toward the other end of the couch, a smug smile on her face. She definitely does not need Zeki's money.

NOW

T HE FEMALE OFFICER pauses as the phone at her hip rings.

"Grady," she answers. She puts a finger up to indicate she'll be just a moment, then walks into the kitchen to take the call.

So that's her name, Officer Grady. Rayna glances around the room again, trying to think of somewhere, anywhere her sister would go to get away. But she keeps coming up blank.

Because until last night you guys barely talked, her subconscious reminds her.

Rayna knows their drifting apart has been mostly her fault. After all, she's the one who left the bulk of the texts unanswered in the beginning. And then Remi stopped trying after awhile. And honestly, Rayna can't blame her. Kinda hard to keep texting someone who never texts back.

Officer Grady hangs up the phone and returns to the couch. "Sorry about that, where were we?" she asks as she picks up her iPad once more.

"Um, well, Remi called me in tears because she found out John was married."

"Uh huh. And did she say how she found out?"

Rayna nods, the conversation flashing back to the front of her mind once more. "Yes, his wife came over here last night and paid her a visit."

"Interesting." Officer Grady begins wildly typing notes. "Did Remi say anything about the wife or what she wanted?"

"I mean, she was in tears," Rayna says, pinching the bridge of her nose and shutting her eyes, trying to remember the exact words her sister said, "but I don't think she said why she came over. The name might have been Patricia or something like that?" She taps her finger on her chin. "Maybe Patrice?"

The officer nods. "Alright, that gives us something to go off of. Now, does your sister have any enemies?"

"No, none, everyone loves her. I'm the hated one." Rayna crosses and uncrosses her legs, glancing at the clock on the wall. It's almost eleven, she's already been talking to the officer for an hour.

"None at all? Most people have at least someone who doesn't like them."

The scene from months ago before she moved out comes to the front of Rayna's mind. "Actually," Rayna hates to do this, but finding Remi is more important than avoiding her boyfriend's anger, "she never really got along with my boyfriend, Zeki Arnold."

"Did they argue?"

She shakes her head. "Nothing of the sort. It was actually a bit more awkward than that. Remi had never been a fan of him, and then a few months ago he was drunk and mistook her for me. That's why I moved out of this apartment actually."

"You used to live here?" The officer doesn't even look up from her iPad.

Rayna rolls her eyes. "That's what I just said."

"And where do you live now? We will need to check out the room where you last saw your sister."

She bites her lip as she realizes they'll need to see the guest room. And Rayna grimaces as she remembers its current state.

"I live on the other side of town. I'm happy to have an officer come check it out, but—"

"But what?" Grady pries.

Rayna's embarrassed now. "My boyfriend tore apart the guest room this morning. I'm not sure, if there was any evidence in the first place, if there will be any left."

"And does your boyfriend tear apart rooms of the house often?"

This is starting to feel like an attack, and she can feel herself becoming defensive. She tries to repress it and remind herself she's only helping Remi, but it's difficult.

"No. Zeki is great, he just, uh, had a bad morning." She realizes after she says it how fake it sounds. Zeki is definitely on the suspect list now.

Officer Grady slides her iPad into a pouch. "I think you and I better head to your place and have a look at this room. Can you call Zeki to meet us there?"

Rayna winces, but agrees. Calling Zeki is never easy.

Both of them rise from the couch, and Rayna goes to slip on her shoes.

Officer Grady stands by the door. "I never properly introduced myself, by the way. I'm Detective Grady. My partner, Detective Brown, is going to follow in his car."

Rayna nods, glad to finally get their names, although she didn't realize she's been speaking to a detective this whole time. As they step out the door, Rayna decides to ask a question that's been bothering her the whole time. "So do you and Detective Brown work a lot of missing persons cases?"

"Some," Grady replies curtly, opening the passenger side door of an unmarked police car for Rayna.

"And do you usually find the person?" Rayna asks hopefully as she slides in and buckles her seatbelt.

Detective Grady looks Rayna straight in the eye before answering.

"I'm not going to lie to you. Detective Brown and I, our main job is homicide."

NOW

S HE'S BEEN IN here for almost a month. She's sure of it. If only she had a way to see the daylight and mark off the sunsets to be sure.

Her stomach growls, at a volume she's never heard before. Hunger is beginning to have a new meaning. Not that Remi has ever been picky, just conscious of what's good for her body and what isn't. She obviously isn't a vegan, but she's always gravitated towards all organic foods, and kept her meat consumption to a minimum.

What she wouldn't give right now for some chicken wings. Or even a package of one of her most detested foods, Oreos. She'd eat the entire thing.

She's out of water again, and God hasn't reappeared with more. She's tried praying again, but to no avail. Her mind has questioned if there's a possibility maybe it isn't the Christian God. Maybe it's the Jewish one, and He became offended when she said "in Jesus' name" at the end of the prayer. Maybe she should try again without it. Does Buddha get offended? Is that even possible?

As her thoughts spin over all the religious lore she's absorbed over the years, her ears perk up at a sudden scratching sound.

"Hello? Who's there?" she calls out.

No one answers.

Remi begins to crawl forward on her hands and knees, looking for the source of the sound. On her first loop of the small room, she encounters nothing. She sits back on her heels to listen.

This time when the sound comes, she thinks she can tell where it's coming from. Moving forward to the nearest wall, she places her ear on it. At first it's cold, but her ear quickly adapts. She begins to slide along the wall.

As she approaches the corner, she hears the sound again, loud and near her ear—just on the other side of the wall.

"Who's in there?" she whispers, mostly to herself. The scratching stops. *It's probably just a mouse,* she reasons.

Just to be sure, she continues to slide around the perimeter of the room with her ear to the wall. As she comes to the spot she thinks is directly opposite from the scratching, she hears something similar to the ocean.

"Running water?" she asks out loud to no one in particular. "Am I by a river?" Of course, there is no answer, so she continues her listening expedition. She doesn't encounter anything else interesting and is soon back to the scratching noises.

"Hello, mouse family. If you are mice, that is. If you're not, and that sort of thing offends you, I'm sorry." Remi realizes she's whispering to a wall and chastises herself for a moment. But then she shrugs her shoulders and continues, "if you're not a mouse, maybe a cat or something, maybe you could get me help?" She mentally slaps herself at how dumb and crazy she's being, but for once she feels like she's doing something besides sitting around.

The scratching noises stop again. And Remi sits down and leans on the wall.

"I'll just wait here while you go get help, ok?" she lets the noises know. They don't start back up.

Remi touches the two empty water bottles by her feet. She fiddles with them, stacking them on one another to pass the time. It's pretty boring with only two water bottles, but she doesn't know what else to do.

While she's fiddling with the water bottles, she remembers a time when she was really little. She and Rayna were playing hide and go seek. Remi had climbed in her parents closet on a shelf, and buried herself in clothes.

Rayna looked for minutes, then hours for her sister. Remi used the time to take a nap. When she woke up and returned to the living room (she had forgotten they were playing hide-n-go-seek) her parents were aching with worry, asking her where she had been and why she hadn't come out when they called. Remi never liked being yelled at, and this intimidated her so much she started crying. She never ended up revealing her hiding spot.

That was the end of hide-n-go-seek for the twins, though. Rayna never wanted to play it again. In fact, Remi distinctly remembers that as a turning point in their childhood. It was the last day of their doing everything together. Sure, they still played together often, but it created a rift between them.

Their parents became even more concerned when, a month later, Remi came home from school with an imaginary friend.

Rayna was always popular, even in kindergarten, surrounded by her little posse of friends. Remi struggled, and always relied on Rayna to be her best friend. Kindergarten proved to be difficult, as Rayna wanted to gravitate toward new people, away from her sister. Their parents didn't know what to do.

Remi didn't mind at all, really. She liked her friend Zoza. They did whatever she wanted all the time. Her parents indulged her, setting a place for Zoza at the table and even making her a plate of food when Remi insisted. Her father found it especially hilarious.

"So Remi, where does Zoza sit in school?" he asked as they ate dinner one night.

Little Remi shrugged as she munched on her pasta. "She waits outside and plays on the playground all day. Zoza doesn't have to go to school."

"And why is that?" her father presses, trying to restrain his laugher.

Remi doesn't even hesitate. "She already knows everything."

"Ah I see." He chuckles. "Well maybe she can help me with a problem. Can you ask Zoza what the square root of twenty five is?"

"Sq-Square root?" Remi stutters, never having heard the word before as she was only five.

Her dad nods. "Yes, square root of twenty five."

Remi turns to the chair next to her and begins whispering. After a moment of silence, she turns back to her dad. "She knows but says she doesn't need to tell you."

"And why is that?" he prods.

"Because you're not in charge of her."

Her dad didn't stop laughing for a full five minutes.

Remi smiles at the memory. At the time, she didn't know what her dad found so funny. Now she laughs along with him.

Luckily, she finally outgrew Zoza, but much later than her parents anticipated. Zoza went everywhere with Remi until almost fourth grade. And even then, Zoza only disappeared because other children started to bully her.

Remi closes her eyes and reminisces about Zoza. She never told anyone, but Zoza looked just like her and her twin sister. Only young Remi considered her a *real* twin, because she actually liked all the things young Remi liked. Even hide-n-go-seek.

And Zoza won every single time.

BEFORE

T HE SOUND OF her alarm wakes Remi and she rolls over to quickly shut it off before it wakes John. She isn't quite fast enough, however, and his groan reaches her ears.

"It's Saturday."

"I know," she whispers back. "I need to get some work done."

"No," John protests as his arms snake around her waist and he buries his nose in her hair.

As comfy as she is, Remi knows her work can't wait. She gently pries off his arm.

"I have to."

John grunts an unintelligible response.

By the time Remi stands up and slides on her yoga pants, he's already sound asleep and snoring softly. "Men," she mutters under her breath with a quiet laugh.

She's rooting around in her drawer, looking for a T-shirt, when she hears a flush from the bathroom down the hall. Daisy must be awake, too.

Remi grabs her computer and slips silently into the hall, closing her bedroom door behind her. The hallway is empty, but as Remi turns the corner into the kitchen, she finds her roommate sitting quietly at the table in her bathrobe, drinking a cup of coffee.

"Coffee's fresh." She motions to the pot on the counter.

Remi helps herself to a cup. "Thanks." She looks around for the ceramic hippo that holds the coconut sugar she usually likes to put in her coffee, but the container doesn't seem to be on the counter. Too lazy to look, she shrugs and takes a sip of her coffee black.

"You're up early," Daisy comments from her spot at the table.

Remi raises an eyebrow. She's up early quite often, she's more curious as to why her roommate is just sitting at the table, not appearing to do anything. "I'm normally up quite early. Why are you up this early?" It sounds a little more accusatory than she means it to, and she quickly gulps her coffee to try and hide her awkwardness. This is why she doesn't have friends.

Daisy shrugs. "Couldn't sleep."

"My twin and I often have trouble sleeping, but we usually stick to watching TV or reading and avoiding the coffee." She motions to the cup in her roommate's hand.

"I'm not really planning to go back to sleep," she responds dismally.

Remi tops her cup off and heads to the table, setting up her laptop. "Work today?" she asks as she keys in the passcode to her work database.

"You know it." Daisy swirls the last of her coffee in her cup and then tosses it back in one large gulp as if it's a beer.

Strange, thinks Remi. If she were more into social situations, she probably would ask if something's wrong. But she decides instead she should keep quiet.

Daisy rises from the table, setting her used mug in the sink. Without another word, she turns and heads down the hall to her room. Remi hears the sound of the door closing behind her.

Really strange.

Remi quickly buries herself in her work, completely zoning out of the world around her. This happens often when she gets really into projects. Jonathon has yet to let her know the outcome of the audit, but she hopes to find out when she goes back to work Monday. For now, she's distracted with making sure the tax documents her team prepared for a company are completely in line.

There are a few mistakes here and there, probably from Jared, but when she gets to the line regarding charitable donations, her eyes widen a bit. The number is a lot larger than she remembers it being when they started the return a few days ago. She quickly minimizes it, and opens the spreadsheet the CEO sent her personally.

Sure enough, the number has almost doubled.

Giving her team members the benefit of the doubt, Remi quickly types up an email to the CEO, asking if there have been any changes or last minute donations he forgot to notify her of. For this particular return, she's supposed to be the point of contact, but he may have called when she was away from her desk, or pushed the wrong extension and spoken to either Jared or Lyle. All things aside, they really are a team.

She knows her email will probably go unanswered until Monday, so she skims the rest of the document to make sure everything else is in order. The company has been set to get a four figure tax return from the start, but with the change to the charitable donations amount, they're now set to get a five figure tax return. She'll just have to wait.

She's so into her work, she doesn't notice John is in the room until he clears his throat.

"Morning," he mumbles, heading straight for the coffee pot. He pours himself a cup, then begins looking around for Remi's sugar container.

"Morning," she replies, quickly noticing he's encountered the same dilemma she did. "I know, I couldn't find the sugar either."

John's more desperate than she was, and begins opening all the cupboards. He looks each one up and down before closing it. Remi watches from her place at the table, quickly saving her work and closing her laptop.

"Ugh," John groans, obviously giving up his search as he gulps his coffee black. "Yuck."

"Black coffee is the worst," Remi comments as she stands and heads for the fridge. She almost always makes breakfast on Saturday mornings, and today is no exception. Pulling out eggs, bacon, and English muffins, she turns and sets the oven to broil.

Her boyfriend slouches himself into the spot at the table previously occupied by Daisy, mumbling about how he wants sugar for his coffee.

Remi rolls her eyes. "I'll find you some sugar." She opens the cabinet that holds her baking supplies and begins to shift things around. She doesn't have any backup coconut sugar in here, but she does have some brown sugar. She grabs the bag and a spoon and places them in front of John.

"What's this?" he grumbles, his mind not yet fully awake.

"Brown sugar," she calls over her shoulder as she begins to separate and butter the English muffins.

"Blech," John replies like a little kid. "I want your coconut sugar."

"And just what did you do before you met me? I know you don't have any coconut sugar at your house."

"Before you I got plenty of sleep," John replies, and they both start laughing. Remi cracks the eggs in the pan as John relents and puts a scoop of brown sugar in his coffee.

Bacon, eggs, and muffins are Remi's favorite breakfast, and she's a pro at cooking all three things at once. So much so, she's done with the meal in a few minutes. She scoops a massive pile of eggs onto Johns plate, and puts half as much on hers. Each plate gets two strips of bacon and an English muffin.

She carries the plates over to the table and they both dig in.

"Did you get your work done?" John asks between bites of bacon.

She shrugs. "For the most part." She wants to tell John about the anomalies she found, but once again she keeps her mouth shut. She's never sure how far these confidentiality contracts reach.

"Want to go do something fun today?" he asks as he crams the last of his English muffin in his mouth.

"Sure." She nods, glancing down at her plate that's barely been touched. She isn't as hungry as she initially thought. "Did you have something specific in mind?"

A Cheshire cat grin spreads across John's face. "I was thinking someone might want to go...bowling." He emphasizes the last word, knowing the effect it'll have.

"Bowling?" Remi clarifies, her face lighting up like a Christmas tree.

Bowling is one of Remi's favorite indoor activites. She isn't very good, but she loves to give it a shot. And she absolutely adores the snacks.

"What are we waiting for?" she asks enthusiastically, dumping the rest of her food in the trash and putting both their plates in the sink. "Let's go!" She's practically jumping up and down in excitement.

John smiles. He loves when Remi gets excited about something as simple as bowling. "Put your shoes on, and I'll go change and we can go," he says as he turns and heads back to the bedroom.

Remi heads to the door, sitting down to slip on her pair of socks and her sneakers. She's on cloud nine.

John returns shortly, dressed semi-casually in nice jeans and a polo. "Want to go get an early dinner tonight? We can get tapas?" he asks as he slides on his socks and shoes.

Remi smiles. "Man, you are just spoiling me today!"

"Anything for my girlfriend," he replies, opening the door for her to walk through.

As Remi turns to make sure she has all her essentials, keys, wallet, and phone, she glances around the apartment and her eyes catch on something on top of the cabinets.

Way up high, in the area above the cabinet but below the ceiling, is her ceramic hippo bowl. The one that holds the coconut sugar.

"John," she asks as she closes the door and they make their way down the stairs. "Why did you put my coconut sugar on top of the cabinets?"

He looks confused. "Uh, I definitely didn't. That makes zero sense."

"Huh," Remi replies, confused. She isn't tall enough to put things there, and definitely wouldn't store her sugar up there. She makes a mental note to ask Daisy later. For now, she's too happy about the day ahead to let something stupid like coconut sugar get her down.

When they reach the ground level, Remi giggles as John holds out his arm for her to grab onto. "M'lady, may I escort you to the metro?"

"Why yes, sir, you can," she replies, her accent not nearly as smooth as John's.

They head down the road toward the train station, Remi on cloud nine as she considers the day ahead. She can't imagine how her life could get any better.

Or worse.

BEFORE

"I REALLY DON'T want to go out to dinner tonight," Rayna says, looking down at the three dresses Zeki has laid out for her.

"I already promised my buddies that we'd be there," he replies as he buttons up a white collared shirt.

Rayna sighs. "I wish you would've asked me."

Zeki rolls his eyes in annoyance. "I'm sorry I assumed eating dinner with me and my friends wouldn't be too much to ask."

She doesn't say anything back. She doesn't feel like going out to dinner tonight, but she especially doesn't feel like fighting with Zeki.

It isn't dinner that's the problem, it's that Rayna knows these friends of his. They're judgmental, and she has a feeling they don't like her very much. Not only that, but looking down at the dresses Zeki deemed "appropriate" for the evening's activities, all three are ones she considers uncomfortable. She keeps them in the corner of her closet because she doesn't want to wear them much.

"You know, it wouldn't hurt you to make friends. Jay's wife is a great person once you get to know her."

It's Rayna's turn to roll her eyes. "She's great if you consider liking Starbucks and dogs personality traits."

"You love dogs."

"But that's not all I talk about," Rayna snaps. This evening is already not going as planned. Her hand hovers over the skin-tight blue dress she knows she can't breathe in, and the black strapless dress she knows she'll be pulling up all night. She's already eliminated the red halter that requires a stick-on bra. She doesn't feel like messing with that. Not tonight.

It's been a long day. Daryl messaged her and asked her to come in for a last-minute shoot. Rayna agreed, but the shoot went long, meaning she had to rush home and change into her sweats as quickly as possible before

Zeki got home. She had just sat down on the couch with her conveniently opened bag of chips when he walked in the door. And then he immediately demanded she get ready for dinner.

Rayna hasn't even had a chance to shower this time, and she feels gross.

Zeki walks into the bathroom attached to their master bedroom to fix his hair. She lets out a breath she didn't even realized she's been holding. Since when has she become such a hermit, she wonders. She used to always love going out.

"You still haven't decided? You're going to make me late." Zeki returns to the bedroom and sits on the bed to put on his nice pair of shoes. Rayna finally picks up the skin-tight blue dress and puts it on.

It's a little tighter than she remembers it.

Zeki must notice, too, because he raises his eyebrows as he watches her inspect herself in the mirror. "Maybe you should go with the black one, babe?"

Rayna looks down to see her breasts popping out over her dress, and her small stomach pouch, accumulated over the past couple months of sitting on the couch, sticking out. "Nah, I like this one," she smirks.

She can tell he's unhappy with her answer, but with a glance at his watch he apparently decides to let it go. "Alright, well let's go."

"But my makeup." Rayna points to her face.

"Do it in the car," Zeki tosses over his shoulder as he heads down the stairs. She sighs and grabs her makeup bag. He's insistent tonight.

They drive to the restaurant in silence. Both of them feel the tension in the car, but neither of them truly wants to argue. There'll probably be a big fight when they get home.

Zeki parks the car in front of a fancy steakhouse, one of Rayna's least favorite places to visit. For some reason, eating a giant hunk of meat like a caveman just doesn't appeal to her.

They walk in arm in arm, a fake smile plastered on each of their faces. The other two couples are already there, and they all introduce themselves and give fake hugs and handshakes. Rayna is sick of these types of meetings.

There's Zeki's friend Jay, and his wife Julie—whom they've met and dined with before—then there's Mark and his wife Katie, who have apparently met Zeki previously, but this is Rayna's first time meeting them.

The host leads them to a large semi-private booth in the back of the room. Rayna doesn't mind being trapped in her seat, so she slides in first. Katie slides in directly across from her, and her husband slides in right next to Katie. He gives Rayna a funny look.

At least I won't have to discuss Starbucks and dogs the whole dinner, Rayna thinks smugly to herself. Julie has chosen a seat all the way at the other end of the table. They all look at the menu in silence.

"So," Jay speaks up, "how's the restaurant business these days Rayna?"

Rayna plasters a fake grin on her face. "I quit, actually."

Julie's ears perk up from all the way at the other end of the table. "Oh, really? Where do you work now?"

"Nowhere, I'm just staying home." Back in the day, Rayna would add that she was working on her fashion design career, but that's no longer the case. Rayna honestly has no idea what she wants to do anymore.

Zeki elbows her. "Rayna wants to get into fashion design, isn't that right dear?"

"Not anymore," she replies loudly, no longer caring if she embarrasses him. A silence follows.

"Well," Katie starts, obviously trying to save the evening that Rayna's ruining, "I just got a promotion at work, I'm officially the head nurse on my floor!" A round of congratulations follows. Mark is still looking at Rayna with an odd look on his face.

"Yes?" Rayna asks, making eye contact with Mark.

He shakes his head. "I feel like I've seen you somewhere before."

Rayna smiles, this sort of thing happens all the time. "You might have, I have a twin sister Remi, and she works in finance."

He looks perplexed. "Maybe that's it. I work in finance as well, at the Peterson firm."

"Interesting," Rayna replies, even though she's not interested at all.

Katie is now looking at her funny, too.

Rayna decides to ignore them and turns to look at Zeki, who's deep in conversation with Jay.

The server approaches to take their order.

Everyone around the table pretty much orders a steak and some sort of potato. Rayna orders the fish, and now everyone's giving her strange looks. This is why she didn't want to come to dinner in the first place.

"I need to go to the bathroom," Rayna announces rather loudly, sort of embarrassed that she chose to sit on the inside of the booth. But she can't take everyone ostracizing her anymore. Zeki and Jay stand up so she can climb out.

In the bathroom, she doesn't even bother going in a stall, she simply looks in the mirror and plays with her hair.

She checks her phone. Then she takes a few mirror selfies.

She must be taking too long, because soon Katie comes into the bathroom.

"They sent me to look for you," she announces as she heads into a stall.

"That's nice," Rayna replies. "Well, you found me."

Katie doesn't seem to get her sarcastic humor, because she doesn't reply, she just flushes and exits the stall to wash her hands.

"I've seen you before too, you know."

"It was probably my sister Remi," Rayna clarifies again. For living in such a big city, this happens a surprising amount.

"Nope." Katie pops the 'p' as she says it. "It was definitely you. I'd recognize those nails anywhere." She nods her head toward Rayna's currently red sparkle nails with diamond accents on the ring fingers.

"Okay...well sorry I didn't remember you then." Rayna is unsure where this conversation is going.

"Oh, you never met me. I recognize you from your videos."

"M-my videos?" Rayna feels her face drain completely of color.

Katie smiles, knowing she has the upper hand. "Oh yes, Mark and I thoroughly enjoyed that one you did with Mondo." She winks.

Rayna stands there open mouthed. She doesn't know what to say. This is her worst nightmare coming true.

"Zeki is a lucky guy. But I'm sure he already knows that." Katie dries her hands and holds open the door. "Shall we?"

Rayna heads mutely towards the door, turning to Katie the minute they were out. "Please don't tell Zeki about the videos."

"Oh, he doesn't know?" Katie seems flabbergasted.

"Uh, not yet." And hopefully not ever, Rayna adds in her mind.

"Sure honey, your secret is safe with me." The two of them begin walking back to the table. Just before they're in earshot of their friends she turns to Rayna and whispers, "but my silence is going to cost you."

Rayna gulps. Cost her what?

Before she can ask, everyone notices them approaching and begins to stand up so they can slide back in. The appetizers Zeki ordered for the table have arrived.

Rayna feels too sick to eat.

"You okay?" Zeki whispers in her ear when he notices her empty plate.

"I'm fine, just not feeling a hundred percent," she whispers back, noticing that across the table Mark and Katie are having a whisper session of their own. She grimaces as she considers what it could be about.

"Well, we already ordered so we have to stay for dinner, but we won't linger long, okay?" Zeki promises, placing a hand on her thigh.

Rayna nods. It's times like these when Zeki is sweet and gentle with her that she wonders how she could possibly have done what she did. Is doing.

When she looks up she notices both Katie and Mark staring at her with dumb grins on their faces. Great. Now Mark knows.

Rayna pulls out her phone under the table, keying up Remi's number in the text message app. She begins typing a message before she pauses, then back-spaces the entire thing. She wants to tell her sister what's going on, but how can she? Remi would be so ashamed. Rayna closes her text message app and slides her phone back in her purse.

She's on her own this time.

NOW

Rayna leads the detectives up the front walk and to her front door. It's locked, so Zeki probably isn't home yet.

She pulls out her key and slides it into the door. "Zeki?" she calls out as she pushes the door inward. "Zeki? Babe?" she tries again.

There's no response.

"I don't think he's home," she says over her shoulder to the detectives as they step through the door behind her.

"Did you call him?" Grady asks as she flips on the lights and surveys the living room.

Rayna nods. "Yes, but it went straight to voicemail."

"Did you guys have a fight this morning?" Detective Brown asks as the two of them begin poking around. Rayna feels nervous about having her things examined, but she has nothing to hide. Well, besides the fact she just discovered her boyfriend is a drug dealer this morning.

Suddenly, she has a moment of panic. Why did she let the detectives come over? What if they find his stash? He would kill her. What if the detectives think it's her stash? Perspiration breaks out across her forehead.

She doesn't know what to do. It's obviously too late to tell the detectives they can't look at the room Remi was staying in, but Zeki...

Who matters more? Remi or Zeki? her subconscious asks her.

"Remi," she answers, not realizing she says it out loud until both cops turn to look at her.

Oops.

"I mean," she tries to correct, "yes, we argued, but it was very minor, a normal couple argument." Rayna isn't very good at brushing things off. "Remi was staying in the room upstairs." She turns and leads them to the guest room. When she pushes open the door and flips on the lights, she winces as she realizes it's worse than she remembers it. The room looks like a hurricane blew through.

Grady lets out a low whistle. "What happened here?"

"This isn't all from Remi," Rayna tells her. "When I woke up this morning Zeki was tossing the room looking for something he lost. We argued because he thought I moved it."

"And just what was he looking for?" Brown asks as he slides on a pair of latex gloves.

Rayna thinks fast. "A picture his mom sent him of the family when he was little." She mentally pats herself on the back for that one. "There's no digital copy," she adds for good measure.

Grady doesn't bother slipping on gloves. Instead, she turns to Rayna. "I'm not going to lie to you, we probably can't get anything from this room. We need your boyfriend to come home so we can interview him about what the room looked like before he tore it apart."

Rayna nods.

"Does anything in this mess look like it belongs to Remi?" Detective Brown asks as he tiptoes over the clutter on the floor. Rayna looks around.

She often keeps her off-season clothes in the spare closet in order to keep the main closet in the master bedroom more open. All the clothes tossed on the floor appear to be hers, but honestly, Rayna has so many clothes she can't be certain. She kneels down to inspect a dark blue hoodie on the floor.

"Don't touch anything!" Detective Brown shouts, crossing the room quickly and using his gloved hand to push Rayna's hand away from the hoodie. Rayna shakes her head.

"It's mine. I thought I'd take a closer look." She sighs. "Honestly, my sister and I are so identical we wear so many of the same clothes—" Rayna's mind comes to a dead stop.

Remi's shoes.

She was wearing Remi's shoes.

Her mouth is so dry she can't even find the words to tell the cops where she's going, she just turns and runs down the hall to the master. She opens the door and flips on the light, pointing to the shoes haphazardly tossed at the end of the bed.

Detective Brown steps into the room and picks up one of the wedged sandals with a gloved hand. Both detectives look at her expectantly.

Rayna collapses to the ground before either detective can catch her. Tears slide down her cheeks at the site of the shoes.

"They're Remi's," she whispers. "I woke up wearing Remi's shoes."

Detective Grady kneels down next to Rayna. "And why were you wearing her shoes?"

"I don't know," she answers honestly. "Remi and I wear the same size, so in the past we'd switch clothes all the time. Back when we lived together." She wracks her brain for a reason, but comes up empty. "I can't for the life of me imagine why we switched shoes last night."

Detective Brown pulls a plastic bag out of his pocket and places the shoes inside. "What shoes were you wearing when you left the house?" he asks.

Rayna scratches her head. She has so many pairs of shoes. She furiously wipes the tears from her eyes and walks over to the closet, surveying her shoe organizer. These are just the closet shoes, she has another organizer down by the front door. There are no shoes missing from here.

Still unable to communicate fully, Rayna stumbles through her sentence and motions to the door. "I have to, check...by the front door," she musters. Both detectives follow her.

As she surveys her collection of shoes, she's shocked she didn't notice it before. Her favorite pair of gold sparkly slide on sandals is indeed missing.

"Size eight gold sparkly slide on sandals. They're the shoes I was wearing. And I think I know why we switched."

Both detectives look at her expectantly, not saying a word.

"My shoes were flats. Remi's were wedge sandals. She got too drunk to walk in heels, so I probably switched out our shoes so she wouldn't fall flat on her face."

Detective Grady jots down notes while Detective Brown types something in his phone. Just as they look up to ask her more questions, the sound of the garage door opening reaches their ears.

Zeki is home.

NOW

WHEN SHE OPENS her eyes again, Zoza is there.

"Zoza, I didn't know you were still around," Remi whispers as her oldest friend leans down to run her hand over Remi's hair. It's a comforting gesture.

Zoza doesn't say anything, she simply sits next to Remi in silence.

"How long have I been here?" Remi asks.

Zoza shakes her head, she doesn't know either.

It's still pitch black in the room, but for some reason Remi can see her childhood friend with ease.

"Do you think Rayna's looking for me?"

Her friend shrugs again.

"I hope she is," Remi mumbles. Everything seems surreal all of a sudden. Maybe this is a bad dream she'll soon wake up from.

Remi sits up and picks up the two empty water bottles still situated near her feet. She hasn't been given another one. Maybe she should pray to God again.

"Did you bring any water with you?" Remi asks.

"No, I don't drink water," Zoza replies, in a voice unfamiliar to Remi. In fact, it sounds nothing like the voice of her childhood friend. Or maybe, has it been so long she's forgotten what she sounds like? Remi shakes her head and pulls at the roots of her hair.

"I'm not crazy," she says out loud to herself.

Zoza looks at her, her eyes unblinking.

"You're not real! Get out of here!" she shouts, pushing in the direction of her imaginary friend. She pushes so hard she loses her balance and falls. When she looks up again, she's alone in the room.

She puts her ear back to the wall, listening for the mouse family. But there's no sound.

Remi sits back on her heels wondering how long she can take this.

Maybe being alone isn't as great as she thought.

"Zoza?" Remi calls out into the pitch black. Her friend doesn't reappear.

She climbs to her feet, intent on walking around the room to stretch her legs, when suddenly a square of light appears in the middle of the ceiling.

Remi's eyes burn, she's been in the dark so long. She squints through her lashes to see what's going on, just in time to see a what looks like a ladder being lowered into the room.

And there's a figure climbing down the ladder.

REMI

BEFORE

Rᴇᴍɪ's ᴏɴ ᴄʟᴏᴜᴅ nine all weekend. It seems as if nothing can damage her elated mood.

Until she walks into work on Monday morning.

At first, everything seems normal. She checks in with the secretary up front, and heads to the break room to slip her packed lunch into the fridge.

Then she heads for her desk. Immediately, she knows something is wrong. All of her drawers are open, and the large calendar that takes up most of the top of her desk is ripped up. As she inspects it more closely, she notices many of her pens and things littered about the floor.

"What the..." she mutters as she leans down to inspect the extent of the damage.

She hears a snicker and pops her head back up. Both Lyle and Jared are at their desks working quietly. Are they the ones that did this?

Remi begins to gather all of the odds and ends littering the floor. Most of her pens are broken, or separated into pieces, the ink cartridges strewn about.

As she pulls open her top drawer to put in the collection of pens she's gathered, she notices with absolute horror that the desk is filled to the brim with shredded paper. All her documents have been shredded.

She slams the pens down on the mess occupying the top of her desk and heads straight for Jonathon's door, only to be stopped short by a note saying he'll be out of the office on Monday and will return Tuesday. Figures.

Remi turns and heads back to her desk, noting from afar that Lyle and Jared seem to be whispering something. She narrows her eyes.

Picking up the trashcan that sits right next to her desk, Remi quickly sweeps her destroyed calendar into it. Even torn up, it fills the entire trash can. Without a thought, she reaches over and grabs Jared's trashcan and dumps the mess of the top drawer into it, effectively filling it as well. She places it back in its place next to his desk. He watches in silence, his eyes narrowed.

She narrows her eyes right back at him as she looks in her two other desk drawers. The top one, where she normally keeps pencils, pens, and her calculator, is empty. Mostly because the contents of this particular drawer now inhabit the floor. The calculator is alright and still functioning, but Remi will definitely need to buy some new pens and highlighters.

As she leans down to check out the state of her last drawer, she distinctly sees a look pass between Jared and Lyle, followed by Lyle covering his mouth with his hand and stifling what's probably a fake cough. They definitely seem guilty.

She glances back down at the drawer, finding it, like the one above it, also empty. However, this is much more serious, as this is the drawer that holds all her files.

The drawer is normally locked, with a key that only she and Jonathon have. She inspects the locking mechanism. It isn't terribly fancy and appears to have been jimmied.

Remi takes a deep breath and tries to not let it get to her. All her files are backed up on her work computer as well as her laptop. It will not take long to print out new hard copies. She's fine.

Keeping her face straight so Lyle and Jared won't know how much they got to her, Remi opens her computer and logs in to her work email address. Quickly, before she can lose the nerve, she sends an email to Jonathon about the desk destruction, and sends a carbon copy to both herself and HR. She can't wait to see what HR has to say about all this.

After sending the email, Remi unlocks her phone and begins to type up a quick text to John. When she finishes reading the message, she reads it through and realizes how crazy she sounds. She can't send that. She quickly deletes the text and sets her phone down again.

She turns back to her computer and logs in to the assignment system they all work out of, checking the documents that need reviews or calculations. She selects a few and begins her work.

It's hard without a working pen, and after a few minutes of trying to process numbers without scribbling them down, Remi heads to the secretary to see if she can borrow some supplies.

The young woman is on the phone when she arrives at the desk, and Remi waits patiently for her to finish.

"How can I help you?" the woman asks as soon as she hangs up.

Remi smiles. "Something happened to my desk, and I was wondering if you had a couple pens and a notepad I could borrow?"

"Oh no!" The secretary immediately opens her desk drawer and rummages through. Handing Remi two pens and a stack of pink post-it notes. "What happened to your desk?"

Remi shrugs. "I'm not sure, but it was rummaged through and a lot of my things were destroyed."

"Should I call security?" The young woman already has her hand on the phone.

Remi shakes her head. "No, I think it was just a practical joke thanks to my desk mates. They think they're so funny."

The secretary moves her hand away from the phone. "Who are your desk mates?"

"Jared and Lyle."

"Ah, yes, Jared can be a joker sometimes." The secretary smiles fondly as she says Jared's name, leading Remi to believe she probably knows him outside of work to some degree.

"Yes, he is," she agrees, to keep the peace. The secretary is obviously on Jared's side.

"Well, let me know if you need anything else. I have a supply closet for general use. Not much in it besides pens and printer paper, but you're welcome to whatever you find in there."

She smiles. "Thanks, I appreciate it."

"No problem." The secretary smiles as Remi heads back to her desk with her newly acquired supplies. It's nice of her to offer the supply closet, but the pens she gave Remi are the cheap ones that come in one hundred packs. Great for companies, but definitely not for Remi. She'll hit the office supply store on her way home.

The rest of the day passes uneventfully, and silently, as it seems no one in the office other than the secretary wants to talk to her. Remi has always been a loner, but people do usually say hello when she walks into the break room to take her lunch. Today, no one says a thing.

Probably because they saw your desk and now think you're nuts, her subconscious reminds her.

Remi shakes the thought out of her head as she slides her messenger bag with her work laptop over her shoulder and heads for the door.

As she steps in the elevator, her phone starts to ring. She glances at the screen to see who it is and sighs in dismay, as it's "private caller" once again. Remi lets it go to voicemail. She doesn't have time to deal with whatever idiot is crank calling her.

She makes her way to the Office Max conveniently located only blocks from her office. She picks out new pens, pencils, highlighters, and a new calendar. She has to admit, as much as she hated having her desk vandalized, she absolutely adores picking out office supplies.

Remi pays for her purchases, then rushes back over to the train station just in time to catch the last express train. If she took half an hour longer she would have to take the normal train, which has twice as many stops.

She sits on the train in silence, looking out the window as the city speeds by. She thinks about texting Rayna, but she doesn't know what she would say to her, either. They haven't spoken in weeks, and Rayna would think she's nuts to worry about a few crank calls. She does text John, though, and he says he'll pick up dinner and be over in a bit. He's such a great guy.

Remi steps off the train at her stop, her messenger bag still over her shoulder and the giant bag of office supplies draped over her other arm. Perhaps buying the large desk calendar on her way home from work wasn't the brightest idea after all.

She lugs her stuff the couple blocks to her apartment, turning the corner just as John is stepping out of his car with a pizza in his hands.

"Great timing," she comments, lifting her heels so she can give him a peck on the lips.

"I know." He smiles back, following her up the stairs to the apartment.

They step inside quietly, just in case Daisy's sleeping. Remi has yet to figure out her roommate's hours, but they're strange for sure.

She sets her bag down on the kitchen table so she won't forget to grab it when she heads into the office tomorrow. Then she goes to the cabinet to grab plates.

She opens the wooden cabinet door, only to step back in surprise. The cabinet is empty.

She closes it, and then opens it again. But nothing is there. All the different varieties of plates that usually inhabit the cabinet are gone.

Remi turns and opens the cabinet next to the one that held the plates, to see it's full of its usual contents, mugs and glasses.

"That's odd," she whispers to herself. She just did the dishes last night. Maybe Daisy used all the plates today?

The sink is empty. Remi leans down and slides open the dishwasher. Also empty. Where are all the plates?

"John?" she calls over her shoulder, going back to stand in front of the empty cabinet.

"What?" he calls back, walking into the kitchen behind her.

"Did you move the plates?"

He stops walking when he's behind her, staring at the empty cabinet. "Um, I certainly didn't move all of them," he answers.

He steps over to the side and does the same action Remi just did, opening the cabinet that holds the cups. Seeing that those are there, he takes it a step further and opens the next cabinet over, which usually holds Tupperware. That cabinet, too, is full to its normal capacity.

Following her boyfriend's lead, Remi reaches down and begins to open the lower set of cabinets, only to find them all full of their usual contents as well. How odd.

"Let me go ask Daisy," Remi mutters. She heads down the hall, leaving John to stand and stare at the empty cabinet.

As she's walking down the hall, her phone buzzes once more and Remi picks it up to see it's once again listed as 'private caller.'

She huffs and presses talk. "Hello?" she grumbles into the mouthpiece.

Once again, all she hears from the other side of the line is heavy breathing. Remi doesn't even bother saying hello again, she just hangs up and knocks on her roommate's door.

"Daisy?" No answer. "Sorry to bother you." She knocks again.

Still no answer.

Remi opens the door just a smidge. Daisy's room is empty. She opens the door a little further and glances around. Everything looks exactly as it did on the day Daisy moved in. In fact, it looks nearly undisturbed.

"Daisy?" she tries once more, for reasons beyond her own understanding. But when there's once again no response, she closes the door quietly and heads back down the hall.

John is in the pantry grabbing paper plates.

"What'd she say?"

Remi shakes her head. "She wasn't home."

John cocks an eyebrow. "That's odd. Did she take all the plates with her?"

She glances back at the empty cabinet again. Remi owns two full sets of dishes, each set complete with eight each of salad, dinner, and dessert plates. It'd be pretty heavy to transport them all.

"Maybe." She sighs, giving up. "I'll have to ask her later."

John slips an arm over her shoulder and leads her back to the living room. "Think of it this way, you won't have to do dishes later."

Remi shrugs. "I guess you're right, I just prefer to save the environment."

"Well guess what, we can watch Planet Earth, will that make you feel better?"

She laughs. "I guess that's fine."

John dishes them each up a slice of pizza and a breadstick, and they sit back on the couch eating in comfort. They end up watching Planet Earth until ten, when Remi's eyes start to close of their own accord.

"Guess I better head to bed." She stands and gathers the trash, glancing at the front door, which has remained closed all night. "Guess I'll have to ask Daisy about the plates tomorrow."

John nods and takes the trash and leftover pizza from Remi's hands. "You go to bed, babe, I'll clean up and be there in just a moment." He leans over and gives her a kiss.

Remi smiles and walks down the hall to bed, stopping only at the bathroom to briefly brush her teeth. When she arrives at her bedroom, John passes her as he heads to the bathroom, giving her another kiss on his way.

She strips off her clothes and steps into bed. Her eyes droop of their own accord and she's asleep before John returns from brushing his teeth.

RAYNA

BEFORE

IT's still dark in the room when Rayna rolls over to check her phone. She can't tell if the darkness is due to it being night, or just because of her blackout curtains. Her phone says 4:00, which is completely unhelpful. She unlocks it and goes into the clocks app to find out for sure. Yep, it's four in the afternoon, she's slept all day again.

Rayna leans back on the pillows, debating if it's even worth getting up now. It'll be bed time in a few hours anyway.

Zeki's side of the bed is empty, but she can't bring herself to care.

She looks at her phone screen, devoid of messages and notifications of any kind. She doesn't have any friends.

Rayna pulls up her texting app, scrolling through the messages until she finds her sister's name. The last text they exchanged was over a month ago, and she isn't sure what to say. She finally decides to stick to the basics.

RAYNA: Hey. How's the roommate?

It doesn't take long for her sister to respond, which is slightly unusual considering she should still be at work.

REMI: I barely see her, which is great I guess?

RAYNA: What else is going on?

She watches as the little gray bubble indicating Remi is typing pops up. It stays up for a few minutes, and Rayna mentally prepares herself for a novel.

REMI: Not much, John and I went bowling this past weekend.

That's it? That's the novel? Rayna rolls her eyes and types back.

RAYNA: You and bowling LOL

REMI: Yep, what are you up to?

Rayna sets the phone down on top of the comforter as she debates what to say. What can she even say? That her life is falling apart and it's her own damn fault? No, she can't say anything. She picks up the phone again to type in her nonchalant response. As she's typing, another message pops up on her screen.

DARYL: Need you 2nite. U around?

Rayna doesn't even have to think about it.

RAYNA: No. Busy.

She switches back over to her message to Remi, figuring that will be the end of it, but another message quickly interrupts her once more.

DARYL: Plz. They want u.

Rayna rolls her eyes and ignores the message. He'll figure it out eventually. She switches back to the text to Remi for the third time.

DARYL: Cmon u owe me.

When she sees the message, Rayna screams in anger and tosses the phone against the wall. She doesn't even care if it breaks. Who is this guy? Saying she owes him!

She sits in silence, waiting for Zeki to come ask what the noise was, but he never appears. He must still be at work.

Rayna sort of wants to watch TV, but she and Zeki don't have one in their bedroom, and she doesn't feel like heading downstairs. Getting out of bed is futile at this point. She closes her eyes and tries to drift back into dreamland, but it's worthless, her body doesn't need any more sleep.

She debates getting out of bed. But then she doesn't. That's where Zeki finds her hours later.

He walks into the room and flips on the light, giving her an incredulous look when he notices she's still in bed and obviously undressed.

"Did you even shower today?" He wrinkles his nose in disgust.

Rayna rolls her eyes and debates pulling the blanket over her head like a little child. "I didn't do anything today, therefore I'm not sweaty and can't possibly smell," she retorts.

He steps over to the closet, obviously somewhat annoyed, and begins to strip out of his work clothes.

"I can't believe I have to work all day and all you do is sit on your ass."

Rayna rolls her eyes. "You're the one who told me to quit all those months ago."

"Yeah, but I assumed you would do something. Clean the house, cook, grocery shop, anything but lay in bed all day," he calls angrily from inside the closet.

"Hey, I do plenty around here!" She feels her rage boiling.

"Oh really, like what?" He pops his head out of the closet as he slides a t-shirt over his head. He's already replaced his work slacks with basketball shorts.

"I do laundry." Rayna can't lie, she really doesn't do much, but she does at least make sure she does the laundry once a week.

"Oh, whoop dee do." Zeki rolls his eyes and heads over to the door. As he does, he passes her phone lying on the floor. He picks it up and glances at the screen.

Uh oh.

"Who the fuck is Daryl?!" Now he's seething.

Rayna tries to think of what the text could possibly say. She hopes it doesn't give anything away. She crosses her arms across her chest.

"If you must know, I was looking at jobs and Daryl is an old patron from the restaurant who said he may have one for me."

"Oh, really?" Her boyfriend cocks one eyebrow. "And what sort of job is this?"

"I didn't really get that far," Rayna lies.

"Then why is he saying he will pay you double this time, hm?"

Crap. She wracks her brain, trying to think of something, any sort of excuse. "I worked for him back in the day before I met you. He's offering me double what he used to pay me." It rolls off her tongue easily. Phew.

Zeki chucks the phone at her head and it's only thanks to her quick reflexes that she ducks. "Well, either take the damn job or start doing something around here. I swear to God, if I come home and find you in bed again..." His rant fades as he heads down the hallway. Rayna isn't sure if there's an end to the threat or not, but she really doesn't want to find out.

She picks up her touchscreen phone from where it landed on the bed, touching the screen to make sure it still works. It does.

As much as she wants to hate Zeki for the fight that just happened, she understands. It's probably infuriating for him to spend all day at the bank, then come home at six p.m. to see she hasn't even gotten out of bed yet. She'll try to do better. She can watch YouTube videos and make recipes. That will probably make him happy.

She sighs and slips out of the bed, pulling on a pair of sweats and a t-shirt she's pretty sure is hers. She glances toward the en-suite master bath, debating taking a shower, but decides against it. Sounds like too much work.

She glances at her phone screen, debating what to do. She really doesn't want to work for Daryl anymore. She just can't. Every time she leaves that hotel she feels absolutely horrible. Scratch that, she feels absolutely horrible all the time these days, it seems.

Rayna looks in the mirror, touching the bags under her eyes. No matter how much she sleeps, they're always there. Her hair isn't perfectly done like it used to be. And she hasn't put on her signature eye makeup in months. In fact, besides dinner the other night, she hasn't really done anything regarding her appearance in months.

"Alright girl, pull yourself up. Whatever this is you think you are doing, it has to stop." She chuckles at the fact that she's talking to herself, but she hopes it will help.

She follows it up with a few deep breaths, like her mother used to make her take when she was angry. She can do this.

Tomorrow she'll start looking for jobs, and if things go bad, she can always go ask for her old restaurant job back—she left on good terms.

She won't need to work for Daryl anymore. The money was great but this feeling isn't worth it. She's done this before.

But you've always had Remi to help, her brain reminds her.

"So what?" She looks at her reflection again. "You don't need Remi. You can do this on your own. You can." She adds a slight growl at the end of the sentence. Actually, it's more like a pathetic whimper, but she'll make it a growl.

Tomorrow. Tomorrow is the day she'll start turning her life around.

NOW

S HE SITS AWKWARDLY on the couch while the two detectives stand. They're all waiting for Zeki to walk through the door.

They wait a few minutes, and nothing happens. He doesn't walk in. Rayna feels something isn't right.

"Uh, we had a fight, maybe he doesn't want to come in..." she says quietly as she crosses the living room and opens the door connecting with the garage.

It's empty.

She doesn't notice the detectives have walked up behind her until Detective Brown says, "he probably saw the cop cars. I bet they spooked him."

Both of them push past Rayna and look out the open garage door and down the street. The car is nowhere in sight, meaning Zeki probably didn't even pull into the garage at all.

They turn to look at her. "Why would your boyfriend not want to come home?"

Rayna sighs. "I told you, we had a fight this morning. Maybe he thought I called in a domestic violence?"

"Did he hit you?" Grady obviously doesn't believe this excuse.

She shakes her head. "No, but you saw the room."

Both of them continue to stare at her. They don't believe one word she's saying.

Rayna glances up at the ceiling. She knows what she's about to do will change her life forever. She pinches her eyes shut and interlaces her fingers.

"Zeki thought Remi...uh...stole his drugs?"

"Maybe we better go inside and sit down."

Rayna doesn't realized her hands have started shaking, but when she looks down she can see she's trembling. What's wrong with her?

She nods and follows the detectives back to the couch. Once she's situated, the questioning begins.

"How long have you known your boyfriend was into drugs?"

"I swear," Rayna takes a deep breath, "I just found out this morning when he was tearing up the room."

"You had no idea? No indication?" Grady speaks to her with a firm tone, and Rayna has a feeling she isn't on her side anymore.

"He told me he was a banker. I mean, I guess he always made plenty of money, but I just assumed..." She trails off, unsure where she was going with the sentence. "Oh, God. Do you think he took Remi?"

Neither of the detectives speaks. They glance at each other, then turn their attention back to her.

"Do you think he took Remi?" Detective Brown cocks one of his eyebrows.

She drops her head into her hands. "I...I don't think so. I mean..."

"You said Remi and Zeki had never gotten along."

Cold realization rolls over her entire body. Does Zeki hate Remi that much? No. It isn't possible.

She shakes her head. "I mean, they don't get along, but I can't imagine Zeki would hurt her. He knows how much she means to me. We're twins, after all..."

Detective Grady's phone rings from her pocket and she turns and walks to the kitchen to answer it. Rayna continues to stare at the empty doorframe, hoping it's good news. Detective Brown continues to observe her silently.

Finally, Grady walks back in, hanging up her phone. "We need to head back to the station."

Detective Brown nods in acknowledgment.

"What? Why?" Rayna asks pleadingly.

"There's been some new developments," Grady clarifies, "and we would like you to come with us."

Now, Rayna isn't dumb, she's seen cop shows. "Am I under arrest?" It sounds more feeble than she intended.

Grady shakes her head. "No. We would just like to ask you more questions. You can leave at any time. And if anything changes, we will notify you."

She feels like that's a sort of round-about answer, but it doesn't seem she's in serious trouble or anything, so she stands and heads to the door to slide on her sandals.

The ride to the station is uneventful. Neither cop speaks, and Rayna has a feeling that's because they don't want to discuss whatever this 'new development' is with her.

When they arrive, she's led inside to a waiting room with a couch, a soda machine, a water jug, and a stack of magazines. How homely. They tell her to make herself comfortable, then they leave the room, shutting the door behind them.

Rayna looks around at the white walls and scratches at her hand nervously. She picks up a magazine, but she can't seem to focus on any of the words. All she can think of is her sister.

She tries closing her eyes and relaxing. She tries to summon up Remi in her mind like she's seen in all the movies. She pictures her sister and tries to see if she feels any different. Nothing happens. Nothing comes to her.

She and Remi have never shared that twin ESP thing everyone talks about, so Rayna isn't surprised she can't sense anything now. Growing up, her parents always tried to test it, but even though they looked alike, their brain waves must've been on completely separate wavelengths. Try as they might, they could never communicate or sense things about each other. And that hasn't changed.

With a sigh, she pulls her phone out of her pocket, only to see there were no texts or notifications on the screen. Zeki is in the wind, and she doesn't really have any other friends.

The door to the room opens and a tired-looking John is pushed through. Rayna feels her eyes narrow.

"You! This is your fault!" she yells before she even realizes what she's doing. She launches herself at him.

He artfully dodges her attack. "Whoa, whoa, settle down. I've been cleared. That's why I'm in here with you."

Rayna is still seething, but she takes a couple of deep breaths. "Cleared?" she mutters through gritted teeth. "How?"

John sighs and sinks down onto the couch. "I have an alibi."

"Oh really, who?" She's still furious.

"Patrice, my, uh, my wife. I went to her place after seeing Remi last night."

"You asshole," Rayna yells, her anger fully renewed. Her hands are in fists at her side. Assaulting John will not help her right now, and she knows that.

"Listen," he says, holding up his hands, "it's not what you think."

"Oh, so when you say wife you don't mean you've been cheating on my sister for years?"

"No, it's—" John runs a hand through his dark hair. "We got married really young, and we've been separated for years. I was about to go through divorce proceedings when I met Remi, and well, I swore I would tell her but I just fell in love so fast, and then it was too late and—"

"And you're an idiot."

He nods. "That, too."

"So just when were you going to tell her?" Rayna crosses her arms, notices she's still standing, and sits down awkwardly on the other end of the couch.

"I thought Remi was a fling. I never thought two years later I'd still be here." He lets out a breath. "Patrice and I don't talk, I mean I assumed she'd found someone else. But then she called me up last week, wanted to fix things." He looks up at her. "I, of course, said that wasn't possible. She started asking why, and well, I've known her for a long time and I started telling her about Remi and... God I fucked up," he grumbles.

"And what?" she presses.

"I went and saw a lawyer earlier this week to have her served divorce papers, and, well, she won't sign them. She really wants to fix things. I was just about to take things to the next level, where I divorce her anyway, when I guess she decided trying to ruin things between Remi and me was the easiest way to get what she wants."

This story still doesn't add up to Rayna. "Why does she suddenly want you back after three years?"

John looks down at his lap, taking another deep breath before continuing. "My mother loved Patrice, but my dad trusted my judgment. When we got married, my parents updated their wills and left everything to the two of us collectively as one unit. Anyways, fast forward a couple years and my parents meet Remi. My dad realizes she's perfect for me—much less drama than Patrice—so recently, a couple weeks ago, he goes and has their wills updated, leaving everything just to me and any offspring I may have. And well, even though my mom is happy with Remi, I guess she felt some sort of loyalty to Patrice and called and told her."

"So she wants the money?"

"My parents are old, they had me when they were nearing fifty, and, well, they're not in great health. Patrice knows that, and I think she just wants to prolong the marriage to get her share. Which of course is making me want to end it all the more quickly. I was going to tell Remi...but then you know what happened."

Rayna nods. "I'm still mad at you for lying in the first place, and you're definitely on my shit list, but I'm not as mad at you as I was last night."

John presses his lips together in frustration. "I appreciate the half forgiveness but all I can think about is Remi. What if she doesn't make it and the last thing we did was fight over a lie I'd been telling for years?"

"Don't you dare say that," she seethes.

"Say what?"

"Remi is fine." Rayna feels her hands clenching into fists once again. "I just hope this isn't your fault and she ran away because she was pissed at you."

He shakes his head. "You know as well as I do it's not like Remi to run away. She always faces her problems head on."

Rayna doesn't say anything. He's right.

"Maybe your shithead boyfriend kidnapped her."

She gives him a look. "And why would you say that?"

"Zeki and Remi were enemies and you know it."

"Zeki wouldn't hurt a fly," Rayna argues, but her words aren't even convincing to herself.

John raises his eyebrows. "You sure about that?"

She doesn't get a chance to answer before an officer Rayna hasn't met opens the door.

"Hello John, Rayna," he acknowledges them both, then slides into the room, coming to sit on the sofa between them. "I'm Officer Leary." He shakes each of their hands in turn. He opens the cover of an iPad in his arms. "Have either of you met Daisy, Remi's roommate?"

He looks at Rayna first and she feels color creep up her neck. "No," she mumbles, embarrassed. "I should have. I promised I would, but things got away from me recently." She feels her eyes welling with tears as guilt fills her heart.

Leary doesn't seem to take any notice and turns to John.

"Yes, I've met her a few times."

"Do you have any information on her, last name, where she came from, where she works?" Leary is making notes in his iPad.

John shakes his head. "I didn't know her all that well, but she seemed to work a lot wherever it was she was at."

"Did Remi have her sign a rental or lease agreement?"

His eyebrows furrow. "Remi was a big paperwork girl so I imagine so, why?"

Leary closes his iPad and looks between the two of them. "She hasn't returned home yet and there are no personal effects in the room. We are just trying to find her to talk to her."

Both of them nod, making eye contact.

"If Remi did have a rental agreement, it would be in her desk or filing cabinet in her room," John volunteers.

The officer nods. "We have people looking there now." He stands. "If either of you think of anything else, I'm just down the hall. Grady and Brown should be in to check on you in a bit."

And with that, the door closes once more.

Rayna feels her eyes drooping as her adrenaline from all the events of the night starts to crash. Her mind is still wired, but she leans back on the couch and closes her eyes.

"How can you sleep at a time like this?" John accuses.

"I'm not sleeping," she responds, "just resting my eyes."

"Oh, God," John mumbles.

Her eyes snap open. "What?"

"Remi used to say that all the time!" He puts his head in his hands, distraught.

Rayna has never been good at comforting people, and she feels really awkward sitting there not knowing what to do or say. Luckily she's saved when the door opens once more and Grady pokes her head in.

"Rayna, I need you to come with me."

She stands and follows the officer out of the room.

NOW

H ER EYES ARE unaccustomed to the light, so the figure leaning over her is as indistinguishable as a shadow. She squints, trying to get her bearings.

"God, is that you?"

There's a chuckle from somewhere in the room. Are there two of them?

She feels a foot in her side as the shadow uses his foot to try to shift her.

"Didn't take her long to go nutso."

"It never does."

Remi can't tell where the voices are coming from. She can only see the one shadow, but wait, are there two?

The shadow closest to her picks up her empty water bottle collection. "Well, she drank all the juice."

"Give her some more."

"You sure?"

"Positive."

Remi's head hurts from the brightness of the light, so much so she starts to miss the darkness. For some reason she feels like she should be getting up to run, but for the life of her she can't remember why she wanted to run in the first place.

"You know, she's different than I remember."

Remember? Has she met the shadow before?

"Toss me another water. We probably gotta feed her something soon."

"Here's a protein bar."

She hears a crunching sound that, for some reason, makes her smile. She vaguely remembers being concerned about something, but now she can't remember what. She's still squinting through slitted eyelids as the shadow retreats. The ladder is withdrawn from the light, and it's once again dark.

Remi realizes she's lying on her back, but can't find any of her former energy to get up and explore. Even rolling to her side seems like too much work.

She stretches her arms out in either direction as if she's making a snow angel, and her fingertips brush something cool.

Water!

She shifts a tiny amount to wrap her hand around the bottle. Using all her strength, she lifts her head and chugs the water.

As she sets the bottle back down, her hand encounters something else. It's rectangular and crinkly. Ah! The protein bar!

Her hands are shaky as she rips open the packaging. Vaguely, her sub-conscious reminds her she must not eat too fast. Remi wonders where that thought came from, but decides it's better to not ignore it. She nibbles small bites of the bar. It tastes like something she can't place, but at this point any food to calm her raging stomach is a godsend.

After finishing the bar, Remi lowers her head to the ground once again. She'll remember what she needs to remember later, she's sure of it...for now...what she really needs is some sleep...

BEFORE

O N WEDNESDAY MORNING Remi takes the train to work as normal, excited about all the new office supplies she set up at her desk yesterday. Although she was initially upset that her desk was destroyed, she has to admit getting new supplies felt great.

Walking into the office, she nods to the secretary, makes a pit stop in the break room to stow her lunch, and heads to her desk as usual. She sits down and smooths out the wrinkle that has appeared in her brand new calendar. Glancing at the day, she notes there are no appointments or meetings scheduled, which means more time to work uninterrupted. Which is a blessing in an office as big as hers.

Remi boots up her computer, glancing out of the corner of her eye as both Jared and Lyle arrive for their work days and take their respective desks. She didn't have time to talk to Jonathon yesterday about what happened on Monday, but she intends to make a stop at his office today.

She pulls up the spreadsheet she's currently working on, pulling the matching document from her shoulder bag. She begins the tedious process of transcribing the document into the spreadsheet, double checking to make sure all her numbers match.

Time passes quickly, and before she knows it, her stomach is growling to remind her it's lunch time. Remi slides the document she's working on into her desk drawer, then heads to the break room to grab her packed lunch. Jared and Lyle's desks are already empty, and she secretly hopes they chose to go out today so she won't have to see them in the break room.

Her prayers are answered as she walks into the break room and finds it empty. At least she can eat her lunch in peace. Remi opens the fridge and shifts around the myriad lunches, looking for the brown bag with her name on it. She shifts some more but doesn't see her lunch bag. Has someone moved it off of the second shelf? Remi quickly searches through the top shelf and the bottom shelf, but she still can't find her lunch.

Something is wrong. Remi always packs her lunch, and she distinctly remembers setting it on the second shelf this morning. She packed a Tupperware of leftover lasagna from last night. She wouldn't forget about lasagna.

Remi stands up and closes the fridge, before opening it again and searching once more. It's no use, her lunch isn't there.

She begins to look around the employee break room. There's a coffee maker on a counter, with cabinets filled with supplies. She opens every single one but finds nothing more than the usual cups, plates, and plastic utensils. She opens the freezer above the fridge, but finds it barren except for a tray of ice cubes, which she's sure hasn't been used in decades. The center of the room is occupied by a long table surrounded by a dozen chairs. Remi surveys them all but finds nothing sitting on or under any of them.

All that's left is the corner by the door, which is filled with a water cooler and large trash can. Remi walks over to the trash can and peers inside.

She's obviously late for lunch, as the trash is already filled with various stinky remnants of food, but there, peeking out from behind a half eaten quesadilla, is a brown paper bag, and Remi can just make out the large RE printed on the front. She doesn't have to dig in the trash to know that's her lunch. Someone threw it away.

Remi groans and sits down at the table in frustration. Why can't Jared and Lyle just leave her alone? The prank calls she can handle, but destroying her desk and her lunch? Now they're going too far.

Blinking back tears, Remi hurries over to Jonathon's office, keeping her head down in case anyone were to see the angry flush in her cheeks. She doesn't want people to know she let Jared and Lyle get to her over some lasagna.

The door to Jonathon's office is closed, and Remi knocks lightly twice and then listens for him to tell her to come in.

There's no sound from the other side of the door. Feeling like an idiot, Remi crouches down and looks through the half inch of space between the door and the carpet. She can't see much, but she can tell the office is completely dark. Jonathon isn't in.

With a sigh, Remi turns and begins to head back to her desk, but as she does, something catches her attention.

It's Jared and Lyle, they're by the secretary's desk and they're laughing at something that must be really funny. As Jared leans over to catch his breath from laughing so hard, Remi notices there's a third man standing right behind him.

It's Jonathon. And he's also laughing, obviously in on the joke.

Feeling like she's been utterly betrayed, Remi rushes back to her desk, slamming her documents in her shoulder bag as fast as she can while simultaneously powering down her computer. She needs to get out of here, and now.

As she turns to leave her desk, she notices Lyle and Jared returning to theirs. Remi keeps her head down and walks out without acknowledging either of them. Bypassing the elevator, lest she run into someone else she would rather not see, Remi darts down the two flights of stairs to the floor HR operates out of. She pushes the door inwards to a quiet hallway. She glances each way to verify no one is coming, then she slides down to the floor to catch her breath.

She probably sits there for about five minutes, just breathing deeply, when she hears a door slam down the hallway. Remi quickly stands and brushes off her clothes, slipping her messenger bag strap over her shoulder once more. She begins to walk down the hall towards the HR office.

As she approaches the office, she notices the door is open a crack and she can hear voices from within. Remi stands with her back up against the wall, waiting patiently for whoever is talking to finish.

She doesn't mean to listen in, but suddenly she realizes she recognizes one of the voices. It's Jonathon.

"Yeah, I don't know what's going on with her lately, but she's leaving the office early often and it's starting to affect her team."

Wait. Is Jonathon talking about her? Remi feels her breath stop.

"I understand, Jonathon. I'll try to call her in here to talk, but you have to understand, leaving early a couple times is not a fireable offense. In fact, in her contract, as long as the work is done and she's in here five days a week, there are no stipulated hours that she has to occupy that desk," answers a female voice belonging to the HR director.

"I hired her, and now I'm telling you this isn't working," Jonathon replies angrily.

"And I'm telling you Jonathon, her record is squeaky clean. I can discuss her performance with her and issue her a warning, but you can't fire her over this."

Remi can't believe what she's hearing. Jonathon is trying to fire her? Why?

Suddenly, everything clicks. Remi went to him when she found someone stealing money. He insisted he would take care of it. She hasn't heard anything since, and now, now he's trying to get rid of her. Jonathon is the one stealing from the company.

As the realization hits her, she knows she has to get out of there, and now. As quickly and as quietly as she can, she rushes back to the stairwell door and slides inside. She's on the eighth floor, but she doesn't care, she runs the entire way down the stairs and rushes through the main lobby. Once she's outside she doesn't stop, she practically runs all the way to the train station.

She doesn't relax until she's seated on the train in the furthermost available corner seat.

What is she going to do? Her manager is stealing from Johnson Finance. Who can she even tell?

BEFORE

I T'S BEEN NEARLY three weeks since her revelation. And Rayna has yet to find a job.

She still has the money from her last video, but it's dwindling, and fast, mostly because she lied to Zeki and told him she asked for her job back at the restaurant, when in fact she didn't.

The harassing messages from Daryl have only increased. When she first discussed this with him, he insisted she could leave at any time, just do one video and be done. Now his tone has completely changed and he's insisting she owes him another video.

Rayna does the dishes as she promised she would, planning what she's going to make for dinner. She's told Zeki that things aren't good at the restaurant these days so she isn't making much. He believes that, at least.

Rayna just hates lying. She hates that she has to pretend to leave for work every night, then go sit in the Starbucks down the street until it closes at ten. Then she slowly makes her way home and thinks of stories to tell her boyfriend about how work was.

The truth is, she has tried to get her job back, but they told her it's too slow right now, and to come back in a few months. But Rayna knows she can't afford to wait that long.

As she loads the dishwasher and presses start, she tries to think of a way she can 'quit' her fake job again. But nothing is coming to her.

How did she get this far?

It all started when you stopped living with Remi, her mind nags her.

Rayna wants to disagree, but she can't. If she were living with Remi, her sister would never let her go down this path.

Is that why you stopped talking to her?

Rayna pushes the pesky thought away.

Her phone buzzes from its spot on the island. Rayna dries her hands and picks it up—fully expecting it to be another text from Daryl.

Instead, she's surprised to see an unknown number instead. She clicks on the message:

555-970-8556: Hey it's Katie, Mark's gf. We really enjoyed dinner the other night.

Something is off, Rayna can feel it, but regardless, she saves the new number as a contact in her phone and types out a reply.

RAYNA: Hi Katie. What's up?

Katie's reply comes through so fast that Rayna knows she must've already had it typed out.

KATIE: I want you to come to a party with me tonight.

Rayna looks at the message. She hasn't been to a party in awhile, and that would be a nice change rather than sitting at the Starbucks all night... Oh crap, Katie probably wants Zeki to come! That would ruin everything.

Rayna begins to type out a polite declining message, when another message pops up on her screen, interrupting her typing.

KATIE: Just you. No Zeki. Remember you owe me.

That's weird. She doesn't want Zeki to join. Maybe this is a girl's party? The thought makes Rayna's heart pick up in pace. She always loved parties back in the day, and she really does need to get out... Before she can change her mind she quickly types her reply.

RAYNA: Sure. Just tell me when and where to meet you.

Katie texts back an address with '9pm' tacked on the end. Rayna tells her she'll see her there, then closes the texting app on her phone. She'll still have to lie to Zeki about why she'll be home late.

Rayna quickly pulls up her banking app and checks to see how much money is left. There's still almost a thousand dollars. She can just tell Zeki she's supposed to work a private party and that she'll be home late. As long as she comes home with a couple hundred dollars, she's sure he won't question it.

She heads upstairs, excited to pick out what she's going to wear tonight. It's been so long since her last party, she doesn't even know where her party clothes are stashed. Rayna flips through everything hanging in the master closet, and doesn't see anything there. Thinking back, she hasn't been to a party since before she moved in—meaning she probably never unpacked them.

Quickly she rushes back down the stairs and out to the garage, to the stack of boxes in the corner with her name on them. She quickly opens each box until she finally finds the one filled with her mini skirts, skimpy halter shirts, and cute crop tops. Oh, how she has missed these outfits.

After heading back upstairs with an outfit tucked under her arm, she tries it on and models it for the mirror. She's gained some weight in the last few months, but she has to admit she still looks good.

Glancing at the clock, she realizes it's almost four in the afternoon, and Zeki will be home at any minute. She quickly slips her black button-up server shirt over her top and takes off the skirt—tucking it in her purse for later—and slides on her black slacks. Then she heads into the bathroom to put on makeup.

That's where Zeki finds her when he arrives home an hour later.

"Your makeup looks nice," he says as he walks in, giving her a peck on the cheek.

"Thanks." She smiles and continues to line her eyes with her black eyeliner.

"Seems a little overboard for waiting tables, if you ask me." He starts unbuttoning his work shirt.

"I'm working a private party tonight. I won't be home until late." She's shocked at how easily the lie slides out.

"That's good. You'll make extra money for it right?"

"Of course," Rayna replies as she finishes the eye liner and starts applying her mascara. She's almost done.

Zeki doesn't say anything else as he slides on his basketball shorts and heads back downstairs. Rayna figures she'll find him in front of the TV.

With a sigh, she begins to pack up her makeup bag, realizing she doesn't have time to cook dinner as she originally planned. Her fake work shifts start at six p.m.

She quickly sticks a few makeup touch-up items into her purse and zips it closed. She then realizes she can't leave wearing the sparkly gold sandals she wants to wear to the party, so she grabs a larger purse and transfers her essentials, piling them on top of her heels. Then she slides on her work loafers and heads for the door.

She passes Zeki on her way out. "Don't wait up, the private party doesn't start until nine." It isn't totally a lie.

"I won't," he responds, not even glancing up from the TV. Wow, things have changed.

Before she can change her mind about it, Rayna leaves, locking the door behind her.

NOW

RAYNA IS LED to a cement room with a table and one way mirror. Definitely some sort of interview room, she figures. She's seated at the table across from Grady and Leary.

"Am I under arrest now?" she asks. Can't be too careful around the police.

"No," Detective Grady answers as she turns the file on the table toward Rayna. "We are here to talk about Zeki."

"Did you find him?" she asks hopefully.

Grady shakes her head. "No. But can you tell me more about him?"

"I mean, I thought he was a normal guy until this morning, now I'm not sure anything he told me is true." Rayna puts her head in her hands. She really thought she was above being fooled like this. Apparently she was wrong.

"Can you tell us where you met Zeki?"

She nods. "At a party, almost four years ago now."

"What kind of party?" Leary interjects as he appears to take notes on his iPad.

"A house party of sorts." Rayna cringes as she remembers her most recent house party experience. What she wouldn't give to make that a night she can't remember.

"Did you ever meet any of his friends?" Grady asks, glancing down at the papers on the table.

Rayna nods. "At a dinner a few times. They weren't really my favorite but there was Katie," she mentally grimaces at the name, "her husband Mark, then Jay and Julie." She hasn't seen the last two since their dinner months before, but she assumes they still talked to Zeki.

"Do you have any last names?"

She wracks her brain. "Sorry, but...no..." She's a horrible girlfriend. She should know her boyfriend's best friend's last name.

"Any indication that any of them, Zeki included, were selling and/or using?" Officer Leary doesn't even look up from his iPad, he just continues to type.

"Zeki, no. I'd never even seen him handle drugs before. I had no idea he even knew how. I don't hang out with Jay and Julie much, but Katie and Mark...they were definitely using."

"Using what?" Detective Grady asks.

Rayna tries to push the intruding memory away. "Cocaine. And before you ask, yes, that is exactly what Zeki was apparently selling."

"Is Zeki his full name?"

"I think so." Rayna actually isn't sure. It's becoming very apparent to her that she doesn't know her boyfriend of three years at all. But the more she thinks about it, the more she realizes that they haven't talked, or even been intimate, in almost three months.

"You think so? And you dated how long?" Leave it to Officer Leary to be judgmental.

"You're right, I'm dumb. I just realized I don't actually know who Zeki is. I've been spending the past year so wrapped up in myself and my problems, I've barely talked with him." She leaves the being intimate part out, but she's sure the police can connect the dots.

"So what have you been wrapped up in?" Detective Grady sets down the file in her hands. Rayna catches a quick view of Zeki's smiling face in a mug shot before she looks away. That's another thing he never told her.

"I've...well..." Rayna figures now is the time to be honest with herself. "When I moved out of Remi's place, I fell into a deep depression. I quit my job. Most days I didn't even get off the couch." She sets her head in her hands and closes her eyes. "Zeki tried to encourage me to get out and do things, but I didn't make it easy." She decides leaving out her porn stint is best for everyone.

"And how do you feel now?" Leary asks, setting his iPad down. He's probably worried she's going to off herself or something.

"Better," she acknowledges, not wanting to go into the nitty-gritty details with these strangers.

"Good to hear." Leary picks his iPad back up. "And I know I asked you earlier, but you never met Daisy, correct?"

She nods. "Correct."

"Did your sister say anything about her? Any personal details that might help us find her?"

Rayna shakes her head. "My sister and I, well, the past few months we haven't talked as much as before. And now I'd do anything to go back and do it over." She fights back tears.

Neither officer says anything, they just look at each other and stand up. Rayna follows suit.

"We are going to take you back to the waiting room now. Hopefully we will find Zeki here shortly and can finally make a little leeway on the case." Detective Grady holds open the door for Rayna, then leads her back to the waiting room. Rayna can see on the clock that it's almost four in the morning, and her body knows it, too.

Detective Grady must read her thoughts, because she motions to the couch in the small waiting room. "You're welcome to lie down. If we don't find your boyfriend soon, I'll have an officer take you home. You have to understand, we will be staking out your house until we find him, though."

Rayna stifles a yawn. "I understand." She makes her way to the couch and lies down. She's just begun to drift into dreamland when the sound of the door opening brings her back to reality. She looks up to see Detective Brown leading John into the room. John nods at her and then politely takes a seat on the floor, leaning his back against the wall.

She doesn't really feel like talking, but she decides to make polite conversation anyway. "How did your interview go?"

"Fine." John's eyes are closed as well. "Detective Brown is nice. I just wish I had more information to give."

"Information?" Rayna mumbles sleepily.

"Yeah. They're really trying to find Daisy. I described her to them but I really don't have any personal information."

"I thought they were looking for the lease?" Rayna can feel herself perking up a bit as she recalls the earlier conversation. Maybe sleep isn't as close as she thought.

John nods. "They found it. Problem is, everything on it is fake."

Rayna sits up. "Everything?"

"Yes. Even the name, Daisy McMullen, doesn't exist in their database. Not to mention the social, prior address, and all the references aren't real."

"I thought Remi vetted her carefully?" Rayna's fully awake now.

"I thought so, too," he agrees. "I can't imagine what could've happened to let this slip through."

"Do you think Remi was distracted?" she questions.

John shakes his head, his eyes still closed. "She was on top of it as always." Suddenly his eyes and nose scrunch up as if he smells something bad.

"What?"

"I just remembered. Some weird things started happening when Daisy moved in."

"Weird things?" She sits up on the couch, staring directly at John. He opens his eyes and nods.

"Yeah, some stuff went missing."

"Stuff where?"

"In the house. Some things were just moved first, then stuff, like dishes, was straight up missing." They both seem to come to the same conclusion at the same time, and John jumps to his feet and heads for the door. "I'll go tell the officers."

Rayna watches quietly as John leaves the room. Remi never mentioned the missing things around the house, nor any doubts about the new roommate. It makes her wonder what else Remi forgot to mention…

NOW

Remi has grown quite accustomed to dreamland. In fact, she's beginning to enjoy it more than the reality that meets her when she wakes.

She's right in the middle of a new dream. Well, it isn't really a dream, more of a memory. She's on the swings outside of her elementary school. She's trying to swing as high as she can, but her little legs can only pump so fast.

Suddenly, she feels a pair of hands on her back. She turns around to find her sister standing there, ready to push her.

"I can help." She smiles sweetly.

Remi doesn't say anything back, she simply nods. With her sister's assistance she begins to swing higher and higher.

And then she's falling, she reaches around her to try to grasp anything she can—

Remi jolts awake. It's still dark in the room she's in. But something has changed.

A hand touches her face, making her jump and try to move away, but her back is already against the wall.

"Such a beautiful girl. Shame you ended up here."

She tries to clear her head, tries to focus on where she's heard that voice before, but it's no use. Her head is filled with mush. Her arms and legs are lead, her lips glued together. She isn't sure she's even awake at all anymore. Zoza stands in the corner, a hand raised to her lips in the "shh" motion.

There are more sounds, as whoever is in the room with her stands up and begins to move away. She hears the sound of footsteps on the ladder as she drifts off, back to her same dream.

She's on the swing, trying to get just a little bit higher...

"Why did you leave?" her sister asks her from her spot behind Remi.

"I didn't," she replies as she feels the warm sun on her face, "I'm right here." Why does Rayna think she isn't there?

"Come back, Remi."

She turns to find her sister is no longer pushing her on the swings. Now where has she gone?

The sun is no longer in the sky, the playground cast in shadow. There are no other children around. The swing comes to a slow stop.

The playground is getting darker and darker...

Then it's pitch black. Is she still in her dream?

BEFORE

S HE PUSHES OPEN the door to her apartment and steps inside quietly. It's late and she doesn't want to wake Daisy in case she's sleeping after a work shift.

Remi slips off her Toms and sets them in the shoe organizer by the door. Her work laptop is still in the messenger bag slung over her shoulder. John called her while she was on the train. He could tell she was upset, and suggested they meet for an early dinner before she headed home.

They met at the French restaurant down the street and ordered a Beef Wellington to share. It was delicious, though it didn't do much to help with her stress over work.

She debated telling John about her work revelation, but decided against it at the last minute. She needs to try to figure this out on her own first.

As she starts to head down the hall toward her room, she passes the kitchen, and figures she had better set the timer on the coffee maker for the morning. Even though her career could be coming to an end, she'll continue to show up for work until it does.

With a sigh, she flips on the kitchen light, pinching her eyes closed as the fluorescents momentarily blind her. When she opens her eyes, she zones in on the counter the coffee maker usually inhabits.

It's empty.

That's odd. Remi is a regular coffee-aholic, and she never puts the coffee maker in the cabinet.

Calm down, it's not the end of the world, she thinks to herself as she leans down and opens the cabinet where she keeps all the small kitchen appliances.

It's completely bare.

The cabinet usually holds her toaster, can-opener, and blender. None of which are there. Remi sits back in shock. Where is all her stuff disappearing to?

Pulling her phone out of her pocket, she checks the time to see it's already almost ten p.m. As much as she wants to look into this tonight, she still needs to send an email before she can go to bed.

Remi stands up and shuts off the kitchen light, shaking her head in confusion. It's all too much, the crank calls, her stuff disappearing, the fact that her boss is stealing from the company and is now trying to fire her to cover it up. When will she ever get a break?

Passing Daisy's room, Remi makes a split second decision and knocks on her door.

"Daisy?" She listens to see if she can hear movement from the other side of the door. "Daisy, you home?" she tries again.

When there's no response the second time, she slides open the door and glances inside. The room is dark and the bed sits perfectly made on the other side of the room. There isn't any sign her roommate has even been home in recent days. Remi sighs and slides the door shut.

She debates texting Daisy. After all, she does have her number. But at the same time, she's afraid of coming off as an overbearing landlord. She can ask Daisy about her stuff the next time she sees her.

As she pushes open the door to her own room, her phone begins to vibrate in her pocket. Glancing at the screen, Remi sees the words "private caller" and rolls her eyes. She tosses the phone on her bed without answering it and heads over to her desk.

She sets up her computer in its usual spot and opens it up to begin her work. First, she makes copies of all the files she found, downloading one to a flash drive, and the other to her hard drive. After she ejects the flash drive, she signs in to her email account and begins typing.

It takes awhile to get it just right, but finally she feels it's done. Sliding open her desk drawer, she pulls out her new hire file from when she was first hired at Johnson Finance. She turns to the back page and begins to type in all the email addresses she finds there. She has never met anyone higher up in the company than Jonathon, and she only hopes one of these people will have the authority to do something.

She takes a deep breath and presses send. Hopefully she'll still have a job after this. Picking up the flash drive, she pulls out an envelope from her desk drawer and slides it inside. Now she just needs to think of somewhere safe to keep it. Who does she trust?

The answer comes to her instantly, and Remi seals the envelope and fills out the mailing address. She doesn't bother putting her address in the left-hand corner. She places a postage stamp in the right-hand corner. Glancing at her phone, she notes it's already past eleven. No matter, this has to be done.

Grabbing her phone and keys, she makes her way back down the hallway and out the front door. The mailbox isn't far, but Remi is nervous enough to glance over her shoulder as she walks. When she reaches the mailbox, she grips the envelope tightly, lets out the breath she didn't know she was holding, and drops it inside. Remi looks around, then quickly makes her way back to her apartment. Her phone begins to vibrate in her hand again. The screen lights up with "private caller."

Even though she knows she shouldn't, she lifts the phone to her ear. "Hello?"

"I'm going to kill you, bitch."

Then the line goes dead.

BEFORE

THE HOUSE IS in a nicer part of town. Not that Rayna and Zeki live in a "bad" part of town, but they definitely don't have a gate and security guard in front of their house, either. The house isn't a massive mansion, but it certainly isn't small. It has the hard edges of modern homes. And the door is twice the size of a normal one, with a massive metal handle to match. It reminds Rayna somewhat of a castle.

"Name?" the security guard asks as she approaches the gate.

"Rayna Casell," she replies, trying to steal a glimpse of the clipboard in his hands. He quickly moves it toward him and away from her view.

"Come right in." He presses a button and the gate swings inward.

Rayna makes her way up the cobblestone walk, marveling at the incredible detailing. Whoever's party this is, they definitely have money to spend.

She reaches the double-wide door and raises her hand to knock, but then notices it's open a crack. She can't help but look around to see if there are any instructions or notes or anything. There aren't, so she pushes the door open and steps inside.

The house is just as marvelous on the inside as it was on the exterior. The walkway has a high ceiling that's lit by the most beautiful chandelier Rayna has ever seen. She can hear laughter coming from the kitchen, so she slips off her shoes and sets them in the pile growing by the door at the foot of the double wide staircase. Everything about this house is double what she's seen in any other house.

Turning the corner into the kitchen, she's met with twenty or so blank stares.

"Hi, uh, I'm Katie's friend Rayna."

One of the gentlemen standing by the massive island in the middle of the kitchen shifts his wine to his left hand, approaching Rayna with his right hand outstretched. "I'm Hugh, nice to meet you. Katie went to the washroom, but she should be right back."

As soon as he finishes speaking, the conversation in the room picks up once more.

"Thanks, Hugh, this is a beautiful house you have," Rayna says as she observes the impressive kitchen. Black granite countertops sparkle in the lighting, and the large island is filled with every sort of hors d'oeuvre imaginable.

"Thanks. You must thank my wife, Melanie, the interior was all her." Hugh notices her eyeing the food. He picks up a small china plate and hands it to her. "Here, help yourself to whatever. Water is in the fridge, and see my bartender Jack if you want something a little stronger." He winks at the last word, then quickly turns his attention back to the man on his other side.

Rayna looks over to the corner of the room to find a wet bar situated with a bartender behind it. She's sure her mouth is permanently agape as she makes her way over.

She's almost reached the bar when Katie intercepts her.

"Rayna! You made it!" Katie squeals as she embraces Rayna in a hug.

Rayna just stands there awkwardly. After all, this is only the second time they've met. Seems a little too soon for hugs, in Rayna's book. She leans back and takes in Katie's party attire. She's smartly dressed in a black midi skirt paired with a red lace bralette that barely keeps her decent. The heels she wears are gold and sparkly, matching well with Katie's platinum blonde hair. Rayna notices a faint smudge of white powder beneath Katie's left nostril.

"Hi...Katie..." she mumbles in slight confusion. Did Katie really think she wouldn't show up?

"Good! You found the alcohol! Let me handle this!" She approaches the bartender, a five dollar bill held crisp in her manicured hand. "Jack, can you be a dear and make my friend and me two white gummy bear shots? Then after that, we'd each like a prickly pear spritzer."

"Sure thing, ma'am." The bartender smiles and begins pouring various liquors and juices into a shaker.

"What's a prickly pear spritzer?" Rayna asks, feeling a little dumb that she doesn't know.

Katie laughs. "Prickly pear is the food of the gods. It's a plant that grows on a cactus in somewhere like Arizona I think… Anyways, it's Jacks specialty." She smiles and winks at the bartender in a flirtatious way that makes Rayna wonder just how well she knows this bartender. As if realizing how that sounds, Katie quickly elaborates. "Jack is Hugh's permanent bartender. He's here for all the parties, and Hugh throws them about once a month."

"Once a month?" Rayna asks, wide eyed.

Katie nods. "Yep. He works from home, so I think he gets bored not seeing people on the reg. Plus, why have a massive house like this if you can't show it off all the time?"

"What does Hugh do?" Rayna asks as a shot glass is placed in her right hand.

"He's some sort of software engineer." Katie motions to the shot glass in Rayna's hand. "Bottoms up."

Rayna tosses back the shot, tasting the familiar sweetness of pineapple juice along with the burn of vodka. She hasn't taken a shot in years, and it instantly warms her stomach and reminds her of the party days of her past.

Before she knows it, the empty shot glass is removed from her hand and a frosty glass filled with a bubbly purple liquid is placed in it instead. She holds it up to the light and inspects the way the drink seems to sparkle.

"That's the secret," Katie whispers. "No one knows just how he gets them to sparkle like that."

Rayna looks over her shoulder at Jack, who's cleaning a glass. He winks at her.

"Come on." Katie pulls Rayna's arm. "Let me introduce you to everyone."

She pulls her back toward the kitchen and begins pointing people out and saying their names. She's going so fast, Rayna can hardly keep up, much less remember the names she's tossing towards her. Various people stand as they're pointed out, and make eye contact or nod politely at Rayna. She tries to nod politely in return.

"And this," Katie turns to a man standing by the side, "is Roger." The man is tall, towering over six feet. He's slim, with tan skin and a hard jaw line. He has light brown hair that doesn't quite match his dark skin tone.

Katie reaches over and whispers something in his ear. A smile spreads across his face.

"Why Rayna, it is a pleasure to meet you. I must say, you must've charmed miss Katie here, as this is the first time she has brought a guest to one of Hugh's parties."

Rayna's brow furrows. "You don't bring Mark?" she asks.

Katie shakes her head. "These are my friends, and, well, Mark isn't really into partying."

She nods in pretend understanding, sipping at the drink in her hand. Katie is right, it is delicious.

"So Rayna, what do you do?" Roger asks politely, taking a drink from the bottle of Corona in his big hand.

"I'm actually between jobs right now, but I used to be a server." She takes another nervous drink from the glass in her hand. Roger makes eye contact with Katie and snickers.

What is that about?

"A server, what restaurant? Maybe I've seen you there before."

Rayna mentions the name of the steakhouse, observing suspiciously as Katie and Roger seem to have a silent conversation. What's going on here? Before she can ponder it further, she finds another shot glass in her hand.

She turns and sees a smiling woman. "Hi, I'm Melanie, Hugh is my husband. Welcome to our house." Melanie clinks her own shot glass with Rayna's as Roger and Katie hold up theirs as well.

Why are they giving us shots? Rayna wonders as she tosses her second shot back. She's going to need to slow down. She won't be able to explain to Zeki why she came home drunk from work.

Conversation flows easily as the three women make their way around the room. Katie seems much more at ease than she was at dinner. Rayna wonders if it's due to her being around her friends, or if it's the influence of alcohol.

She continues to sip her drink as Katie jokes with Melanie about something that happened a few months ago. Rayna feels really out of place. It doesn't seem like Katie really needs her there, and she wonders why she was invited in the first place.

"So, Rayna, what do you and Zeki like to do for fun?" Melanie asks, obviously trying to keep her engaged in the conversation.

"Uh," Rayna realizes she doesn't actually have much of answer. She scrambles quickly to think of what would be a normal activity for a couple to do. "We like to go...out..." She mentally winces at how dumb that sounds.

If Melanie notices, she doesn't show it. "Nice, anywhere in particular? Hugh and I are a fan of Crocodile downtown."

She takes another nervous sip of her drink. Her glass is already almost empty; that isn't good.

Katie seems to notice her predicament and quickly interjects, telling Melanie about their night out as a group. Rayna inspects the bottom of her glass. It's been awhile since she's had much to drink, and she can already feel her senses becoming a bit fuzzy.

"Did you like the Prickly Pear Spritzer?" Melanie asks.

Rayna nods. "It was different, I've never had anything like it before."

"Jack and I spent a long time perfecting the recipe. Now it's top secret information." She winks.

Another shot is placed in Rayna's hand. Katie has one in her hand as well. "Cheers!" Katie calls out, clinking her glass with Rayna's.

Instead of drinking it as she did the past two, Rayna discreetly dumps the shot into her already empty glass, then places it down on the table next to some other seemingly empty glasses.

Katie seems to immediately notice the lack of drink in Rayna's hands. "Let's get you a beverage." She pulls Rayna toward the bar, her grin a little lopsided. "Jack, can you be a doll and make us some more shots? Oh, and a margarita." She leans on Rayna's arm and stares at Jack in a way that leads Rayna to believe Katie is becoming quite intoxicated.

Jack makes eye contact with her. She mouths 'no shot,' to which he nods briefly before beginning to add liquor to his shaker.

A moment later he hands her a salt-rimmed margarita, complete with a mini umbrella. Katie picks up her drinks, downing the shot almost immediately and setting the glass back down.

"C'mon Rayna, let's go meet my friendssss."

Katie is definitely drunk now. Rayna smiles and nods, following her back to the kitchen.

"Hey everyone!" Katie says as she walks into the kitchen. Everyone seems to be involved in their own side conversations and no one acknowledges her. This doesn't faze Katie, she simply walks over to the island and grabs a fork from next to the food spread. She bangs her fork on her margarita glass unceremoniously. "Hey!" she yells again.

This time she gets a response, at least from the group of people standing in a small circle near the island. "Yes, Katie?" asks a guy whose name Rayna can't remember.

"Let's go to the hot tub!" She's speaking in a much louder than normal voice, but doesn't seem to notice.

"Sure, let me go turn it on," Melanie pipes up from the other side of the room.

Rayna can feel herself start to get nervous again, and she leans in close to her friend's ear. "I didn't bring a swimsuit," she says quietly.

Katie doesn't seem fazed. "That's okay, just go in naked, after all, you do *porn*."

The room falls silent at Katie's last word. All eyes are on Rayna. She can feel the heat creeping up her neck.

"I...uhh..." She doesn't know what to say. Her hands start to shake.

"Oh, come on, I'm sure everyone here would like to see," Katie continues, too drunk to see the distress she's causing.

Luckily, Melanie notices Rayna's predicament. "Alright everyone, there're two bathrooms down the hall if you need to change for the hot tub, or feel free to use the guest room to the left! Katie, can you and Rayna come to the bathroom with me?"

It isn't the best save, but it's as good as she's going to get. Rayna quickly grabs Katie's hand and follows Melanie up the stairs. Katie stumbles multiple times. Rayna is practically carrying her by the top.

"I love you guys sooooooo much," Katie gushes as they pause in front of what Rayna assumes is Melanie's door. Rayna looks between to two women in front of her.

"Maybe I better take Katie home," Rayna suggests as Melanie opens the door and leads them into a beautifully decorated beach-themed master bedroom. Katie sighs and lies down, face first, on the bed.

Melanie nods. "That might be best. I'm sorry to see you leave so early, though."

Rayna shrugs. "I think it's better if I do leave, I uh...already caused enough drama." She motions to the door. Although she's embarrassed, she's relieved to notice she doesn't feel the same shame she did at dinner weeks before.

"You really don't have to, trust me, no one here is going to judge you." Melanie smiles sweetly. "Lots of us have had unique jobs at some point. A job doesn't make a person."

"Thanks." She debates staying at the party longer, but one look at Katie and she knows her friend needs to get home. "I appreciate the invite, but I'd really better get Katie home. How did she get here?"

"Her husband always drops her off."

Rayna nods and crosses the room to tap Katie on the shoulder. A muffled "hmf?" comes from her nearly limp form.

"Katie, can you dial Mark on your phone? It's time for us to leave," Rayna presses sweetly. She isn't used to being the motherly type in these situations. Usually she's the one passed out on the bed. In fact, she was always the one passed out on the bed, until today.

"Okay." Katie pops her head off the comforter and clumsily pulls her phone out of her bra. She begins to repeatedly try to type in the password, but she keeps getting it wrong. Rayna sighs and takes the phone from her hand.

"What's the password?"

Katie giggles. "Seven, seven, seven, one."

Rayna doesn't see anything funny with that, but she types it in and begins looking through her contacts to find Mark. Melanie steps into the bathroom, presumably to change into her bathing suit.

She finds Mark's name and presses dial. The phone is picked up on the third ring. "Hey, babe."

Now Rayna feels awkward again. "Hi Mark, this is actually Rayna, I'm at the party with Katie and she needs to be picked up."

"Oh, she okay?" His demeanor changes immediately.

"Yes, she's fine, just a bit intoxicated." She hears the sound of keys jingling in the background.

"I'm on my way." The line goes dead.

Rayna takes a deep breath and sits on the bed. She was right, this party was such a bad idea.

Melanie steps back out of the bathroom, clad in a cute yellow bow tie bikini. Rayna feels immediately envious of her flat stomach and visible six pack. She thinks briefly of her body's current state and admits she needs to get back into shape. She isn't fat by any means, but the weeks of sitting on the couch are definitely starting to show.

"I'm going to head out back, can you guys find your way out okay?" Melanie asks.

"Of course." Rayna smiles. Even though the party isn't her thing, she really does like Melanie.

"Good. It was great meeting you. I really hope you'll come to another party."

"I'll try," she replies, but deep down she knows she probably won't be at another party of any sort any time soon.

Melanie waves and turns to head down the stairs. Rayna pulls out her own phone and pulls up her text message conversation with her sister. She hasn't responded in weeks.

RAYNA: Hey. Sorry I didn't get back to you. Miss you tons.

She types out the message and looks it over. It doesn't sound like her, that's for sure, but at this point she isn't even sure what *does* sound like her anymore. She presses send. She pulls up a word game on her phone to play while she waits for a response.

Remi usually responds to texts very quickly, so Rayna is surprised when her phone still hasn't buzzed ten minutes later. It's then that she notices the time. It's past midnight, Remi will already be in bed.

Well, at least I tried, she thinks.

"Hello? Rayna?" calls a male voice from downstairs.

Katie doesn't show signs of moving, and her breathing is even. She's probably asleep.

"Up here!" Rayna calls, hoping he'll know what that means.

A disheveled Mark appears in the doorway. It looks as if he tossed his clothes on in a hurry, his jeans wrinkled and his polo shirt only half tucked in. His hair is askew. Rayna is a bit taken aback; it looks like he's been drinking as well, though it didn't sound like it on the phone.

"Thanks for calling me, Rayna." He starts walking toward the bed. His steps are slow and deliberate, making Rayna nervous.

"Uh, yeah, she was having a great time, then she uh, just passed out, er—" Rayna is cut off as Mark reaches the bed and leans in over her. Rayna tries to scoot back, but instead ends up in on her back with Mark looming over her. He leans in to her ear, effectively trapping her below his body as he breathes his alcohol-tinged breath in her face.

"You know, Zeki is a real nice guy. Think he would let me take you on a date?" He smells putrid.

"I don't think so," she rasps out as she tries to get as far away from his foul-smelling breath as possible. "I don't think Katie would like it either."

"Psh." The way he says the sound sends spit flying into Rayna's face. She reaches her hand up to wipe it off, but finds there's barely any room, as Mark is now just inches from her face. "Katie doesn't mind sharing me."

"Uh, are you sure?" Rayna asks, trying to buy time to figure her way out of this mess.

"Uh-huh." Mark hiccups and falls to the side, allowing Rayna to finally sit up straight.

She stands to try and put as much distance between her and Mark, but before she knows what's happening he grabs her hand and pulls her into a kiss.

Rayna nearly retches at the smell of him so close to her nose, and quickly pulls back from his embrace. As she does, her eyes come into contact with the wide open eyes of Katie.

And she is not happy.

"I need to leave," Rayna stutters as she wrenches her arm from Mark's vice-like grip. She turns and runs from the room. She nearly trips on the top step of the double wide staircase, cringing as she catches herself on the banister. It takes her a minute to pull open the massive door and duck out into the night. She runs down the driveway to the gate, still hearing the sounds of laughter coming from the backyard.

TWO

145

NOW

S HE BURSTS INTO the briefing room, slightly embarrassed that she's late, but she has a good reason. All eyes are on her.

"Sorry everyone, what've we got?"

Detective Leary, the head detective on the case, shakes his head. "That's what we were just saying, we've got basically nothing."

"Nothing?" she questions, sliding into a chair next to her partner Brown.

"Nothing. We caught the boyfriend of the twin, Zeki, a few hours ago trying to board a plane to Mexico. Brought him in for questioning. Turns out, he had no idea Remi was even missing, he was fleeing purely based on the drug dealer confession to the girlfriend."

"Are you sure?" Grady knows she sounds combative, but feels it necessary to ask.

"Very. Had an alibi for all of the hours since she's been missing. Turns out he spent the night at a party, dealing. Everyone there accounted for him. After the fight with the girlfriend, he headed straight to the bank to withdraw money, then to the airport. All accounted for. Lawyered up pretty fast, so we didn't get many details."

"Why flee then?" It's Brown who speaks up this time.

Leary shrugs. "I'm not one hundred percent sure, but my guess is, he expected the girlfriend to turn him in. Honestly didn't seem like much love lost there—considering he confessed, then immediately prepared to jump ship."

Grady makes notes on her iPad. It seems Zeki and Rayna haven't been on the same page with their relationship. She makes a mental note to ask about it later.

"And the roommate, Daisy," Leary continues, "she's in the wind, and it's a fake name, fake previous address. And all the numbers she filled out for references are no longer in service."

"That's why I was late, actually," Grady interjects. "I just spoke to the boyfriend of the victim, John, and he said that in the last few weeks a lot of things have gone missing from the apartment."

"Such as?" Brown asks from beside her.

She flips her iPad to the notes she just took. "Looks like a stack of plates, a coffee maker, and some other small kitchen appliances."

"That's odd," says one of the other officers from where he leans on the wall.

"Very," Leary agrees, "but let's take it as a clue. Brown, do me a favor and look into past reports of petty theft. I don't know why small kitchen appliances could ever be worth anything, but I've been surprised before."

Brown nods and flips his iPad case closed. "Will do."

With that, it seems like the meeting has ended, as many of the officers in the back begin to exit. Grady stands as if to leave.

"Grady, wait a minute," says Leary, motioning for her to come closer to him.

"Yes, sir?"

"I'm not buying that this girl didn't have any enemies. Pull phone records, look at her social media, whatever you have to do. Someone was out to get this girl, I just know it."

Grady nods. "Yes, I agree one hundred percent. So you've decided this isn't a random kidnapping?"

Leary shrugs. "I think it's way too carefully planned to be random. This girl was taken from her home and no one saw or heard anything?"

She thinks for a moment. She's seen it happen before, but she doesn't want to disagree with her boss. "I'll do my best to look into it, sir."

"Thanks, Grady."

She nods in acknowledgment, then heads for the door. Although she isn't quite as sure that this isn't a random kidnapping, she does know one thing. The quietest people often have the most dangerous enemies.

NOW

THE OUTSIDE AIR burns Rayna's bloodshot eyes as she leaves the precinct and heads toward the subway station. The sun is barely rising, making everything appear in a pinkish hue.

She can't believe she's leaving the station without her sister. She was so sure this was just a misunderstanding, and that they would find her and she would be home by sunrise.

Rayna doesn't know where to go. She could go back to the house she lives in with Zeki, but she knows the cops have tossed the place. It isn't even really home for her anymore, anyway. She thinks about going to the place she shared with Remi, but then she knows she'll feel more ineffective than she already does. Finally, she decides to go to the only place she knows she can relax: her parents' home.

Suddenly, Rayna realizes they may not even know Remi is missing yet. Everything that went down in the past few hours started at ten p.m. Her parents are usually in bed by nine with their phones on silent. They have to wake up at five for their respective jobs.

She reaches into her pocket to check the time on her phone, and as if on cue, the phone vibrates in her hand and her mother's number illuminates the screen.

"Hello?"

"Oh my God, Rayna! I just woke up and I saw the message from the police. Remi is missing!"

Rayna takes a deep breath. Dealing with their over-dramatic mother is never easy. "I know, mom. I just left the police station."

"The police station! Why? Did they find her? Do they know where she is?" The questions come rapid fire without any room for response in between. Her mother is clearly about to hyperventilate.

"Mom, I was just talking to them, the police don't know anything yet.

Can you hand the phone to dad please?" At least her father will be able to discuss things rationally with her.

"Hi, honey," her dad's voice says over the line. "Now tell me what's going on."

"Dad, Remi is missing. They have no idea what happened to her."

She can hear her father's sharp intake of breath over the phone line. "When did this happen?"

"The police aren't sure. Remi and I went out last night, then she stayed at my place. She never made it home this morning." Rayna stops walking at the top of the empty steps leading down into the train station. "Listen, dad, I'm about to get on a train, but I'm headed your way. I'll be there in fifteen."

"Okay, we will see you then," he responds somberly, and the line goes dead.

It's almost twenty minutes later when Rayna arrives at her parents' front door. They live on the opposite side of town from the police department that's handling Remi's disappearance. Their house isn't in the nicest part of town, but there are definitely worse neighborhoods out there. When Rayna confronted them about maybe moving to a better subdivision, her parents stood their ground. Their house was paid off and they didn't intend to "die in poverty" because they bought a new house at a late age. Rayna has to admit, they did have a point.

The door is opened just as she raises her hand to ring the doorbell, and her mom immediately pulls her into a bone crushing hug.

"Hi mom," she squeaks out as best she can, as all the air is expelled from her lungs.

Her mom can't even seem to find words, instead she simply bursts into tears. Her dad quickly ushers the two of them inside and closes the door.

"What did the police say?" her father questions without even bothering with formalities.

"They aren't sure. They have a couple leads, but so far nothing has panned out." Suddenly, Rayna feels a little weird telling her parents about the details of what happened last night. She isn't sure Remi would want them to know about what occurred between John and her.

"What leads?" her dad asks, just as Rayna knew he would.

She makes the split second decision to skip over the details about John. Those are Remi's to tell. "Well…" She opens her mouth to explain about Zeki, but then realizes she doesn't want to tell her parents about her romantic life, either. Instead, she chooses the safe route. "Remi had this new roommate, and it turns out all the information she had provided was fake."

"Fake?" her mom sobs.

Rayna nods.

"They find out who this roommate actually is?" Her dad sinks down on the couch next to her inconsolable mother.

"Not yet." Rayna tries to supress a yawn. "I've been up all night. Mind if I get some sleep and we can talk more later?"

"Sure." Her dad motions to the stairs. "The guest room is still set up." By guest room, he means her old room that they've barely redecorated since she moved out with Remi years ago. She nods and heads toward the stairs.

"Oh, and some mail came for you, I put it in the drawer by the sink."

Rayna nods and heads into the kitchen. Although both girls moved out years ago, many of their old acquaintances and schools only have this address, so they sometimes receive mail here.

She pulls open the old oak door by the sink and removes the pile of letters occupying the front half of the drawer. The first one looks like some sort of credit card application. Trash. Second one is a letter from the alumni association at her college, probably just looking for donations. She tosses that one aside as well. The third letter is addressed to Remi, so she sets it back in the drawer.

As she looks over the fourth and final envelope in her hand, something odd about the third letter she just set down catches her eye. Something is off, but she can't figure out what.

She shakes off the feeling and with a sigh she tears open the fourth envelope to find a notice from the library the girls went to as a kid. The letter should actually be addressed to Remi because Rayna lost her library card about a week after they got them, so for years they just shared Remi's.

The letter is just thanking Rayna for her book donation. Which is odd, as she doesn't remember donating any books lately. She's so tired she can't focus any longer. Instead she slides the letter from the library back in the front of the drawer and stumbles upstairs to bed.

She doesn't even bother changing, instead she lies across the bed in her clothes. She doesn't even have a chance to turn off the lights before she falls into a deep sleep.

In her dream she's an eight year old again, in the neighborhood library with Remi. They're both dressed in one of the matching outfits they wore in their youth. Rayna looks down to see she holds books in her small hand.

"Where's your card?" her sister whispers as she approaches with a stack of books twice the size of her twin's.

Rayna looks around. Everything looks large and exaggerated. "I don't know," she professes, looking ahead at their mother standing by the check out desk. She can't believe she lost her new library card so soon.

Remi looks down at the stack of books in her sister's hands, then at the ones in her own. "I know, I'll go first, then give my card to you. They'll never know."

The clerk scans Remi's books, then her library card, then hands it back to her. Rayna comes to stand right next to her and quickly grabs the card from the hand behind her back. She looks up to see their mother's attention is drawn somewhere else. Good, she hasn't noticed.

Rayna places her books on the desk next, and watches as the clerk scans them. Next comes the moment of truth, as she reaches out her hand holding her sister's card. The clerk scans it, then hands it back, as she does, Rayna's eyes are drawn to the handwritten name at the bottom of the card. It's Remi's name, printed, as the girls are still learning cursive and haven't quite mastered it yet. The writing looks familiar. And just like that, Rayna's brain jolts.

She sits straight up in bed panting, shaking her head to clear the after-dream fugue that clouds her thoughts. After taking a minute to find her bearings, she jumps off the bed and makes her way down the stairs as quickly as she can.

When she rounds the corner into the kitchen, she finds her parents sitting at the table drinking coffee. Someone else is there, too, someone she doesn't recognize.

"Rayna, you're awake. This is our neighbor Carol." Her father motions to her. Rayna can't get her mouth to move to exchange pleasantries, she's still half asleep. "And this is our daughter Rayna." Her dad adds, noticing her predicament.

She half waves as she heads back to the drawer she went through just hours ago, sliding it open carefully as if something is going to jump out at her. The two letters are sitting right where she left them. She moves the letter addressed to her and picks up the one addressed to Remi.

The handwriting on the letter. It's Remi's own.

Why would she send a letter to herself? Rayna wonders. She flips it over to check the back. There's no return address.

She's so engrossed in what she's doing, she hasn't noticed that her father has come up to stand behind her.

"That's Remi's."

Rayna shakes her head. "She addressed it to herself, dad, that's her handwriting." She points at the address on the envelope with a shaky hand.

"I better call the police."

That's her father, always the one with his head on straight.

Rayna squints so she can make out the postmark in the upper right hand corner. It's dated two weeks ago. "Wait, dad, I don't think this is a ransom note, Remi sent this to herself here two weeks ago."

Her dad stops mid-dial. "Why would she do a thing like that?"

"I don't know," she responds as she slides a finger under the flap and tears the envelope open gently. Glancing inside, she notes the envelope is empty, except for a flash drive. She dumps it into her hand and holds it up so her dad can see it.

Without a word, he turns to finish dialing the phone.

A GIANT WAVE of water breaks through Remi's dream. She's back at the library, her refuge as a small child.

She chokes as a small amount of water enters her lungs.

A male voice speaks. "Get up."

Remi tries to stand, but her legs betray her and she stumbles back to a kneeling position. She continues coughing, trying to dislodge the water in her airways. She squints, trying to get the man in front of her to come into focus. Her mind is still so fuzzy from all the drugs.

The man takes zip ties out of his pockets and slides them around her wrists. Remi wants to ask questions, but her tongue is useless in her mouth.

He once again pulls Remi to her feet, and again, she stumbles back to the ground. Her legs are like jelly, she wonders just how long she has been sleeping. It has certainly been awhile since she's stood up.

With a huff, the man stands and tosses her over his shoulder in a fireman carry. She briefly thinks this might be her moment to escape, but realizes none of her limbs want to respond to her brain. She's basically a rag doll.

She watches, upside-down, as the man carries her up the ladder into a nicely furnished room. There's carpet, a wide screen TV, and a plush looking couch. Remi looks back at the hole they just emerged from, confused. Just where are they keeping her? Her eyes are telling her it's a trap door of some sorts, but that can't be right. What sort of house even has a trap door?

The man tosses her on the couch like a sack of potatoes, looking toward another man in the room. "She coming?" he asks.

"Yeah, any minute," the other man replies. Once again, Remi tries to survey their features, but her brain still swims as if under water.

"She doesn't look so good," one of the men says.

Remi tries to open her mouth to say she's fine, but then everything goes black.

NOW

S HE SITS AT her parents' kitchen table as the police interview her parents in the other room regarding the envelope. She knows it's most likely futile; her parents don't check the mail every day, as they often don't receive much. When they did get the letter, they saw Remi's name and set it aside as always.

Detective Grady comes to sit next to her, with bags under her eyes to match the ones under Rayna's.

"So how did you come to open the envelope?" She observes Rayna with curious eyes.

"I recognized her handwriting," she replies. Grady holds up the plastic evidence bag, which now contains the envelope.

"Did you see what was on the flash drive?"

She shakes her head. "No, I saw it was a flash drive and my father called you guys right away."

Detective Grady nods and pulls her phone out of her pocket. "I just got a call a few minutes ago. Apparently the flash drive is full of documents, spreadsheets and the like, that Remi used for her job. Did you know anything about that?"

"No, Remi was always much more mathematically gifted than me. When I look at a spreadsheet the numbers just float in front of my eyes and they don't make any sense."

"Did your sister mention she was having trouble at work?"

"No," Rayna groans in desperation. "I had such a rough few months, I kind of fell out of the loop and I feel terrible about it. There's so much I didn't know."

Grady is silent for a moment, then pulls out a yellow manila envelope. She opens it up and lays its contents in front of Rayna.

They're call logs for her sister's phone.

"See this here?" She points to the listing "private caller," which has been highlighted in pink at various times on the sheet. "Whoever this was seemed to call an awful lot."

Rayna squints, looking at the times. It seems a lot of the calls occurred after her sister was home for work for the evening. She flips through the sheets, seeing other numbers interspersed between. The private caller called quite a bit in the last few weeks. She sets down the papers and raises her eyes to meet the questioning look of Grady.

"I don't know who that could possibly be. My sister," she takes a deep breath, "she didn't really have many friends other than her boyfriend. Really, I don't know who would call her like this."

The officer nods, sliding the papers into a stack and putting them back in the envelope. "We found Zeki."

Rayna waits for the usual pitter-patter of her heart that comes with her boyfriend's name, only to notice the feeling is absent. *How long has she not felt her heart race at the thought of her significant other?* "And?" she asks.

A hint of a smile shows on Grady's face. "He confessed to drug charges. But he's accounted for almost all of his hours since Friday night at ten p.m., so we've ruled him out as a subject." The officer's smile fades quickly. "Since his house was acquired through illegal dealings, we will be repossessing it. I'm actually here to take you to get anything of yours out of it."

Rayna feels a lump form in her throat. "O-okay," she rasps and gets shakily to her feet. They walk through the living room to the door. As they step outside, she realizes she hasn't told her parents she's leaving. "I, uh, need to—"

Grady cuts her off. "Don't worry, I told them we'd be back in a bit."

"Did you tell them about the, uh, the—"

"Drugs?" she volunteers. "No, I figured you can let them know what you want to know later, since Zeki has been cleared in this investigation."

"Thanks," she mutters quietly as she slides into the passenger side of the car.

"No problem. I know how tough parental relationships can be."

Rayna doesn't respond, she simply looks out the window as the city flies past. She catches a glimpse of her reflection in the side mirror and shudders. Her hair is unkempt, her eyes red rimmed and dark, her skin oily. This still doesn't seem real. Actually, her life for the past few months doesn't seem real. How has she gone from the happy-go-lucky popular girl to someone who can barely stand the look of herself in the mirror?

Grady doesn't try to make conversation as they pull up in front of the house Rayna once called home.

As she steps out, she takes a mental picture of the modern two story she thought would be her home through her marriage and maybe the home of her children. Well, that dream is gone.

The pair make their way up the stairs and Grady watches as Rayna grabs a duffel bag from the closet and begins filling it with her favorite clothes and shoes. There are too many outfits for one bag, so she grabs a second wheeled suitcase and fills that as well. There are still more things, but Rayna realizes that many of the clothes were gifts from Zeki or are remnants of her old life she doesn't want. It's time to leave those behind.

She heads into the bathroom next and grabs her makeup bag and toothbrush. She'll buy everything else new when she figures out where she's going.

And just where is that? her subconscious asks her. Rayna doesn't know. Honestly, she'll probably just hang with her parents for awhile like the quintessential college dropout.

With a sigh she turns to Detective Grady, who is still waiting patiently by the door. "I guess this is it," she says as she slings her duffel bag and makeup kit over her shoulder and begins to wheel the suitcase toward the door.

"Are you sure? Because once the techs come in here and tear the place apart looking for drugs, I can't guarantee we will be able to get anything back for you."

She takes one last look around and zeroes in on her jewelry case on the dresser. She quickly picks it up and stuffs it in her duffel bag. "Now I'm sure," she replies.

They make their way down the stairs and back out to the car. As they step in, Detective Grady gets a phone call. She steps out of the car to take it, and Rayna watches as she paces back and forth while she's given information. When she's finished, Grady slides into the driver side.

"That was the station. The forensic accountants finally finished analyzing the files on that flash drive."

"And?" Rayna prods, practically sitting on the edge of her seat.

"Did your sister mention anyone by the name Lyle, Jared, or Jonathon?"

She squints at the list of male names; they mean nothing to her. "No, why?"

"They were your sister's coworkers, and they have just become suspects. I can't give you too many details, but I'll be dropping you off at your parents' then heading to the station. If you think of anything about the three of them, you let me know."

Rayna nods and turns her attention back to the window. How has she missed this much of her twin sister's life?

S HE STEPS BACK into the station, giving the woman manning the front desk a nod before heading to her own. Tossing her jacket over the back of her swivel chair, she collapses into it with a huff of frustration.

"Anything new?" Leary looks up from the paperwork on his desk. He looks just as disheveled as she feels.

"Nada. The twin just maintained the same story, she didn't know anything about her sister's work, nor the men I mentioned."

"Seems odd, doesn't it?" Leary questions as he leans back in his chair, placing his hand on his chin and rubbing an imaginary beard.

Grady nods. "Very. What twin barely speaks to her sister? We talked to the parents, and they both said the girls were glued at the hip through both primary and secondary school. They even lived together in college."

"But then something had to happen." Leary leans forward.

Grady pulls up her notes on her iPad. "According to Rayna there was an issue with the boyfriend, Zeki, did we confirm that with him?"

"No, he clammed up once the lawyer showed and advised him to remain silent. They took him down to central booking. Probably going to spend some time in jail, unless he gets a really good lawyer. Which, with the drug money, who knows what sleaze this guy is going to find."

Grady shakes her head in disdain. "So we are back at square one as far as the relationship between the girls is concerned."

"Pretty much." Leary pulls up his own notes. "Boyfriend John seems very forthcoming. Told us all about how Remi had found things missing all over her house, he mentioned there had been some crank calls..." He trails off as he evaluates the paper in his hand.

"Funny you call him forthcoming," Grady pipes in.

"You wouldn't?"

"He forgot to tell his girlfriend he was married. That definitely isn't very 'forthcoming' to me," she elaborates, leaning back in her own chair.

Her eyes droop slightly of their own accord. She only managed to sneak in a few hours of sleep in the early morning. And all of those hours were in the employee break room, which is far from comfortable.

"True. Where's he at, anyway?"

"His apartment," Grady rattles off the address on her iPad. "Got a couple of plain clothes officers sitting on him."

"Good," Leary agrees. "Now tell me about this work debacle."

Grady checks her watch. "Well, the three gentlemen in question should be in here at any moment, but basically the work on the flash drive we found showed that Remi had discovered that there was someone stealing from her company. She had it narrowed down to two people, took the info to her boss, then found out about two weeks ago that her boss was in on it. Turns out, over a hundred thousand dollars has gone missing over the past year and a half."

"So do we think all three are guilty?" Leary is scribbling down notes of his own.

"Definitely not. I'm no forensic accountant, but I personally think it's the boss and one of the accountants. For some reason I don't think three of them would be in cahoots like this. And one hundred thousand doesn't seem like an amount high enough to keep three people happy, especially since it was taken over such a long period of time. I think if there were three of them, they would take more."

He nods. "I guess we will split them up for interview and see what comes of it. Make sure we triple check all of their alibis."

There's a pause in their conversation as both of them mull over their individual thoughts.

"I still think the twin is hiding something," Grady interjects.

"Oh yeah?" He sets down his papers, his full attention on her.

"Yeah, seems like she's keeping something back. Her answers...well it's not that they seem dishonest, it's just that they seem...not all there, if that makes sense?"

"Makes sense, but listen, you're too tired to look into this more now, I can see your eyelids slipping down from here. Go catch a couple hours rest in the break room and I'll wake you up when the three stooges are brought in."

He's right. She is too tired to deal with this now. She nods in agreement, then heads to the break room for a quick nap.

Leary shakes her shoulder to wake her, much too soon for her liking. But she quickly gets up and uses the mirror to freshen herself up.

"They here?" she garbles.

He nods. "In three separate rooms. They've been here for an hour actually, just letting them sweat it out a bit before we take a crack at them."

An hour? Grady checks her watch and realizes she's been asleep for almost three. "Think they'll lawyer up?" she asks as she tries to straighten the wrinkle that's appeared on her shirt.

"The boss? Definitely. The two suspected henchmen? I'm not sure. Honestly, for corporate accountants they don't seem all that bright. They left quite the paper trail which Remi caught onto. Our accountants were easily able to trace the money and the amounts from her detailed notes."

She nods, then opens the door to head into the hallway. "Anything else I missed?"

Leary shakes his head. "Nope. Still sitting on the vic's apartment trying to wait for this sketchy roommate to show up. Zeki will be spending the night in jail before his bail hearing tomorrow...and I think you're up to date otherwise."

"No calls from the twin?"

"You mean random confessions? Nope. But the parents did call trying to see if there was any update."

Grady exits the room and heads for her desk, stopping by the office printer where a picture of the girls has printed out. It looks like it was taken when one of them graduated college, as one is wearing a cap and gown. The other is wearing a pale blue cocktail dress with a white cardigan. Grady stops and picks up the picture.

"Shocking, isn't it?" Leary is right behind her.

"Very. They look like the same person."

Setting the photo back on the printer for whatever officer printed it out, she grabs her iPad off her desk and heads toward the interview rooms. "Which one am I taking?" she asks.

"You get, uh..." He flips through his phone for a picture, showing her briefly before turning his phone back around to look up the name. "...Lyle Roberts. Says here he's thirty-two and unmarried. Has been at Johnson Finance all of his working career. Social media accounts are pretty dry, can't find any evidence of a girlfriend." Leary finishes just as Brown walks up behind Grady. He smells nice and fresh, as if he just got out of the shower.

"Brown is going to take Jonathon, the boss. I'll be in with Jared." He motions to an interview room at the end of the hall. "Remember, Mirandize them, be their friend, see what we can get out of them. But if they lawyer up, stop talking immediately."

"Will do," Brown replies as he heads for the nearest interview room.

"But if they do lawyer up," Leary continues, a certain gleam appearing in the corner of his eye, "make sure you take your sweet ass time calling that lawyer."

The three of them laugh, then straighten themselves up as they prepare to go into their respective interview rooms. Three other officers come down the hall, prepared to watch from the outside and be their backup if needed.

With a quick breath to compose herself, Grady plasters a fake smile on her face, then ducks into her interview room. *Here goes nothing.*

S HE WAKES TO the face of a strange man right in front of her. Surprisingly, she doesn't open her mouth to scream. Instead she tries to move backwards, but finds she's up against something sturdy. She turns to find another man behind her.

"Well, she's awake," the one in front of her says.

"Yeah, no thanks to you. I told you to lower the dose on those pills."

"Whatever."

Remi blinks as the two men bicker. Her mind is clearing from the fuzz for the first time in days. She begins surveying her surroundings, trying to figure out just where she is. The man seated directly behind her holds her wrists tightly. Remi becomes aware of pain in her shoulders. It's the first pain she's felt in awhile. She knows whatever they gave her is definitely wearing off.

"I thought you said she was coming," grumbles the one behind her. Obviously he's growing tired of holding her wrists. He loosens his hold slightly, allowing Remi to relax her shoulders. It's still painful, but not nearly as much as it was before.

"She is," the other one snaps back. "She called and said she was on her way like thirty minutes ago."

"Ugh."

Remi surveys the man in front of her. He's short, probably about her height, but it's hard to tell as he's sitting down. He isn't the skinniest, but definitely isn't fat, either. Stocky is probably a more appropriate word. His skin is light, but with a tinge of something. Perhaps he has a tan. Or a distant relative was from somewhere else. His clothes are average, a basic colored tee and what look like cargo pants. His shoes are worn tennis shoes that obviously needed to be replaced long ago. Remi gets a feeling that neither of the men has much money.

She wants to turn around and get a good look at the man holding her wrists, but she knows they'll think that suspicious. One thing is for sure, though: neither of them is wearing a mask. Which means they aren't worried about her turning them in. If she wants to get out of here alive she needs to think of a plan.

"Gah. Next time I get to sit there and do nothing and you get to hold her wrists!" He tightens his hold again and Remi gasps in pain.

"Dude, she's like a twig, don't tell me you're having trouble controlling her. Plus it's not my fault you cut the only zip-tie we had off of her when she passed out!"

The two of them continue to argue, and Remi zones out again to survey the room. The carpet is white, and stretches wall to wall. She's on the floor now, not on the couch like she was when she passed out. The couch is cloth covered and worn looking. Although this room appears to be an auxiliary TV room, it doesn't seem to belong to someone with a lot of money. It seems homey, and very middle class. There are no windows, making Remi think it's definitely a basement room.

"Swap me!"

"No! We took this job because of you, so now you have to deal with her!"

"She wouldn't have passed out if you hadn't over drugged her!"

Remi rolls her eyes. The way the men are bickering reminds her of how she and Rayna used to bicker when they were younger. It makes her think that the men could possibly be siblings.

She searches her memory for anyone she might have pissed off. The first people who come to mind are obviously Lyle and Jared. But these two men are definitely not them. And they keep referring to a "she." Remi can't think of a female she could have possibly pissed off. She doesn't even really have many female friends. And none who could possibly be mad at her.

Suddenly her bladder reminds her it's there. And she needs to go. Bad.

"—It's not my fault you invested all our money in that shotty offshore—"

The men are still bickering, but Remi really needs to go.

"Um." It comes out as a whisper. She clears her throat and tries again. "Um, I need to go to the bathroom."

The men stop mid sentence and look at her, then at each other. The one in front of her speaks first.

"Well what are you waiting for? Take her to the bathroom."

The man holding her wrists groans and drags them both to their feet, almost yanking Remi's shoulders from their sockets.

He lets her toward a corner of the room that has been out of her field of vision so far. He opens a small, thin door and tosses her into the dark room. She stumbles as he lets go of his hold on her wrists.

"Hurry up," he says before closing the door behind her.

Remi feels a sense of déjà vu as she is completely enclosed in the dark room. She stands there for a moment rubbing her wrists, until her bladder once again reminds her it has been way too long.

She begins to feel along the side of the wall for a light switch, but can't find anything. She realizes this is taking way too long and quickly gives up on looking for a lightswitch. Instead she feels around for the familiar shape of the toilet.

She has just sat down to use the toilet when the man begins banging on the door.

"What's taking so long? Hurry up!" he shouts again.

Remi tries to go as fast as possible, but it has been way too long since her last bathroom break. She tries to think back to the last time but she can't remember. Maybe while she was in one of the drug-induced comas in the cellar? Remi suddenly realizes she has no idea how long she has been here. It feels like days. But it could have been longer, after all, she was out for much of it.

The door slams open and the man grabs her wrist before giving her a chance to wipe.

"Pull up your pants," he snaps at her. Remi does the best she can with one hand. She probably looks like a mess, but she supposes it doesn't matter anyways. Not like she's trying to impress anyone anyway.

With that thought, a sudden image of John fills her mind and a small nudge of longing fills her heart. She is definitely still mad at him, but a part of her misses him too.

The man drags her back to the couch, taking a seat and roughly shoving her down on the floor. Then he wrenches her hands once again behind her back. The other man sits on a beanbag on the other side of the room, staring at them.

"You comfy?" he sneers.

"Fuck off," the man holding her wrists replies. Remi prepares for them to start their bickering where they left off, but the sound of the door above makes them pause.

Suddenly, the man on the beanbag stands up and walks over to the bottom of the stairs. The man holding her wrists sits up straight. Just who is this woman?

She hears the sound of footsteps coming down the stairs and the two men share nervous glances. The woman turns the corner and Remi quickly observes her appearance.

Unlike the men, she's concealing her identity with a thin Mardi Gras type mask that covers her eyes and nose. Her blonde hair reaches her shoulders and looks glossy and healthy. She's dressed well, obviously endowed with more money than the two henchman she has watching over Remi. She wears a designer pantsuit, leading Remi to deduce she just came from a job of some sort. Maybe she does work in the office Remi works in? Maybe she's in on the money stealing operation at Johnson Finance. Maybe—

The woman leans down in front of Remi's face. Moving it from side to side as if she's doing an inspection.

"Well hello, Rayna. Have I got plans for you..." the woman sneers as she steps back.

Her words take a moment to register.

Rayna?

NOW

S HE KNOWS WHAT she's doing is a bad idea. She's seen some of the cop shows her sister loves. Vigilantes never actually help the cops, they only get in the way.

Even as those thoughts register, she can't be persuaded, as she finishes getting dressed and heads to the bathroom. She inspects her face in the mirror, trying to decide what she should do. She has bags under her eyes, which is expected considering her lack of sleep over the last two days. She could put make-up on them to conceal them, but that doesn't seem like something Remi would do. She decides to leave them as they are and heads down the stairs toward the door.

"Where are you going?" her mother asks tearfully from the couch. Rayna doesn't think she's stopped crying since Rayna arrived here yesterday.

"For a walk, mom," Rayna fibs, knowing her mom won't let her leave if she knows otherwise.

"Okay dear, be careful." Her mom sounds suspicious, but Rayna is an adult so she can't prevent her from going out—even though Rayna knows that's exactly what she wants to do. If it were their mother's choice, she and Remi would have never moved out at all.

Rayna walks down the street toward the subway, her mind running over her plan again and again. It isn't even a good plan, but sitting around doing nothing doesn't seem like a good idea, either. She has to try and help Remi somehow.

The trip across town to her sister's apartment takes about half an hour. When she walks up to her old home, she looks around quickly before slipping her key in the lock and turning the knob.

Inside is a wreck. The police have overturned everything. The couch cushions are scattered across the floor, pictures are missing from the fireplace, and finger print dust coats every surface. Rayna closes the door behind her. Time to set her trap.

While she was bored in her room, she did some research. She found Patrice's Facebook, and with that information, and thirty dollars, she was able to do a phone number look up. Now it's time to make a phone call.

She dials, and the phone rings in her ear.

"Hello?" a woman answers.

"Hi, Patrice right? This is Remi...I, uh, want to talk." She crosses her fingers as she speaks the line out loud. The police haven't quite aired her twin's disappearance yet and she hopes no one has told Patrice what's going on.

"Oh, hi...I don't think there's anything for us to discuss. I want you to stop seeing my husband." The woman is definitely becoming less welcoming by the second.

"I will, I promise," Rayna lies. "But I found....something out about John I need to share with you. It's my duty as a woman." She cringes as she adds that last part, but it sounds like something Remi would say.

"What?" Now she has Patrice's full attention.

"I don't want to discuss it over the phone. Can you come over to my apartment? I promise it will be quick."

"Uhh..." She hesitates.

"It won't take more than five minutes," Rayna says reassuringly.

"Okay," Patrice agrees reluctantly. "I'll be there in half an hour." And with that the line goes dead.

Rayna smiles, proud of herself, her plan is right on track. She looks around the room and cringes. She needs to fix this. If she opens the door and Patrice sees the room as it currently is, she'll definitely run for the hills before she can be interrogated.

She quickly rights the pillows on the couch, then heads to the kitchen to grab a paper towel. She isn't able to completely wipe the fingerprint dust from all the surfaces, but at least it isn't as smudgy looking as before.

Rayna is so busy cleaning, she jumps halfway out of her skin when the doorbell rings. "That was fast," she mumbles to herself as she takes one last look around the room she just speed cleaned. Not too shabby, she thinks as she heads for the door.

She looks through the peephole, surprised to see a man standing on the other side of the door. Her eyebrows knit together as she opens the door. "Yes?"

The man looks up.

It takes her a moment to recognize him not in his uniform, but when she does, she's even more confused. "Detective Brown?"

"Ms. Casell?"

"Yes?"

"We've been looking everywhere for you." A smile breaks out across his face. Rayna grimaces.

"I'm not Remi, it's me, Rayna, we spoke last night. Sorry," she apologizes sheepishly. She hates to burst his bubble like this.

"Oh." His expression once again turns flat. "What are you doing in your sister's apartment?" He raises one eyebrow.

Rayna glances at her phone and realizes Patrice will be here any second. She sighs and motions behind her "You might as well come in."

Detective Brown steps inside and Rayna closes the door behind him.

"So are you going to tell me what you're up to?"

For the first time, Rayna takes a good look at Detective Brown. He's taller than her by a few inches, and athletic—but not the overly buff type. He's thin, athletic, which she wasn't able to see through his work uniform, but now that he's in a black polo, the muscles in his arms show. He's shaven and clean, but still has a ruggedness about him. He's definitely older than her, but she guesses he's around thirty, so not by much.

She debates lying to him for a moment, but then she knows she'll have even more to explain when Patrice shows up. "Ugh, fine. I called Patrice, John's wife, and I told her I had something to tell her to try and lure her over here and see if she kidnapped my sister. It's a long shot, I know, but I just had to try—"

He holds up a hand to cut her off. "We already interviewed Patrice. She has an alibi for the night in question."

Rayna knows that means that Patrice probably knows Remi is missing. "But she said she was coming over!" Rayna protests, more to herself than anyone else, slightly crestfallen.

"She did. But that's because she thought the real Remi had resurfaced. She called me after she hung up the phone with you."

Rayna shakes her head. She should have known everything was going too well. A thought suddenly strikes her. "How did you get here so fast? I didn't hear any police sirens."

Detective Brown smiles. "We've had cops watching this place twenty-four seven since you called us Saturday night. When someone showed up and entered with a key, well, my man out there notified me before you even made the phone call."

"Damn. Just make me feel like an idiot." Rayna is embarrassed. She should have known the cops would have something like this set up. She opens her mouth to apologize for wasting his time, when suddenly she hears a key in the lock. "What—"

Brown puts his hand over her mouth and gives her the 'be silent' symbol. Then he pulls her around the corner into the hall so they aren't visible from the door. He whispers quietly into his radio on his shoulder, "Justin, someone is entering the premises. What's your read?"

He doesn't have a chance to hear the answer as the door creaks open.

He moves away from Rayna, mouthing 'stay' as he leans around the corner and steps back into the kitchen. She nods mutely, even though he's no longer even looking in her direction.

"KEEP YOUR HANDS WHERE I CAN SEE THEM!"

The shout jolts her out of her reverie and she peeks her head around the corner to see Detective Brown with his gun pointed at a young woman that has to be about Rayna's age. Rayna stays in her spot, observing as he slowly approaches the woman.

"Do you have any weapons on you?"

The woman shakes her head 'no.' She's obviously just as shocked as they are.

Detective Brown lowers his weapon and begins to pat her down. "Why do you have a key?" he questions.

"I-I live here," she stutters.

"Daisy McMullen?"

The woman sighs. "Yeah." She says it in a way that hangs in the air, incomplete.

"I think we better talk." Brown motions to the couch in the living room just as Rayna steps out from her hiding place.

"Remi, what's this about?" Daisy seems genuinely confused.

"You don't know?" Now Rayna is confused as well.

"That's not Remi. That's her twin sister Rayna," Brown corrects as he leads Daisy to the couch. Another cop appears in the doorway, quickly putting his weapon away as he realizes there's no active threat. The two officers share a moment of silent conversation and the cop takes a defensive stance in the doorway. It's clear they don't want Daisy to leave.

"Where's Remi?" Daisy asks, looking around the room, probably taking in the small changes that have occurred from the police tossing the place.

"Why don't we start with you telling us who you are." Brown's face is stern. He obviously doesn't think she's innocent.

Rayna sits at the kitchen table, trying to stay out of the way, but also eavesdropping. She's pretty sure detective Brown forgets she's even there.

"I'm Dais-"

Brown doesn't let her get any further. "Lie. Daisy McMullen doesn't exist. Try again."

"Am I under arrest?" She fidgets with the end of her fringed shirt.

"Not yet. But if I can't get a straight answer out of you, you're about to be." His response is firm.

She sighs. "Alright, my name is Lena Mullen."

Brown raises his eyebrows and pulls out his iPad. Rayna can't tell if he's taking notes or messaging someone to look up the name.

"And just why are you going under a fake name?"

"I...uh...left an unhealthy relationship. I guess you could say I'm in unofficial hiding." Lena pinches her eyes shut and rests her head in her hands. "I'm from Tennessee. I was hoping that by coming here I would be getting far enough away. But after I had been here a few days, my friends alerted me he had gotten on a plane to O'Hare. So I changed my name and my appearance to hide from him. This was almost two years ago, but everyone got to know me as Daisy, so it just seemed weird to go back. Plus the name grew on me."

"And just where have you been for the past two days?" Brown is still skeptical and not quite buying her story.

"I'm a nurse."

Brown raises his eyebrows and looks down at her outfit, which is a shirt and jeans and most certainly not scrubs.

She shakes her head, knowing exactly what he's thinking. "A private nurse. I've got my license, but after being on the run I just couldn't risk working for the public. I work for two separate families, pretty much on demand as they need me. So my schedule is crazy and I oftentimes end up spending the night either in my car or on the couch of one of their houses. I can provide all the contact info you need."

He nods. "We will definitely contact them." He turns his attention back to the iPad.

"Now...where's Remi and why is she here?" She points a finger at Rayna and Detective Brown starts, as if suddenly remembering she's there.

"When was the last time you saw your roommate?" He's still beating around the bush.

"Ugh," Lena groans, not liking being taken off topic without her question being answered. "I think Wednesday or Thursday? I honestly haven't been home in awhile and it was mostly to change."

"And when you were home last time, what kitchen appliances did you use?"

"What kitchen appliances? Okay this is just getting ridiculous. If I'm not under arrest I'm done talking to you unless you tell me what's going on here." She crosses her arms over her chest, appearing genuinely angry.

Detective Brown stands up and closes the case on his iPad. "That's all for now. I'll need your contact information though. Just in case I do need you to come down to the station and give a statement."

Lena rolls her eyes and types in a phone number on the iPad when he turns it her way.

"Also, you can't stay here—"

"No problem. I'm just here to change and head back to work." With that she stands and heads into her room, closing the door loudly behind her.

Detective Brown walks over to the cop by the door and whispers something in his ear. Then he motions for Rayna to come outside with him. She follows him quietly down the stairs.

When they reach the bottom, he turns to her and opens his mouth as if to say something, but Rayna's anger gets the better of her and she cuts him off.

"That's it? You're letting her go?" It comes out a bit louder than she expected.

"Shh." He looks up toward the officer in the doorway of the apartment. "Don't worry, now that we found her she won't be leaving our sight," he whispers. "Now come with me and I will take you home."

Rayna groans. "I can't go back just yet. It's just so sad there."

Detective Brown doesn't say anything as Rayna heads toward the sidewalk. He stops in front of his car, an unmarked brown Crown Vic. "You sure you don't want a ride?"

"I'm sure," she replies, not meeting his eye. She does want a ride, but not to her parents' house. But then again, she doesn't know where else she would even go. She takes a seat on the curb and puts her head in her hands.

"Uh.." Brown looks around, not really sure what to do in these sorts of situations, then sits down next to Rayna. "You...okay?" he asks.

She nods. "Yes. I mean, yeah I will be. But I don't need help. I just need to figure out what to do." She takes a deep breath and lifts her head, making sure to avoid the scrutinizing gaze of Detective Brown. "Everything has changed overnight. I don't have a home, the only home I would come back to is under police surveillance," she motions to the apartment behind her, "the only person I want to talk to is MIA. I don't have a job, and I just realized, over the past two years I've alienated any other friends I had. I used to be a social butterfly."

He doesn't say anything at first, he simply continues to look forward and let Rayna vent. "That's what they do, you know," he says quietly when she finishes.

"Huh?" She finally turns to look at him.

"Predators. They isolate you. People think predators are psychos who have no friends or family and roam the streets at night, but that's not true. A predator can be anyone, a friend, boyfriend, parent. Anyone who belittles you, changes your life, and then isolates you so there's no way out. They may not trap you physically, but you're stuck there mentally. And honestly, I think that's worse. Physical restraints are easy to escape, you can take classes on how to do it. But mental restraints, well, that's impossible to teach."

They're both silent for a moment, lost in their own thoughts.

Rayna breaks the silence. "You sound like you've experienced it."

He nods. "Everyone's got a story. Even when you're going through the worst thing imaginable, there's always someone who's been in your shoes at some point." He stands and brushes off his pants, reaching into his pocket. "Here's a card for a victim support group."

She reaches out and takes the card. "Support group?"

"Yeah, it's for people who have had a friend or family member go missing. It sounds stupid, I know, but it helps a lot. And who knows, you might find some new friends there." He shrugs and turns toward his car, unlocking the door. "You sure you don't want that ride?"

"I still don't have anywhere to go. But thanks."

"Sure thing." He slides into his car and starts the engine. Rayna watches as he pulls away from the curb, slowly turning over the card in her hand. Once his car is out of sight, she pulls out her phone and looks up the address. It's at a community center a few miles away. There's a meeting in a few hours. She stands up from the curb and looks down the street both ways, preparing to cross, and heads toward the center early.

As she does, she notices movement out of the corner of her eye. It's Daisy, and she's leaving the apartment. Rayna watches as another unmarked police car peels out after her. She's happy they're keeping a good eye on Daisy, something about her story just seems off.

Rayna's so busy observing the situation in front of her, she doesn't notice another unmarked police car starting his engine just as she crosses the street.

NOW

S HE'S SITTING AT her desk flipping through documents on the case when the screen on her cell lights up with a call from her partner.

"Grady," she answers professionally. Even though he's her partner, she and Brown have never had the joking relationship the TV shows perpetuate.

"How'd the interviews go?" he asks. She can hear car sounds in the background, so she figures he must be driving. Brown had to leave in the middle when they got the call there was movement at the apartment. Grady finished the interviews with a couple desk cops who were on duty.

"Fine. They all talked. Only one asked for a lawyer, and after they conferred, he ended up talking anyway. They admit there was some harassment going on. They claim it was harmless, but it sounds like it got pretty nasty towards the end."

"Nasty how?"

Grady sighs and pulls out the paper she just finished typing up with her notes. "First they crank called her a few times. Then they messed with her work desk. One day, while she was in the break room, they copied her house key and used it to break into her apartment. They claim they only moved things, and they told me where to find all the missing kitchen appliances."

"So, why was this worth their time?" Brown is not a fan of men who mess with women's minds just because they can.

"Well...we assume it was because of the theft. However, we didn't hold any of them, nor question them on the theft—"

He cuts her off. "And just why the hell not?"

She sighs, she isn't happy with this part either. "The DA called the shots. She's planning to prosecute the theft, but she has a feeling that the men know more than they let on. She thinks they may lead us to her.

From what I heard, she may be right, this harassment got really bad at the end."

There's silence on the other end of the phone. He's obviously waiting for her to elaborate.

"The last crank call, about two weeks ago, Jonathon threatened to kill her. Claims it was a joke, but the DA decided not to push it."

"I guess I sort of agree with that." He takes a deep breath. "So are we tailing them all?"

"For now, yes, but I think we are going to pull the tail on some of the other suspects." Grady runs a hand through her hair. She really wishes they had the budget to keep a tail on all of their current suspects, as they haven't yet ruled out a single one, but unfortunately, they don't. In fact, she was going through her papers to make the hard decision when Brown called.

"Keep the one on Daisy/Lena," he interjects.

"I planned on it," she replies, shuffling her papers. "The ones on my cut list are the twin, the boyfriend's wife, and the boyfriend."

Brown is silent for a moment. "I'd prefer to keep them all under surveillance but if we can't I guess cut the boyfriend's wife first?"

"I have to pick two."

He groans. "I really don't trust the boyfriend still, but I also want to keep one on Rayna for her safety. I'm still not sure this isn't one of those creepy twin obsession abductions."

Grady knows exactly what he's talking about, she has gone through the same thought process herself. They've had way too many cases of men abducting twins because of some perverted sexual fantasy. "We can't let him have them both," she agrees.

"Agreed. I'll be back at the station soon. But Grady, listen, I don't like this."

"Me, neither," she agrees dismally.

"I've never seen a case with so many suspects and so many variables."

"I know. We have to be missing something." Grady begins flipping through the papers again. If only something would jump off the page at her.

"We are. It's just a question of what. See you in a bit." And with that, the line goes dead.

Grady holds up the paper with the boyfriend's information. Honestly, the boyfriend is always a suspect no matter what the crime. But John seems genuine. She doesn't like to rule people out based on a hunch, but she sets his info page to the side regardless. She needs to narrow it down somehow.

Next, she picks up John's wife's paper. She doesn't want to rule her out, either; a jealous wife has the perfect motive. And she and John are each other's alibis, how convenient. But did they work together to abduct the girlfriend? She doesn't think so. John seems genuinely in love. She sets her page aside as well.

She picks up the document with Daisy/Lena's info on it. She updated it just moments ago from Brown's notes. She doesn't want to rule her out until they check her work references, but she has a nagging feeling that everything will check out. Plus, the roommate has no motive that she can see. Yeah, she's operating under fake information, but Remi doesn't seem like she would be a threat. She sets her page aside as well.

Left in front of her are the three men she just interviewed, the drug dealing boyfriend of the twin, and the twin herself. The three men have the most clear motive: Remi caught them stealing. But then again, Remi also went missing the same day Zeki's "stash" did. That's also a motive. And the twin? Something is nagging Grady. She looked through the phone history of the victim, and she was shocked at how little the two talked. Rayna claims they're close, but the signs all point to something different. She's the last one to see her sister alive, and the timeline is wide open. Which leads to the question, is she really capable of killing her twin? And if she did, why did she do it?

NOW

F OR SOME REASON, hearing her sister's name out of the mouth of the masked woman gives Remi strength.

"What kind of plans?" she questions defiantly in her hoarse voice.

The woman pulls her face back, as if she's surprised, but Remi can't be sure because of the mask obscuring her facial expression. Whatever happens, the woman snaps out of it quickly.

"Wouldn't you like to know..." she hisses, leaning in even closer than before.

Remi thinks about trying to bite her, but as soon as the thought enters her head, the woman moves her face away from Remi's.

"You'll pay for what you've done." She rises to a standing position and walks towards the stairs.

What has she done? Actually, what has Rayna done to piss this woman off so much?

Another wave of bravery comes over her. "Care to remind me what I'm paying for?" It's out of her mouth before she even considers the implications.

Next thing she knows, there's a stinging sensation in her face and the taste of blood in her mouth. She doesn't know for sure what happened, but she assumes someone hit her. She surveys the three people in the room, her eyesight not as sharp as it was moments before. The woman is rubbing her hand and inspecting her nails. Then it hits her that her own hands are no longer being restrained.

"I can't believe I wasted a nail on you," the woman seethes. Then she turns to the two men, whom Remi has started calling her henchmen. "Tie her to something. Tie her up tight. I don't care if she bleeds."

"But you said no marks," the chubbier of the two men protests.

"That was before," she snaps, motioning to Remi's face.

Wondering why, Remi hesitantly brings her hand up to her face and draws it back down. There's blood. Not much, but it's there. She's also concerned there's a piece of manicured nail in her face as well. The thought grosses her out.

"Photograph everything. Someone will pay for her back." She turns back to Remi. "You may think you are so smart miss Rayna...or should I say Leila? But look here, I don't give a fuck what happens to you, and I don't care how sad your parents are gonna be. Basically, I just don't care. You're nothing to me." She pushes Remi down by her shoulders and walks up the stairs and out of eyesight.

Although she said Rayna means nothing to her, it's obvious that she does in the way she said it. If she didn't really care, she wouldn't bother addressing her at all. Remi doesn't have to be a psychiatrist to know this woman is trying to get a rise out of her. It's the same thing Rayna did all the time when they were kids. Speaking of Rayna, who is Leila? And why has her sister started going by a different name?

She's still going through various mental scenarios in her head, none of them seeming to fit, when the thinner of the two henchmen grabs her by the throat.

Remi struggles to breath and get away, but his hand has a surprising vice-like grip. There's something about the way he's choking her that reminds her of something. But as the air leaves her lungs, so does her ability to string conscious thoughts together.

Just as her vision is starting to go black, he lets go, and she collapses in a heap on the ground, gasping for air.

"So...what was the point of that?" the other one asks from across the room, obviously not amused.

"Shut up," he replies, once again restraining her by the wrists. "Do you have any idea what to do with her?"

"No, but listen, dude, something's not right with this."

"Whadda you mean?" The one holding her wrists is obviously growing tired as he is no longer holding them as tight. Remi wonders what her chances are if she can get away and make it up the stairs. Is the woman still up there? Is she in the middle of nowhere?

"She said we were gonna auction off the girl to the highest bidder. That's how we are getting paid. If she doesn't care about us marking her, that must mean she's not planning to auction her off anymore."

"Hmm..." The guy behind her is obviously about to agree with him.

"So think about it. If we aren't auctioning her, how are we gonna get paid? She definitely doesn't have any money."

"You're right." The guy holding her hands loosens his grip even more, obviously dejected at the thought of not getting paid. "I risked everything for this."

"Me, too." Both men are quiet for a minute as they weigh their options. Remi tries to estimate how fast she can run. As soon as she's about to do it, the man holding her wrists speaks up.

"I have an idea."

"Yeah?" his buddy asks.

"Let's double cross her. She obviously wants the girl. Let's say you and me take her to another location and ransom her back for what we are owed?"

The other man stands and fist pumps the air. "Perfect! Let's wait until she leaves...but wait, where will we take her?" He motions to Remi with his chin. She has to admit she's getting really tired of being treated like a possession rather than a human.

"I have an idea for that, too. What's the last place anyone will ever look for her?"

Remi doesn't like the gleam that comes into the men's eyes.

S HE STANDS OUTSIDE the building, willing her body to go inside, but she just can't do it. Instead, she spends the duration of the meeting sitting outside on the curb.

Rayna isn't sure what the feeling is that's currently consuming her, but she has to assume it's something akin to guilt. She should have been there for her sister. She should have never picked Zeki over her. Remi would still be here.

After another half hour pity party, Rayna picks herself up off the sidewalk and begins to walk down the street. She decides she'll go into the first bar she sees, no matter how divey it is. She's in luck, the first one she passes is an upscale handcrafted cocktail place that the millennials love. She pushes open the too-wide door and heads inside.

It's mostly empty, except for the female bartender and a young couple across the bar.

"Evening, sweetheart, what can I get for ya?" the bartender asks in a sultry southern drawl.

Rayna feels like burying her head in a hole and never coming out—which only means one thing. "Tequila. Straight. Chilled, please."

"Woah." The bartender leans back. "Someone's looking to get trashed." She cracks a light laugh at the end, obviously making a joke.

Rayna isn't in the mood. She tosses the shot back as soon as it's placed in front of her. "Another," she says as she slams it down, her voice hoarse from the onslaught of the alcohol.

"You better slow down," the bartender warns, but she pours her another regardless. Once again, Rayna tosses it straight back. But this time, she doesn't ask for another. She simply fiddles with the glass in her hand.

The bartender must notice she isn't in the mood for conversation, because she's soon across the bar, addressing the young couple. Rayna doesn't care, she likes it better this way anyway.

Soon, she's six or seven shots deep. She really can't remember how many she's had. The world is starting to blur. But she does feel better. She finds herself laughing and joking with the other couple at the bar. And as it turns out, the bartender is actually pretty funny. She finds herself questioning whether she moved down the bar to be closer to the couple, or if they moved to be closer to her.

She has no idea how long they joke for, or even what they talk about, but before she knows it she's sitting by herself staring at the bottom of another empty shot glass.

"It's almost time for me to close," the bartender says with a smile, sliding her a water. "But I have to clean up so you have a few minutes to sober up."

Rayna smiles at the water glass. It's going to take her way more than a few minutes to sober up. She opens her mouth to tell the bartender and instead lets out a large hiccup.

"Need me to call you a ride?" she asks.

Rayna shakes her head. Who would she even call? Her parents? She doesn't have any friends. Remi comes to the front of her mind again, accompanied by another wash of guilt. Great, all that alcohol was for nothing.

She's still debating how she's going to get home when the bell above the door jingles. Rayna continues to stare at her water.

"Sorry, we're clo—" the bartender starts to say, but stops abruptly mid sentence. Rayna looks up to see why, instantly regretting it.

It's Detective Brown, standing in the doorway, his arms across his chest. "I just came to give her a ride." He motions to Rayna.

She tries to stand up defiantly to say she's fine walking, but instead she stumbles into an unceremonious heap on the floor. Then she starts laughing.

The bartender shakes her head. "I'm glad someone's giving her a ride."

Rayna tries again to stand, but ends up half collapsed over a barstool. Detective Brown walks over and helps her get into a standing position where she's leaning slightly on his shoulder. "Alright, I've got you. Let's go."

They walk awkwardly to the car, reminding Rayna of a three legged race, which makes her start laughing once again. Detective Brown doesn't say anything.

He helps her into the front of his car.

"Please don't puke up here and make me regret not putting you in the back," he says as he buckles her in. She's about to respond that she's fine when he shuts the door and walks around the front of the car.

"How—" she hiccups again as he slides into the driver seat, "—did you know where I was?"

He shrugs. "You weren't at the meeting so I began to check all the bars. Didn't take me long."

"How did you know I would go into a bar?" She furrows her brow in confusion. She can't tell if it's because she's drunk, but his words don't seem to make much sense.

"Because that's exactly what I did."

There's silence in the car as Rayna begins to process his words. What he did? Does that mean...

He must be reading her mind, because before she can say anything, he answers her unspoken question. "Yes, my mother went missing when I was in college."

"Did they find her?" she asks in a quiet voice. The tone of the conversation is sobering her up quite nicely. Or maybe it's the fact that she hasn't had another shot in probably over an hour.

"Not alive."

A thick silence fills the car and Rayna considers the implications of his words. Before she can say anything else, he speaks up again.

"Am I taking you to your parents' home?"

She shakes her head. "I would prefer not."

"Then where?" he asks.

She considers for a moment where else she can even go and then shrugs.

"If you don't have anywhere else, you can sober up in the drunk tank?"

She doesn't like the idea of spending the night at the station, but she doesn't like the idea of her parents seeing her this intoxicated either. "Good enough, I guess."

"If you're sure," he says before turning toward the station. Rayna doesn't say anything in protest. After another period of silence she feels a burning question she just has to ask.

"Do you..." she starts and then trails off, not recognizing the scratchy sound of her own voice. He waits patiently as she takes a deep breath and starts again. "Do you ever feel guilty? Like maybe you should have been taken instead?"

"Yes and no." He looks over at her with a somber look in his eyes. "Yes I feel guilty. I think every day if there was something I could have done so that she wouldn't have been taken. But my circumstances are different than yours. My mom was taken by a...sexual predator. They wouldn't have taken me instead. I just wish I would've prevented it."

Rayna nods in quiet understanding. "I just keep thinking that maybe if we still lived together, maybe it would have been me that was grabbed instead."

Detective Brown shakes his head. "You said yourself that you put her to bed in the guest room. She was either taken from there or after she left the house. The same thing could've happened if you had lived together."

She feels the tears trailing down her cheeks as they talk about her sister. Rayna can't remember the last time she was this emotional about anything. It has to be the alcohol. "Still..." She trails off, looking out the window as they pull into the police station parking lot. "She was taken after leaving my house. I feel like it's my fault."

"Hmm," Detective Brown says as he helps her out of the car and up the few steps to the station door. She's more steady on her feet than before, but definitely couldn't walk a straight line if asked.

He leads her into the waiting room where she waited before with John. He's no longer here and she wonders where he went.

"Technically," Detective Brown says with a smile, "I should make you stay in the actual drunk tank, but I think you've sobered up enough to wait in here. Try to get a couple hours of sleep." He helps her over to the couch, and Rayna nods, her eyes closing of their own accord. She's much more tired than she thought. So tired, she doesn't even hear Detective Brown close the door.

NOW

S HE'S SO DEEP into the case, she barely even notices when the clock passes midnight and heads for one. She knows she should probably go home at some point, but something is bothering her about the case, and she feels like if she leaves now she'll lose her train of thought.

She sits there, staring at the pictures of the evidence and possible abduction scenes. But none of them make sense. She's just flipped to the picture of the shoes when her partner walks in with Rayna and leads her to the waiting room. She watches quietly, wondering what's up.

As he closes the door to the waiting room, Detective Brown notices his workaholic partner is still at work and she's looking at him with an inquisitive look. "She was drunk, too much to drive, but not enough for the drunk tank." He shrugs sheepishly, a little embarrassed.

"Why the special treatment?" Detective Grady raises an eyebrow. She's always known her partner to be quite the hard ass, even when it comes to victims.

"I feel for her, you know."

Grady holds up her hand. "Don't peddle that bullshit with me. You've been my partner for four years and we have handled numerous missing person cases. I don't remember you ever giving a family member special treatment in any other instance." She leans back in her chair waiting for him to answer.

He looks back at the closed door, wondering for himself why he bothered to help Rayna. "I don't know. I guess she seems more...alone than most."

"She has her parents."

"I know." Brown walks over to his desk across from Grady's and sits down in his chair, looking at the photo she has sitting on her desk. "I didn't come back to experience the Spanish inquisition."

"I can't help it, I'm a woman, we're nosy." Grady chuckles as she picks up the photo that's caught her partner's eye. "It's the shoes."

"I know," he replies, reaching to take the photo from her. "Something Rayna said in the car is bugging me."

"Care to share?" Grady prods, leaning her head on her hand, elbow on her desk. She's tired, but has a feeling she definitely won't be leaving now.

He studies the photo for a minute. "We were talking about guilt and how Rayna felt it was her fault." He hands it back to Grady. "I told her it wasn't, but then she said, 'she was taken after leaving my house,' and it made me think, what if whoever took Remi literally took her right after she left Rayna's house?"

Grady practically jumps out of her chair as she comes to the realization. "You mean right after, as in, as she stepped out the door, wearing her sisters shoes, so someone would think that Remi was Rayna?"

"Exactly."

"Then we are going about this all wrong. We have spent all this time looking into Remi's life and enemies, when we should be looking into Rayna's!" She nearly yells the last part, then begins shuffling the papers on her desk looking for the correct ones. "I knew we were missing something big. This has to be it!" She pulls out her notepad and begins looking over her notes.

"I think we should let her sleep a couple hours, then interview her as soon as possible," Brown interjects as his partner hands him some files. He can tell she isn't really listening, she's too excited to have found a possible break in the case.

"Put all these away and let's get everything we know about the sister." She sets Rayna's file on her desk and opens it slowly like it's some sort of antique document.

"I'll put these away for you, but then I'm going to get a couple hours of sleep." Brown yawns as he stands with his arms laden with files.

"Sleep?!" Grady exclaims. "How could you think of sleep when we might have just had a major break in the case?"

He rolls his eyes. It has always been difficult to get his partner to put down her work. "Because I'm tired and we can't do much until Rayna wakes up anyways. I'll tell the night lady to make sure she doesn't leave just in case she wakes up before I do."

Grady looks down dejectedly at the file in front of her. She's also pretty tired. Maybe fresh eyes after a couple hours of sleep would help. "Alright, you're right, I'll get a couple hours of shuteye too and then we can interview her together."

"Sounds like a plan," he says as he turns toward the employee break room.

"You're not going home?" Grady asks. She's the one who usually sleeps in the break room.

"After a big break? No way!"

Both of them laugh as they head down the hall. They don't say anything more as they each pick a couch and tuck in for the night.

Grady's phone alarm goes off at six. She groans as she stretches and tries to work the kink out of her neck. These couches really do a number on her muscles.

She looks at the other couch to see Brown doing the same. He's much taller than she is, and appears to be even more uncomfortable. It explains why he goes home to sleep even in the middle of big cases.

Without saying a word, they each get up and take turns using the mirror to make sure they're presentable. Grady uses the toothbrush she keeps in her purse to quickly freshen her breath. Brown shrugs and pops a stick of gum in his mouth.

They head out into the main area of the office where work is just starting up for the day. The night receptionist is just leaving when Brown calls out to her.

"Any noise from Ms. Casell?"

She shakes her head and slides her large purse over her shoulder. "She didn't try to walk by me. Honestly, she's probably still asleep, considering how plastered she was last night." She chuckles.

"Thanks!" he calls after her as she pushes open the office door and heads into the morning mist.

Grady yawns loudly as she starts up her computer. "Are you waking up sleeping beauty or does the pleasure fall to me?" She taps her fingernails on the desk expectantly.

"Go ahead," he replies.

She's surprised, as she thought for sure last night that her partner had a thing for Ms. Casell. She thought he would insist on waking her up himself.

To be polite, she knocks on the door to the waiting room before twisting it open. The light was left on all night, which apparently didn't bother Rayna, who's still sleeping on the couch. She moves slightly as Grady walks into the room.

"Ms. Casell." She taps the young woman's shoulder lightly. It feels weird to refer to her by her last name after referring to her by her first name in her mind.

The woman stirs, but her eyes don't open.

"Ms. Casell," she tries again. This time the woman opens her eyes and blinks a few times and she begins to stretch.

Grady backs up as Rayna sits up and surveys her surroundings.

"You're in the police station waiting room," Grady provides.

The young woman nods. "I recognize it. I remember coming here last night but I sort of thought it was one of my dreams. I didn't realize it had actually happened."

"It did," Grady provides in a flat voice as she watches the young woman pinch her eyes closed and rub her head. "Hangover?" she asks in the same tone as before.

"Most definitely," Rayna replies.

"Well, let's get you some water and Tylenol, and then I'd like you to answer a few questions for me."

"More questions?" Rayna asks as she stands up. She's more sure on her feet than when Grady saw her stumble into the station last night.

"Just a few." It's kind of a lie, but she doesn't want to scare the girl right away with the new direction of their investigation.

"Why? Did something happen?" She follows Grady as they head out of the room and down the hall to an interrogation room.

"No. But we've thought of some questions we didn't ask before. Now please have a seat," she motions to one of the four empty chairs in the room, "and I will be back with water and Tylenol. And maybe if you're lucky, I can snag some sort of breakfast for you."

Rayna shakes her head, placing her hand on her stomach. "Don't bother, my stomach isn't ready for food yet."

Grady nods and closes the door. She walks back down the hall, stopping at the break room for the water she promised, then heads to her desk for the Tylenol. Brown stands up as she walks by.

"She ready?"

"Sort of." Grady heads back toward the interview room. "She's a little too hung over for my liking, but this is just questions about her life so I think she's in a good enough state of mind to answer."

The two of them enter the room together and take two of the available chairs across from Rayna. Grady places the water on the table and the pills in Rayna's hand.

"So Rayna, do you have any enemies?" Grady starts, pulling out both her recorder and notepad.

The young woman groans. "We already covered Remi's enemies."

The officers look at each other. "We know, I want to know your enemies now Rayna, not Remi's," Grady clarifies, hoping the Tylenol kicks in fast.

Rayna furrows her eyebrows for a moment then closes her eyes. "I don't think so."

"No enemies, at all?"

Rayna shakes her head.

Grady is having trouble buying it. Especially since she first mentioned that she was the hated one. Every young woman has at least one enemy, even if it's just a jealous female friend. "You told me a couple days ago that you were, and I quote, 'the hated one.'"

"I didn't mean it like that. I just meant she was always the favorite whenever we met people. And I've been having trouble making friends lately, which I guess reaffirmed my feelings on her being more liked than me," Rayna corrects, a flush on her cheeks.

"Well, let's try something different, who are your friends?"

Rayna thinks for a moment but then shakes her head again. "I don't really have any friends either."

"No friends? Now why is that?" Grady can tell something is missing here. What young woman doesn't have friends?

"I quit my job a few months ago, and I'd had trouble making new friends in our neighborhood. They were all older and we had nothing in common. Zeki was pretty much my only friend, and you already know where he is at."

Both officers sit quietly for a minute, observing the girl. When something finally clicks in Grady's mind. "Rayna, how did you pay for the drinks at the bar last night?"

"You mean like whether I paid cash or card?" Rayna is obviously very confused by their question, which meant she's less likely to be prepared to lie.

"Yes, that's exactly what I'm asking." Brown is also staring at Grady in confusion, wondering what she's getting at.

"I paid with my debit card," Rayna answers with a shrug, the typical twenty year old American answer.

"Can I see the card?" Grady asks.

As Rayna begins to fiddle around in her small clutch for the right card, Grady makes eye contact with her partner. It's clear he's starting to have an inkling what she's getting at, yet is still largely in the dark.

Rayna places the red bank card down on the table in front of them. Grady picks it up and looks at it. "Bank of America, interesting. Zeki didn't have an account at Bank of America."

"If you say so, he never said he had one there but I thought maybe since everything else had been a lie—"

Rayna has started to ramble so Grady cuts her off. "No, I mean I've looked into it, Zeki didn't have an account at Bank of America. So did he send you money to this card? Did he give you cash?"

Rayna, obviously assuming this questioning is still about Zeki and his selling drugs, quickly blurts out, "Zeki never gave me any money!"

Grady smirks. She knew it. "But you quit your job months ago. Seems to me someone living on savings wouldn't be racking up a hundred dollar bar tab."

Rayna is silent, the expression on her face unreadable. Both officers watch in silence. They know from years of experience when someone is about to spill their guts, and this is it.

A single tear slides down her cheek as she sighs and opens her mouth. She closes it, obviously at a loss for words, before opening it a second time. "I...work..."

They wait but she doesn't elaborate. "Where?" Grady prods.

"Part time, various jobs, you know, whatever I can find." Her chatter is nervous and certainly not genuine as before.

Brown tears a page out of the notepad he's using and slides it over to

Rayna. "Can you write down each job that you remember? We will need to look into each one."

Rayna sighs. "I—I can't."

"Why not?" Grady pushes again.

"I—I—was doing..." She looks away toward the wall, obviously having an internal debate on what she'll say. "...videos..." she finally finishes.

"What kind of videos?" Brown sets his pen down, looking straight at Rayna. Grady knows him well enough to know he's shocked, but this is how he shows it.

"Pornography," she says in the smallest whisper. A single tear slides down her cheek. "Please don't arrest me."

Ah, so she's afraid of the legal implications, rightfully so, but Grady doesn't intend to arrest the girl. "We aren't going to arrest you Rayna, but you need to tell me about who you were working for and where. One of these people might have taken Remi."

She shakes her head. "That's the problem, I don't know names or anything. We filmed in a hotel, I would just meet them there when he texted."

"When who texted?" Brown picks his pen back up and once again takes notes.

She shrugs. "I called him Daryl. Probably not his real name, though."

"Last name?" Grady knows it's a long shot but she has to ask.

"No idea." Rayna looks embarrassed.

"And you were paid in cash, I assume?" Brown asks awkwardly. Grady looks at him with a raised eyebrow, then turns back to Rayna.

"Can I have the number you contacted him at? We might be able to find him that way."

Rayna nods and begins to look through her phone. "You really think Daryl took Remi?" she asks, turning her phone so Grady can see the number.

"We aren't sure," Grady responds as she copies the phone number down. "But we have run out of leads on Remi's side, so we need to follow every lead possible."

"But why me? Unless..." Grady can see the young woman connect the dots before their eyes. "...You think I was the one who was supposed to be taken." As she finishes the sentence her face melts into an expression of guilt. She looks at Brown with a look of someone who has been betrayed. "You...you said it wasn't my fault..."

Grady looks over at her partner to see an odd expression that she doesn't recognize come across his face. As if he knows she's watching, he quickly corrects it and his face is once again his emotionless interview mask. "We aren't saying it's your fault, we just need to look at every possible angle. And that means everyone involved in your life."

Rayna sighs. "I never meant for it to get this far. I just didn't want to have to ask Zeki for money. I had savings from waitressing, but when those ran out..." She drops her head down into her hands. "I couldn't think of anything else to do. I only did it a few times. I hated it. It made me feel like trash, but the money was good."

"And the people who were in these...movies with you?" Brown is obviously struggling to keep his emotions hidden. Grady is pretty sure she was correct in thinking he has feelings for the girl.

"I told you before, I only know false names. Daryl was my contact. I would meet up with him and other people would either already be there or show up shortly after. We would film, and then go our separate ways. I don't know of anyone there who didn't like me. Daryl was pretty mad when I said I wouldn't be in any more of his movies."

"And when was this?" Grady asks, quickly scribbling down all the notes she can.

Rayna looks toward the ceiling, counting quietly to herself. "A few weeks ago. He's been hounding me, but Zeki and I's relationship was falling apart so I told him I couldn't do it anymore. But he's kept on messaging me."

"Do you still have the messages?" Brown asks. Rayna nods, presses a few buttons on her phone, then slides it over to them. They both lean in to look at the screen. Grady makes eye contact with her partner but doesn't say anything. They'll discuss the texts later. Grady raises her own phone to take screen shots of what's on Rayna's.

"Do you think Daryl would want to hurt you?" Grady questions, more as a formality. The text messages don't seem threatening, just desperate.

"I don't think so."

"Did Daryl know you were a twin?" Brown passes Rayna's phone back across the table. It takes a moment for what he's saying to sink in, but Grady quickly catches on to her partner's thought process.

"Why would that matter?" Rayna asks, her mind obviously not on the same devious path as the officers'.

"Some people get a little, how do I say it—obsessed—with twins," Grady clarifies for the girl, watching her face for any reaction.

She looks more confused than anything. "When we were kids we would sometimes be harassed. People would wonder if we could have conversations in our minds and feel each other's pain and stuff. But for Remi and I, that never happened. We were pretty much just regular sisters who looked a lot alike. I haven't had anyone zero in on the twin aspect of my life in a very long time. Remi and I have lived mostly separate lives for years. In fact, I hardly even mention it anymore."

Grady nods, finishes scribbling some notes, then looks at Brown. He also completes whatever he's writing then looks at his partner. This is their way of knowing neither of them has any more questions.

"Alright Rayna, you can go home. That's all the questions we have for now."

Both officers stand, but Rayna remains seated.

"I never thought I would be this...lost without her. You guys have to find her."

They look at each other, a sad look on Brown's face. It's Grady who speaks. "We are trying and we will do our absolute best."

The three of them then exit the room, Grady headed for her desk while Brown walks Rayna to the door. They stand just outside and talk for a minute. Grady would give anything to know what they were saying. Maybe she really is too nosy for her own good. She watches as he scribbles something down on the paper and hands it to Rayna.

After another few minutes, he walks back inside, keeping his head down as he passes her desk and heads for his own.

"What was that about?"

"Geez, you're like my mother or something," Brown mutters, obviously avoiding the question.

"You gave her a piece of paper."

"Thanks, Hawkeyes."

"What was it? Your number?" Grady is now leaning all the way across her desk, only inches from Brown's head.

"No." He looks up to find her face inches from his and scoots back, annoyed. She continues to stare at him expectantly. Finally he realizes she isn't going to give up.

"It was the number of a place she can get temporary work. The legal kind."

"And your number?" Grady jokes, trying to lighten his mood, which has been somber since the interview room.

He shakes his head. "She knows where to find me. And the last thing that girl needs right now is someone new in her life. I think she needs to figure some things out first."

"I disagree." Grady sits back down in her chair. "I think what that girl really needs is a friend."

Brown opens his mouth to argue, but they're cut off by the ringing of the phone on Grady's desk. She quickly reaches for it, taking a deep breath before she answers. Their work is never over.

"Grady."

From the other end of the phone line comes the five words every cop learns to dread. "There's been a media leak."

NOW

S HE KNOWS THIS is her chance. And probably the only one she'll ever get.

The two men tied Remi up and put her in the trunk of a car. Well, it's a hatchback car, so trunk isn't quite the right word, but it isn't exactly a seat, either. They've been driving now for almost twenty minutes. Or what she assumes is twenty minutes, her ability to judge time is definitely lacking.

She has no idea how far they're taking her, but she knows the moment they open the back hatch, she needs to be ready.

Her hands are tied behind her back with rope, which she's working furiously to get out of. She knows there's no way she can overpower two men, so her only chance is to surprise one of them with a punch or kick, then run like hell. But her plan won't work if she can't get her hands untied.

"Come on," she mouths silently, willing herself to wriggle harder. Her wrists are definitely bruised at this point, probably about to bleed.

It seems impossible. The rope won't give, and she can't get the rope up or down her arms to be able to reach the knot with her nails. She can do this, she knows it.

Suddenly, the car comes to a stop and she hears the sound of the parking brake engaging. This is definitely not a stop light. Then the car engine shuts off. Remi is out of time.

Her hands are still bound tightly behind her, and she tries to think of something, anything she can do. She needs to get away from these guys, and soon. There's no telling what they'll do now that they've decided to go rogue.

She hears two car doors slam separately, then voices as the two men have a rather long discussion, more like an argument, right outside the car. Remi can't make out what they're saying, but there definitely seems to be something wrong.

The arguing lasts for a few minutes. Then it comes to a sudden stop. It's starting to get stuffy in the car, and she knows they'll either get back in, or take her out, and soon.

Remi decides to take a chance, and positions her body as best she can, ready to kick whoever opens the hatchback door. She readies her ab muscles to pull herself to a standing position if her kick is successful. If it isn't, well, she doesn't even want to let her mind wander down that path.

Finally, she hears some movement outside the door and a shadow passes over her face. She closes her eyes, feigning sleep. She has kept her upper body in the same position they put her in the car in, hoping whoever opens the door won't notice she's shifted her lower body.

This is it, the moment of truth.

The hatchback creaks open.

BAM! She kicks both her feet into the shorter henchman's face as hard as she can. He lets out a yell and falls backwards.

Without pausing, Remi wrestles her way to her feet, which is not easy, and takes a quick look at her surroundings. They're on the shoulder of one of the highways heading out of town. There are grass fields on either side of the two lane road. She doesn't have time to guess which direction is which, because the short man is crawling to his feet.

"Why, you little bitch!" he screams and lunges towards her.

She runs. Faster than she ever has before. Down the road from which she assumes they came, hoping to see another car.

She doesn't look back, but she can hear the shorter man in pursuit. She isn't sure where the taller man went, but she doesn't have time or energy to try and figure it out.

There are no cars coming, and none down the road that she can see. She knows she can't run forever, she'll need to find cover, and fast.

The shorter man is still following her, but she can tell by the sound of his footsteps that he's out of shape and falling behind. But he can definitely still see her, which means she's still as good as dead.

She chances a look over her shoulder to see he's yards behind her. She's definitely losing him.

Why doesn't this state have any damn trees? she wonders to herself as her lungs begin to burn and her legs start to lose feeling. She's going to burn out if she doesn't find a place to hide.

Up ahead, a figure starts to take form on the street in front of her,

someone is walking her way! She's about to call out to him when she realizes it's the other henchman! That's why the shorter one gave up chase!

With absolute panic, she veers off the road and begins running
through the grass. Luckily, or unluckily, the grass is waist high. It makes it
hard to run, but once she's gone about thirty seconds she flops down on
her stomach and holds her breath.

The man was walking with his head down, but there's still a chance he
saw her turn and head into the grass. She waits silently, praying he didn't
see her.

She can't hear him from her position, and she hopes that means he
can't hear her heavy breathing either.

After what seems like sufficient time for him to pass by, she once again
wrangles herself back to her feet. Her hands are now numb thanks to the
rope being too tight. She gets herself into a crouching position and peeks
up over the grass.

The tall man passed right by!

She isn't out of the woods yet, though, she knows it will only take a
few minutes before he meets up with his buddy and finds out she's missing. And he can probably run a lot faster than his friend.

Remi looks around and tries to quickly consider the best course of
action. She could go back to the road and run faster, but more visibly, or
stay in the grass.

She decides to stay in the grass and begins to awkwardly chicken-run
away from the road as best she can with grass hitting her in the face.

Her awkward run isn't nearly as sustainable as her run on the road, and
her adrenaline rush is starting to fade. She knows she needs to get as far
from the road as possible, so she keeps herself crouched down and slows
her pace to an awkward walk.

Soon the walk slows to a crawl, and then she finds herself sitting with
no more energy whatsoever to move. She hopes she's made it far enough.

She doesn't hear any noises or signs of pursuit, and soon, the sun
begins to set and the temperature begins to drop.

Remi tries to use her arms for warmth, but it's no use as they're still
tied up. She needs to keep moving. She wrestles herself back to her feet
and begins walking. She doesn't even know what direction she's headed
in, she just hopes it isn't back into the hands of her kidnappers.

The night comes fast, and it's pitch black. The temperature is uncomfortably cold. Her bare feet are numb. Has she really escaped only to die of frost bite in the countryside?

Just as she's about to call it quits and give in to the exhaustion beginning to take over her limbs, she sees something in the distance.

There's a light.

She musters her last ounce of energy and begins to walk towards it.

NOW

S HE SITS OUTSIDE the police station staring at the piece of paper in her hand for what seems like forever. She knows she should just go over there and get started on a new job. She should, but she doesn't feel like it.

Pulling her almost dead phone out of her pocket, she glances at the screen and grimaces. There are missed calls from her parents and John. She dismisses them all and pulls up her Uber app. She should probably head back before they start to think she's gone missing, too.

Just as she opens the app, her phone screen goes black, the battery giving up on her, too.

Great, just great.

Rayna glances over her shoulder at the police station. She should go back in and ask to use a charger, she supposes. She feels her cheeks flush at the embarrassment of having confessed her recent profession to Detective Brown.

No. She can't face going back into the station, either.

Rayna stands up and brushes off her clothes. They're a mess, wrinkled from sleeping in them all night. Not to mention she still vaguely smells of booze.

She begins her walk to the metro station. She can at least go to a stop a bit closer to her parents' place, then walk from there. Her parents live in a neighborhood similar to the one she lived in with Zeki. Out of the city, and also out of easy range of public transit.

On the walk, she begins to entertain the idea that maybe Remi will never be found. Maybe she's about to be an only child. Then, as if the wind whispers it, she hears Remi's voice in her head.

Don't give up on me just yet.

Rayna smiles to herself. Remi will survive whatever had happens to her, she just knows it.

The metro is empty this time of day, as it's past the morning commute time but before the lunch rush. Rayna's lucky enough to get a seat right by the back of the train, and she watches the train tracks as they speed out from under her. It's sort of a liberating feeling.

She steps off the train and makes her way up the steps toward the sidewalk.

"Rayna?" a familiar voice calls.

She turns to the left to see Katie standing there, outside the metro stop, a brown paper bag in her hand. She looks extremely confused to see her.

"Hi, Katie," Rayna replies and steps toward her friend.

Katie steps back. "Wh-what are you doing here?" Katie glances around the empty sidewalk, seemingly extremely nervous.

Her behavior is making Rayna nervous. So much so that she stops walking when she's still a few feet away. "I'm going to my parents' house," she says guardedly.

"But, I mean...why?" The words come out garbled and clearly not a full sentence. Something is definitely up. Rayna glances around, wondering if her friend sees something she doesn't. Does she really look that bad?

"I had a rough night," she tries to explain her appearance away.

"Yeah, but um..." Katie trails off, obviously running out of words to mish mash together.

"Are you okay, Katie?"

When she says her friend's name, it's as if a change comes over Katie, she stands up straighter and becomes more composed. The flush on her face begins to disappear. "Do you need a ride?" she asks, seemingly back to her normal self.

Rayna still feels apprehensive about her supposed friend's earlier behavior. Why was she so shocked to see her?

She looks around again. It would be rude of her to decline.

"Sure. If you don't mind. Sure you're okay?"

"Yeah, I'm fine, sorry, I was just distracted. Too much on my mind, I guess. C'mon, I'm parked right over here." She motions to a red convertible parked by the side of the road. Rayna climbs into the passenger seat.

"So were you out doing errands?" Rayna asks hesitantly as her friend starts the car.

"Yeah, uh, I was," Katie answers cryptically. Katie pulls out of the parking lot and heads toward the main road.

"My parents' house is in the Little Creek subdivision, if you know where that is," Rayna volunteers, since Katie hasn't asked for directions.

Katie's silent for a moment before she responds. "You know Rayna, why don't you come back to my place and get cleaned up first? I'd hate for you to go home looking like that. And I have some clothes I think that will fit you."

She glances at the clothes she's wearing. She didn't think they were that bad. But maybe they are. "Thanks Katie, but I have stuff to change into at my parents' house. And they're used to me coming home looking like crap. I did it all the time in my late high school years. They'll just shake their heads like normal." Rayna doubts they'll say anything because they're probably too busy worrying about Remi.

"You know Rayna, I really think you should come back to my place." She turns and looks at Rayna for a moment with a serious stare before turning her eyes back to the road.

"Thanks Katie, I appreciate you looking out for me, but really, I should just go home. I've been gone for too long as it is."

Katie's quiet for another moment, then when she looks over at Rayna again there's moisture in her eyes. "Please Rayna, I just really need some company right now. Mark and I are having a tough time and it would be great to have a girlfriend over…" She trails off, brushing away a tear that escapes down her cheek.

Rayna isn't sure what to do. She really needs to get home to her parents and she can't call because her phone is dead…

"Okay I'll come with you, but can I use your phone to call my parents? They're probably worried sick and mine is dead."

"Sure," Katie answers quickly, her somber mood suddenly gone. She reaches into her purse and pulls out her phone, glancing at the screen. It looks as if it lights up for a minute, then the screen goes dark. "Oh shoot. Mine just died too. You know what? Come back with me and we can call from there."

"Okay," Rayna agrees hesitantly. She's pretty sure she saw Katie's phone screen light up. It's odd if it literally just died. But she doesn't want to argue when her friend is having a tough time. "Thanks."

"Anytime, that's what friends are for."

Rayna still feels weird about the entire exchange. Katie's mood has shifted a number of times. Is she really having that tough of a time with her relationship?

The houses slowly become larger and larger as they leave her parents' side of town and head deeper into the suburbs, more toward where the party she attended was. Memories from that night suddenly flash to the front of her mind.

Katie turns off the street into a large driveway. It isn't gated like the house the party was at, but the house still costs easily over half a million dollars. Rayna wonders what Mark does for a living. She winces as she remembers him drunkenly coming on to her at the party.

The girls don't talk as they exit the car and head up the walk. Katie slides her key into the lock and pushes open the door.

Rayna's immediately impressed by the high ceilings and all-white décor, just stepping into the entryway she feels she's definitely too dirty to be there.

Katie slides off her shoes and Rayna follows suit, leaving them just outside the white shoe organizer placed by the door.

As they head into the kitchen, Rayna feels she should say something, apologize for what happened all those weeks ago. "Listen, Katie," she starts as her friend takes down two glasses from a hanging wine glass rack that Rayna is sure cost more than she makes in a month waiting tables. "About what happened at that party, I'm really sorry. I know I shouldn't blame anyone but Mark, he came on to me and—"

"Shh." Katie places her finger on Rayna's lips making her step back a step. "Don't worry about it, it's all in the past now." A wide grin spreads across her face. "Shall we have some wine?" She places an empty glass in Rayna's hand.

Rayna grimaces, remembering the night before. "Actually, thanks but I think I'm done drinking for awhile."

"Aw come on." Katie pouts. "Just one glass? I don't want to drink alone. And I need a glass."

"Alright, one glass," Rayna agrees. Rayna figures she can just swirl it around and pretend to drink it. Katie won't notice.

"Okay I'll even let you go down to the wine cellar and pick one out. Whatever you want and we will pop it open." Katie winks.

"You have a wine cellar?" Rayna's impressed. She's seen in movies that people have them in their houses, but she's never actually been in someone's personal wine cellar.

"I do. Come right this way." She leads Rayna around a corner and down the stairs toward the basement. The room at the bottom of the stairs is not nearly as impeccable as the upstairs décor, in fact it's quite boring, outfitted with a TV and a simple couch.

As if she knows what Rayna's thinking, Katie quickly pipes in, "this is Mark's area of the house. He wanted one place to call his own so I said this could be his 'man den,' whatever that means." She rolls her eyes with a giggle.

Rayna doesn't really know what to say, as when she moved in with Zeki he pretty much did whatever he wanted without consulting her. That's what he always did, now that she thinks about it.

"Here." Katie motions to a trap door in the floor. "There's no light down there but I'll go grab a flashlight, you get started from what you can see with the light from up here."

Rayna watches as she pulls open the trap door and lowers a ladder down like the one her parents had for their attic door when she was a child. She steps down onto the first step, most of her body still above the trap door. "I really can't see anything, maybe you better grab that flashlight first. I don't even think I can get started without it." All Rayna can see is the pitch black beyond a small square of light from the door.

"Here, I'll shine my phone flashlight for you." Katie pulls her cell phone out of her pocket as Rayna steps down two more steps.

Rayna reaches up one hand to grab the phone and then pauses as realization hit her. "But wait, didn't you say your phone was dead?"

A grin spreads across Katie's face, and before Rayna can react she feels a hand push her chest forcefully and she feels herself falling backwards off the ladder. She searches around her for something, anything to grab on to, but her arms merely encounter air.

Until her shoulder hits the ground with a sickening crack. Rayna gasps in pain, unable to move as the sharp knives crawl up her neck and down her arm. It takes her a minute to remember what she was doing.

"Katie!" she calls back up to the square of light, her shoulder throbbing and pain burning her vision. "I think my arm is broken!"

There's a shadow blocking part of the light, probably Katie's head. But the shadow doesn't say anything and the ladder begins to retreat.

"Katie! What are you doing!" Rayna calls out again, scrambling to move, but the shooting pain keeps her from being able to get to her feet quickly. Before she even finishes standing, the light disappears and there's a thump as the trap door is shut.

Rayna finds herself standing, cradling her arm in the pitch black.

"Katie!" she calls again.

She strains her ears, listening for her friend to say this is just some sort of joke, but no sound reaches her ears.

Rayna looks around, unable to see anything. She tries to reach out with her good arm to feel around her, but she finds the minute she lets go of her broken arm, pain shoots up her shoulder. Cradling her bum arm in her good one, she begins to inch her foot forward very slowly, using it to feel the area around before she puts it down. She's really hoping she doesn't run into a wall.

After a few steps, she does encounter a wall, then she walks along it with her good shoulder up against it, trying to feel for something, anything she can use to get out of here.

She comes to a corner, then another, and another. The edge of the room is completely empty. There's no wine, no weapons, nothing.

Rayna slowly lowers herself to the floor, wondering just what she did for Katie to do this to her. Does Katie really hate her that much? Is all of this just because she saw Rayna kiss her husband?

With a sigh, Rayna leans her head back against the wall, beginning to worry about her broken arm. She definitely needs medical attention, she knows that. But she also knows Katie isn't likely to come back here anytime soon. Rayna is beginning to wonder if she's going to come back at all. After all, Rayna knows where Katie lives and what she looks like. And Katie didn't wear a disguise.

Rayna knows enough to know that means she's probably screwed.

NOW

THE DAY IS a flurry of activity from the moment they discover the local news station somehow got a hold of the story of Remi's disappearance.

Like almost every single case this happens in, of course they don't have the right information. Mostly just snippets either heard over a police scanner or from a friend of a friend of a cop. So then the cops' job becomes to have a press conference and give out the right information as soon as possible.

"So are we still withholding that she's a twin?" Grady is seated at Leary's desk with Brown at her side. They're preparing an official media statement.

"I think that's the best course of action," Brown answers before Leary can open his mouth.

"It isn't your call, but yes, if we can keep it under wraps I think that best. We also need to prep the parents. The minute we give out the victim's full name you know they're gonna find the family, twin sister included," he says with a pointed look at Brown.

He nods solemnly. "I know. I just wish it wouldn't have to involve them both."

"That's our other problem," Leary adds. "The minute we release a description we are going to get calls of people who have seen Rayna, not Remi, because even the parents say they have trouble telling the two apart."

"Ugh," Brown groans. "I didn't even think of that."

"Well," Grady ponders out loud, "we could ask Rayna to lay low for a few days at her parents' house."

"That'll lower the call volume, but I'm sure people have seen her out and around this entire weekend. It's really going to hurt us trying to get the media to see Remi as a victim. Especially after the bar debacle I hear about." Leary looks pointedly at Brown, who groans and glares at Grady.

"Hey, he wanted to know how we were able to interview her so quickly." Grady shrugs. "But that's another issue. I think the media already has her first name, which is bad. Because if I'm right about the fact that Rayna was the one meant to be taken and not Remi, we may have just signed both girls' death sentences anyways."

"Because the minute he realizes he has the wrong girl, he's going to dump or kill Remi and try and grab Rayna," Brown finishes for her.

Leary nods. "We've still got the tail on Rayna right?"

"Yep, I've actually been meaning to check in with the guy as soon as we finish the press release." Grady flips to her to do list which, as always, is nearly a mile long.

"Do it before. I want him to be prepared to bring her back to the station ASAP." Leary jots down notes on a sticky pad on top of a mound of papers on his desk. "So Grady is going to check in with the tail and handle the press release. Brown, I want you to prep the parents. Also, maybe we should prep the boyfriend too, just in case. But be discreet. I don't know how deep the media is going to dig but I want to plan for the worst. But don't give them any ideas either."

Both officers nod and stand from the chairs by Leary's desk.

"I'm going to check in with some of our other tails and see if something has developed. We probably need to move manpower around now that our focus has shifted from Remi to Rayna. Did you ever get the phone records for Rayna?"

Grady shakes her head. "Not yet, but I only just asked them when they opened this morning. I usually give them a full business day to get back. I did call this Daryl character. Claims his real name is Daryl but he doesn't have to talk to me or to give me a last name without a court order...and technically he's right."

"So you're also working on a court order?" Leary raises his eyebrows.

"It's typed up, I just need to stop by the judge to have it signed. That was my next step after the press."

"Give it to one of the rookies to take over, you've got enough on your plate, per usual."

"Actually I can take it," Brown interrupts. "The courthouse is on my way to the parents' place, I'll stop by on the way."

"No need," says the front desk secretary, popping her head inside the door to Leary's office. "The parents just walked in the precinct door."

"Let me guess, they saw the news?" Leary grabs his jacket from the back of his chair and slides it on.

"No, worse, they say they haven't seen their other daughter in days." The secretary looks over her shoulder toward the waiting area. Grady's and Brown's eyes meet from across the room. "Should I send them in?"

"Please. And Grady, call her tail and let's get an answer for the parents."

Grady murmurs a "Roger" and heads back to her desk to make the call. Since she's out front in the open area with no private office, it's very easy to see the commotion happening at the front. The parents are obviously distraught.

"Both my daughters are missing and you want me to HAVE A SEAT?" the mother is yelling at the poor secretary.

Grady looks over at her partner, mouths, "fix it," and tilts her head toward the parents. He nods solemnly and heads over to explain that their daughter has, in fact, been with the police the last night and morning.

She dials the phone as the mother's hysterics calm down. The rookie they have tailing Rayna answers on the first ring.

"Yes ma'am?" he asks, obviously having read the name on the caller ID.

"Listen, we need you to bring in the girl. The sooner, the better. Just approach her, show your badge and give me a call if she gives you trouble."

"Uhhhh..."

Grady does not like the sound of that. "Uhhh what?"

"I sort of lost the girl a few hours ago. She got on the metro and the parkway stop and there's no parking there so by the time I was able to park she was already on a train headed somewhere."

"Dammit!" Grady screams, a little too loudly as everyone in the station turns to look at her. She motions to Brown to meet her in the back when he's done escorting the parents into Leary's office. "You need to find her, and fast, shit is about to hit the fan."

"What do you think I've been doing?" he snaps back. "I checked every stop and station I could think of. And this girl is on foot, if she stepped in a restaurant near one of those places I would have no idea. This city is giant."

Grady groans. This is a mess. "I'm going to put out a BOLO on her. Not on the news, but we need her in the station and NOW." She feels a little guilty to be treating a rookie like this but she also can't believe he lost his eyes on Rayna. She hangs up the phone without waiting for his response and storms into the break room where Brown is already waiting.

He doesn't even wait for her to close the door. "What was that about?"

"Rayna's in the wind. I don't think she did it intentionally, but she shook the tail. Hours ago. We are screwed." Grady runs a hand through her hair as she sits down at the table. Things just got infinitely more complicated.

Brown lets out a sound that's a mix between a groan and a growl. "I'll start the BOLO, and stop by the judge's on the way. You prep the parents since they are already here."

Grady doesn't like deviating from her boss's orders, but she knows Brown is just being logical. He does know the girl better than most of the officers and may have an inkling of where to find her. "Ask someone on the way out if they can call to get her phone triangulated."

He nods. "Text me right before you talk to the press. Just so I know."

She agrees and fills a cup up of coffee that's sitting in the pot on the counter. It's probably old, but she doesn't care. Anything to keep her awake at this point.

After a few sips she exits the break room and heads to Leary's office where the parents are waiting. She's happy to make a press release, but she can't lie, she's definitely not excited to deal with parents, she's never been very good at it, unlike Brown. He's a real people person.

She rests her hand on the door knob before slowly cranking it open, bracing herself for the onslaught of questions. Internally she crosses her fingers and hopes they haven't just gotten both of their daughters killed.

NOW

R EMI FEELS LIKE it takes centuries of walking on her now-numb feet to reach the light. For every step she takes, she feels as if it gets further away. But finally, it begins to draw near.

The wind whistles by the side of her face, drying her skin and eyes. Her throat begins to burn. It isn't winter yet, only fall, but the nights are certainly deceiving. She was never any good at guessing the temperature outside, but she figures it has to be right around freezing.

She's eventually able to make out what looks like some sort of small hut with two gas pumps situated outside. The light she saw is the lone street lamp shining down on the little cement oasis. She's never been so glad to see a gas station in her life.

Her pace picks up as she makes her way towards the hut. As she gets closer, she can see the hut is dark inside. Probably closed. Sure enough, as she walks around the side of the hut, there's a sign stating they close at 10 o'clock every day.

Now what? she wonders.

The hut is small, only enough room for a cashier, cash register, and various candy and tobacco products. The windows are glass, and they aren't barred like the gas station further in town. Her hands are still tied behind her back, otherwise she would try to bust open the glass with a rock. Instead, she tries beating her head against the glass, willing it to break.

Of course it doesn't, it's probably bulletproof, and she just ends up with a headache instead.

Remi dejectedly slides down to a sitting position in front of the hut. She's out of ideas. This is it. She can't believe she's come so far to give up in front of a gas station in the middle of nowhere.

You're not giving up! her mind argues. *Take a nap, we can try again in the morning!*

A nap does sound nice, but she remembers from biology class that it's the worst thing you could do, if you're hypothermic like she figures she is right now. To go to sleep is death.

She tries to find the will to climb to her feet and keep walking, but she finds she's so sore she's now unable to move. Her toes and feet are almost completely numb, and she can no longer feel her hands, arms, or shoulders either. It's only a matter of time now.

Sleep it is. "I'm sorry Rayna, I tried. I really did," she whispers into the night before closing her eyes. For once she wishes they were telepathically connected like other twins. But only silence fills her mind as she drifts into dreamland.

NOW

THE PRESS CONFERENCE goes well, as well as could be expected. Of course the minute she finishes she's bombarded by questions, some of which she answers, and some of which she lets be. They already agreed to withhold certain aspects of the case, although it seems some of the reporters already know the answers they're looking for. As of right now, they've only mentioned Remi's disappearance, since they aren't even sure Rayna is missing. Grady just hopes whoever leaked the first chunk of information will now keep their mouth shut.

She reaches her desk and plops down, placing her head on her hands. She's exhausted. But there's no break in sight.

"You okay?" Brown asks as he slides into his desk across from hers.

"If we find these girls I will be." She peeks her head up to look at her partner. He's staring off into space. "Any luck on finding Rayna?"

He shakes his head, not saying anything out loud. Grady has worked with Brown for many years. Even though he claims he doesn't have a thing for the girl, she knows better, there's something there.

Suddenly, his attention is drawn over her shoulder, and Grady spins around in her chair to follow his line of sight.

The boyfriend, John, is standing in the doorway of the police station, glaring in their direction.

"Not this guy again," Grady hisses under her breath as she rights herself and tries furiously to fix her hair.

"At least he cares."

"Appears to care," Grady corrects as they make their way over to the man.

"Any word? I saw the news." He looks at them eagerly. He's clearly worse off than they are, his hair disheveled and his face unshaven. His clothes are rumpled, leading her to believe he probably slept in them.

"If you saw the news, you know there's been no new developments," Brown replies gruffly.

Grady watches John's face fall and instantly feels bad for the guy. The guilt of their last fight is obviously eating at him. "Here, come have a seat, I'll get you a coffee, okay?"

He nods mutely and follows her back to the waiting room, sinking down into the couch.

"I just feel so terrible," he mumbles.

"I know," she replies, debating whether to sit down next to him or remain standing. She decides to remain standing. "You can't blame yourself, though. We believe whoever took her, it was premeditated. She would have been taken whether or not you guys fought."

"I know," he replies. "It doesn't make me feel any better, though. If only I had filed for a divorce earlier."

"That wouldn't have changed the events, John." Grady looks over her shoulder to see Brown approaching with a cup of coffee. She takes it from him and hands it to John, motioning for Brown to leave them be.

"You can't say that. Any small event could've changed the course of everything that's happened." He puts the coffee down and drops his head into his hands.

"That's true, John. But can you go back in time?"

"No," he mutters.

"And neither can I. So it's time we move forward. Now that we've officially made a statement, feel free to hand out fliers and we will begin to organize search parties okay? If that doesn't sound like something you want to do, you can also post on social media, asking people if they've seen her. Sometimes those things really do work." Grady knows anything to keep the families of victims busy usually helps—as it makes them feel like they're helping and keeps them out of the police station and from bothering officers.

John lifts his head, not saying anything but obviously not opposed to the idea.

"I've got to get back to my desk. Feel free to stay here as long as you want."

"Thanks, officer." He stands from the couch. "I think I'll get started right now. Sounds better than moping around."

"Sounds like a good idea." Grady smiles as she watches him leave the break room, checking her watch. It's almost eight in the evening. She walks back over to her desk to see Brown poring over a document.

"What you got there?" she asks, leaning over his shoulder.

"Rayna's phone is off or dead. They can't get it to triangulate." He sighs and runs a hand through his hair. "This is an activity record, shows if the user has used apps like Uber, etc."

"And?"

He shakes his head. "Nothing. Her phone has been off or dead since shortly after I left her on the front steps this morning. I requested the video feeds from the metro station she entered, as well as the one near her parents' house, but we could be digging in a haystack. Those cameras are often times poor quality and aren't always maintained."

Grady is all too familiar with the city's public camera system. It never seems to truly help any of their cases. "I know. I wish they would have better ones."

"I did find something interesting, though." He motions to another paper in his hands, clearly the phone and text log, on which the numbers are highlighted in different colors. The document is mostly blue, with a few yellow and pink stripes. "The blue here is Daryl, and the yellow is Remi."

"So she wasn't lying when she said she and Remi didn't talk often." She squints at the paper, wondering just how far the logs go back.

As if reading her mind, he flips to the next page. "We subpoenaed back only ninety days, but for a twenty-something girl, Rayna sure doesn't use her phone much."

"So she also wasn't lying about not having friends." Grady walks around to her side of the desk and sits down, her feet starting to ache from a day full of walking and standing after a night of not enough sleep.

"I don't think so. But there is this number highlighted in pink here, see?" He points to a line that appears on the first page, and then multiple times on the previous pages. "There were texts and calls from this number, not regularly, but frequently, then they suddenly drop off."

Grady takes the paper from his hands and peers at the number, quickly using her right hand to copy it down on a sticky note.

Brown watches her do so with one eyebrow raised. "I was going to call the phone company when they opened in the morning."

Grady shakes her head. "We may not need to." She flips open her computer and opens a browser window. Sometimes technology really is on their side.

"You're gonna search Facebook at a time like this?" Brown asks as if he thinks his partner's lost her marbles.

"No, you've never seen this before? You can type a phone number in the search bar on Facebook, and if they've got one attached to their profile it will come up." She types in the number and presses enter, the mouse spins in a little circle as the computer searches. "A lot of people don't have their Facebooks hooked to their phone number, but the demographic that does is usually mostly young females." A profile pops up on her screen. "Ah-ha!" she exclaims as she clicks on it.

Brown bumps his elbow as he tries to lean in too quickly to see the screen. "Ow," he murmurs quietly as Grady searches the page.

"Here it is, here's the number." She compares the number on her screen to the phone records in her hand. "That number belongs to a Katie Jackson."

"Pretty common name. Doesn't help us out much." Brown rubs his elbow and leans back in his chair.

"Actually it does, first of all we have a name and a phone number, if she's purchased a house we should be able to find the deed." She scrolls through the public portion of the woman's Facebook page. "She also doesn't have much set to private, and she looks like she came from money so I would bet..." She trails off as she flips through some of the woman's photos.

"Bet what?" Brown asks, obviously slightly astounded at his partner's use of a social media platform during a case.

"That she's got a cute car. Most girls who have cute cars take a picture of them. Which she did. And here it is." She spins her screen so Brown can see the photo.

It's a young, attractive blonde woman standing in front of a bright red Mustang convertible. Brown nods, and pulls up the application to access DMV records.

"Any idea what year?" he asks as he fills out the other portions of the form.

"Eh, I'm not a car person but she posted the picture in 2018 so I'm guessing it would be an 18 or a 19. Let me Google it and see which one looks closer." She turns the computer back her way and begins to type. She stares at the screen, narrowing her eyes in concentration for a moment. "I think it's an 18." She turns the screen his way, flipping back and forth from the Facebook picture to the ones she Googled. Brown nods in agreement.

He types the car make, model and year into the computer then presses send. It always takes a few minutes for this stuff to come back. After a minute, it pops up a result.

"Looks like her. And I have an address."

Grady stands and grabs her jacket. "Type it into the GPS. Let's go."

Brown squints at the numbers in the upper right of his computer screen. "It's past nine, shouldn't we wait until tomorrow?"

"No way. First of all, who even goes to bed at nine, and second of all if she did, I'm sure she wouldn't mind being woken up to find out her friend is missing. I'm sure she'd be concerned."

Brown grabs his coat and follows suit, although he's still apprehensive. "But what if they aren't really friends anymore? After all, the calls and texts stopped about a month ago."

Grady shrugs as they walk towards her vehicle. "Sometimes people just get busy. But we are going to find out either way." They slide into the car and Grady starts the ignition and backs out as Brown pulls up the address in his phone.

"Turn left onto Swanson Street," he tells her as she tears out of the parking garage. "You don't have to drive so fast." He quickly buckles his seatbelt.

"Yes I do," she retorts. "Someone pointed out it's already past nine and I would like to get there before ten. Because showing up after ten would just be way too late." She flashes Brown a sarcastic smile and laughs. He rolls his eyes.

NOW

S HE ISN'T SURE how long she's been in the dark cellar, but it feels like forever. She's tried calling out for help, but gave up pretty quickly as she's sure absolutely no one can hear her all the way down here. Especially in a subdivision like this, where the houses are far apart.

So this is what being kidnapped feels like, Rayna thinks sarcastically. She never imagined she would be in this position, and as she sits there leaning against the wall and cradling her broken arm, she can only imagine her sister sitting in this exact same position somewhere.

She feels guilty for her parents. Now they're going to lose her as well. She tries thinking positive, but every time she shifts her weight and pain shoots through her arm, the negativity returns. She's definitely going to die down here.

Maybe she deserves it. After all, she's been a pretty crappy person to almost everyone around her these past few months. Especially her twin sister. Remi has been there for her through thick and thin. And when things got tough with Zeki, Rayna pulled her typical move and bailed. Just like she's been doing her entire life.

After a few more minutes down that thought path, Rayna rolls her eyes and forces herself to her feet. A pity party isn't going to get her out of here. She already explored the edges of the room earlier, so now she figures it's time to explore the middle. It doesn't seem like a big room, but there could be something there to help her.

She slides her foot slowly across the floor in front of her in the same manner as she did before. She starts at the edge, then turns when she reaches a wall. She giggles a little, imagining how dumb this would look to anyone looking on. As she starts her third row, her foot touches something. She immediately draws it back. She takes a deep breath and inches her toe forward. It encounters something again!

Rayna knows reaching down to see what the object is will be impossible with her arm. She'll have to sit and find a way to rest her broken arm in her lap so she can inspect the object.

She eases herself down on the floor slowly, crossing her legs to sit cross-legged, but leaving one knee higher than the other. She lets her bad arm rest on her knee, then she reaches her good arm out and feels across the floor.

The object moves slightly when she touches it. It's smooth, and obviously lightweight if just a touch can dislodge it. She reaches out again and sets her hand on top.

It's cylindrical, and plastic. She feels its shape as best she can and comes to the conclusion it's probably an empty water bottle.

She uses her teeth to unscrew the cap and lifts the bottle to her mouth. Yep. Empty. She sets the bottle back down and transfers her bad arm so she can stand to continue her search.

Soon she encounters the other wall. That's it. The room only holds one empty plastic water bottle.

But who was drinking water down here? she wonders to herself. *Who else did Katie kidnap?*

But even as she wonders, she already knows the answer.

Remi.

NOW

Tʜᴇʏ ᴘᴜʟʟ ᴜᴘ outside the large house on the nice side of town in no time at all, thanks to Grady's driving.

"Nice house for a single woman," Brown remarks as they pull into the driveway.

"Rude of you to assume she's single," she counters.

"I mean, there wasn't a man in her Facebook profile picture so I, uh..." Brown quickly tries to correct his statement, realizing it came out rude. "Why do you think she's taken?" He tries to distract her from his faux pas.

Grady motions to the two cars in the driveway parked in front of theirs as she steps out. "Two cars, and a two car garage. I mean maybe the garage is full of crap, but somehow I doubt it and I think there's probably at least three cars on this property. And women aren't usually the car lovers if you know what I mean." They walk up the stone path to the door.

"Aren't you the one who just corrected me for assuming?" Brown snaps back as he reaches up and rings the doorbell.

"Touche," she replies as they hear the sound of the doorbell echo throughout the house. "No dog," she comments.

"Strange in this day and age."

"Strange for this city," she replies under her breath as the door creaks open.

The young blonde woman from the Facebook profile picture stares back at them. She's less done up than her picture, but still obviously wearing makeup and dressed very nicely in a cocktail dress.

"Yes, can I help you?" she asks, looking them up and down apprehensively.

They both pull out their badges simultaneously, having done house calls like this a hundred times. Grady does the talking. "Katie Jackson?"

She nods in acknowledgment.

"We are detectives Brown and Grady. We would like to ask you a few questions if that's okay?"

Katie bites her lip and glances over her shoulder nervously. As if on cue, a male voice calls out, "honey, is everything okay?"

"Yeah, everything's fine!" she calls back, then steps out onto the porch, leaving the door open about a foot behind her. "Can we make this quick? I just finished making dinner and I would like to eat it while it's hot."

Grady raises an eyebrow at her partner in an "I told you so" way. He nods and turns to Katie. "Sure thing. We are actually here looking for your friend Rayna."

"Rayna?" He voice raises an octave. "We aren't friends," she says quickly.

Brown makes eye contact with Grady, who continues, "she said she talks to you sometimes, is that not true?"

Katie rolls her eyes. "Okay we were friends for like a minute, then we went to a party together, then she stopped talking to me. But that's it. We were more of acquaintances than anything."

Grady nods. "I understand. So you haven't seen her recently?"

She shakes her head. "Not since I took her to that party about a month ago."

"Sure, and can we get the address for where the party was at? And maybe some of the names of people who were there?" Grady pulls out her iPad, prepared to take some notes.

Katie's eyes narrow. "Why?"

"We are just trying to locate Rayna, that's all." Brown plasters a fake smile on his face as he says it.

"Is she in trouble?" Katie is obviously trying to distract them in order to get off the subject of the party in question.

Grady knows how girls work, and she knows this girl isn't an idiot, so she decides to tell a little white lie. "Sort of. I can't really discuss it with you, but I really need to talk to her."

"I see." Katie's eyes shift from Brown to Grady, then she quickly rattles off an address. "I'm not sure who all was there, but my friend Roger was there. I pretty much just hung out with him and Rayna the whole time."

"And can we get a phone number for this Roger, please?" Grady presses.

As if he heard them talking, a young man appears in the doorway, pulling it fully open. Brown looks at the man, then looks over at Grady with his eyebrows raised.

"And you are?" she asks, assuming her partner must recognize the man or something.

"Mark Jackson, Katie's husband. What's going on here, babe?" He steps out onto the porch, putting his arm around his wife's waist, leaving the door fully open behind him.

"Nothing, they're just looking for Rayna," she replies to her husband. He laughs.

"Something funny?" Brown asks, his voice more stern than before.

"You should try finding her on sexyangeles.com. I think they call her Leila." He grins widely like a Cheshire cat.

Grady and Brown once again make eye contact and Grady flips her iPad closed. "So neither of you have seen her, in person, in the last month."

They both shake their heads no.

"Well if you do, here's my card." She pulls a card out from her pocket and hands it to Katie. "Give me a call at that number please."

"Will do," Mark replies, stepping back into the house, his wife at his heels.

The officers turn and head for their car, hearing the front door of the house click closed behind them.

Once they're in the car, Grady turns to her partner to ask why all the weird looks, but he already has his phone pressed to his ear.

"This is Detective Brown, I need backup." He rattles off the address and continues, "we're going in, exigent circumstances, believe someone is being held against her will."

Grady begins to back out of the driveway, not wanting to continue sitting there in case the couple is watching. She drives down the street at a crawling pace. Brown finishes the backup call and hangs up the phone.

She opens her mouth to ask what's going on, but he starts explaining before she even has the chance to say a syllable.

"I saw Rayna's shoes. In the entryway. They've got her. I know they do."

"Are you sure?" Grady asks nervously.

"Positive. Those are her shoes."

"Maybe they have the same pair? Girls do that kind of thing," Grady speculates, not nearly as sure as her partner.

"They're hers. I saw them on her feet this morning when we were talking. The toe on the left one was frayed. Same as the one I saw sitting in their entry way."

"Shit," Grady mutters. "Well if they do have her we might have just spooked them."

"Park the car and let's head back on foot. I'm not letting them out of our sight."

Grady nods and pulls over, parking the car and double checking to make sure her gun is loaded. She locks the car and slides the keys in her pocket. They're only about two blocks from the house and begin to walk back at a brisk pace.

"You better be right about this." Grady pulls out her weapon as they approach the driveway.

"I know I am. You stay up here, I'll go around back," he whispers as he heads for the backyard, disappearing into the cover of darkness.

SHE MUST'VE FALLEN asleep, because she's suddenly awoken as the room floods with light. It takes her a few minutes to blink as she's blinded from being in the dark for so long.

Once she's able to see, she can make out the profile of Katie standing in front of her. A pillow in one hand. A gun in the other.

"Katie," Rayna says hesitantly. She starts trying to get to her feet.

"Don't. Move," Katie hisses back.

Rayna freezes, trying to discreetly adjust her injured arm, which is not happy at being jostled. "What's wrong, Katie?" Rayna tries to keep her voice smooth and calm, but it breaks at the end, betraying her.

"You. You ruined my life." The gun shakes in Katie's hand and a single tear slides down her cheek.

"I-I don't understand," Rayna stutters.

"It all started after that goddamn dinner. You're the reason my husband is cheating on me."

Rayna is taken aback. She thinks Rayna is seeing Mark? "I'm not, Katie, I promise."

"Shut up! Just shut up!" she shouts, jamming the gun into Rayna's cheek. Rayna winces as the barrel makes contact with her teeth. "I know you are! I saw your pictures in his phone! I saw your texts! I told him to stop and he won't!" She closes her eyes for a second and when she reopens them, Rayna can see they're filled with pure hate. "He won't stop until you're dead."

"Wait—" Rayna starts but is interrupted by the sound of a gunshot. She falls back, a heavy weight on her chest. Pain sears through her. *This is it. This is the end*, she thinks.

Suddenly the weight is lifted off of her and the outline of a man blocks the light.

"Is this heaven?" she asks, slightly confused.

The figure laughs and comes closer to her. "If it is, we're all in trouble."

Rayna relaxes as his features come into shape. It's Detective Brown. She smiles slightly. "I was wondering why my arm still hurt in heaven." She looks around and notices the body of Katie off to the side. Brown is checking her pulse. "What happened?" She's still confused as to how she heard a gunshot and isn't dead.

"Still breathing!" Brown calls over his shoulder as another figure descends the ladder.

"I called for a bus. I have the husband handcuffed to the stair banister. Backup is also on the way," Grady replies as she surveys the scene and approaches Rayna.

"I shot her just as she was about to shoot you," Brown says in a quiet voice, answering Rayna's question. Grady kneels down in front of Katie, taking off her jacket to stop the bleeding in Katie's lower torso.

"Are you okay?" she asks, looking Rayna up and down.

Rayna nods. "Yeah, but my arm or shoulder, or both, are broken I think."

Brown looks at the way she's cradling her arm. "Can you climb the ladder?" he asks.

"I doubt it." She laughs at the irony of the situation.

"Hello?" someone calls out from somewhere above their heads.

"Down in the cellar!" Grady calls back as two faces appear in the trap door and quickly make their way down the ladder. Rayna assumes by the way they're dressed that they're EMTs.

One of the men takes one look around the scene and calls back up, "we're gonna need a backboard!" He then approaches Katie, pulling bandages and gauze from his bag. The other approaches Rayna. More EMTs and cops descend the ladder. The room is small and filling up fast. An EMT begins inspecting Rayna's arm and she cries out in pain.

"Definitely broken. We will need to take you to the hospital for x-rays. Let me see if we can get a sheet set up to pull you outta here." The EMT starts talking to another one that's just arrived.

Brown must sense her unease. "Grady?" He looks at his partner, who's securing Katie's gun and placing it in a Ziploc bag.

"I'll stay with her, you take Rayna up." A small smile plays on her lips.

Brown looks at the EMT. "I can climb the bottom few steps with her with one hand if you have a couple guys up top to grab her from me?"

The EMT nods, pulling a sling out of his bag and slipping it over her shoulder so she won't have to keep holding her arm. Then he motions to another EMT and they head up the ladder. Brown reaches down and slides one hand under her legs. "Now you need to hold on to my neck with your good arm, okay?"

"Yes, sir," Rayna replies, with a smile despite everything that has happened, as she feels his chest against her side.

He moves her and climbs the ladder with ease, stopping at the fifth step where the two EMTs are able to reach in and grab her out. There are two backboards on the floor outside the trap door.

The nearest EMT smiles at her. "I'm James," he says cheerfully. "I'd ask you to shake my hand but," he points at her right hand and Rayna feels a smile coming to her lips again. "Anyways, we need to take you up the stairs. Can you walk or do we need to carry you?"

"I can walk," Rayna answers and James helps her to her feet.

Rayna turns to look at Brown, who's finished exiting the cellar himself and is talking to the EMT. "Grady and I have to stay here," he says, noticing her gaze. "But we will come to the hospital to interview you in awhile, okay?"

She nods as she's led away by James. He leads her through the house she saw briefly before, jolting slightly when they pass Mark handcuffed to the stairs. He's looking at her with confusion in his eyes as two officers Rayna doesn't recognize are talking to him.

James leads her outside into the back of a waiting ambulance. "Your parents will meet us at the hospital, okay?"

She nods mutely, overwhelmed as shock starts to set in. He closes the double metal doors and they're on their way.

They've just finished setting her broken arm and shoulder and outfitting her with the fanciest cast known to man when her parents rush in the room.

"Oh my God, are you okay?" her mom screeches, partially hysterical.

"I'm fine mom, really. I'll be good as new in..." She trails off and looks at the doctor expectantly.

"Eight to ten weeks," he rattles off as he scribbles out a prescription for pain medication.

"That's a long time," Rayna's dad replies, inspecting the contraption on her arm. "Will you be coming home with us, then?"

Rayna nods. "I don't really have another choice with the FBI seizing Zeki's place and Remi's still being a crime scene."

Her father nods knowingly. "You can stay as long as you like."

Rayna hears footsteps and looks up to see Detective Grady entering the room. She smiles when she sees Rayna sitting up and bandaged up. "I see they're taking good care of you." She looks at her parents. "Can I have a minute alone with Rayna please?"

"Uh...sure..." her mom replies, as if she's been helping instead of crying the whole time. The doctor also gives a polite nod and steps out with her parents. Once the door is closed and they're alone in the room, Grady looks at her expectantly.

"Can you tell me how you ended up in your friends cellar?"

Rayna shakes her head in shame. "I thought we were friends, but apparently not. Anyways, I was taking the metro to my parents' house and she was there outside the station by their house and offered me a ride." She takes a deep breath, remembers Katie's confusion, and feels like an idiot, but continues. "I didn't want to ride with her. She seemed really confused and out of it and I think that's because she already killed Remi." As she says the last part, tears start to well up in her eyes.

"Why do you say that?" Detective Grady asks, pulling out her iPad.

"Well she seemed absolutely shocked to see me. I think it's because she'd never met Remi and didn't realize how alike we were. There was an empty water bottle in that cellar—"

Grady interrupts, "we found it and sent it to the lab."

Rayna nods. "Test for Remi's DNA, because the only thing that makes sense to me why Katie would be so shocked to see me is if she had already killed Remi thinking she was me and thought I was a dead person walking." Tears are flowing freely down her face now.

Grady comes over and puts a hand on Rayna's shoulder. "We will find her, don't worry."

"Did Katie say where she is?" Rayna asks hopefully as Grady hands her a tissue.

"Katie is still in surgery. Bullet hit a few major organs, they aren't sure if she will survive or not. I'll let you know when I hear something, okay?"

"Okay." Rayna reaches for a second tissue. "Where's Detective Brown?" she asks, just now remembering he said they would come to the hospital together.

A small smile plays on Grady's lips. "He wanted to come but he has to go through a process since he discharged his weapon today. I think they're about to discharge you but I'm sure we will both stop by your house later once we get news of your sister."

Rayna nods solemnly as Grady takes some quick pictures of her cast on her iPad. "What are the pictures for?"

"In case this goes to court," Grady replies and snaps a few more. "I doubt it will, but you never know." After she's finished, she goes and opens the door and Rayna's parents rush back in.

"The doctor says you're good to go home!" Her mother is dry eyed for the first time since she heard of Remi's disappearance, and a slight smile occupies her lips.

"We will fill your prescriptions on the way home okay?" her dad suggests, yawning and helping her off the table. It's now almost seven in the morning and they were up all night. "I think everyone deserves some rest."

"Wait," Rayna says as they lead her towards the door, "I don't have any shoes."

Grady smiles from the corner of the room. "I'll go grab some hospital slippers for you. Those shoes you were wearing saved your life."

"They did?!" Rayna asks incredulously.

Grady nods. "Yes, Brown recognized them when we went to question Katie. Him and those shoes are the only reason we came back." And with that, she exits the room and heads down the hall to get her the slippers she promised.

She's back within minutes and begins taking off the plastic wrap. Grady then walks with Rayna's parents as Rayna is wheeled in a wheelchair towards the check out desk. The minute the desk woman sees Rayna she startles. The movement doesn't escape Grady's notice.

"Everything okay?" she asks the woman at the desk.

"Yes," the woman clears her throat in embarrassment. "It's just, uh," she looks at the discharge papers in her hand to find Rayna's name, "Ms. Casell looks just like one of our other patients."

Grady nearly drops her iPad. Rayna's mom does drop her purse. "Where, what room, what's going on with her?" Grady snaps immediately into cop mode.

The nurse shakes her head. "I'm not sure. I'll have the doctor come talk to you, Ms. Grady," she says pointedly, as if Rayna and her parents are about to get information they aren't privy to.

Grady doesn't argue, she just nods then turns to Rayna's parents. "I'm going to head down to intake. Wait out in the waiting room for me. We need to confirm it's her first."

Her dad nods excitedly and begins to turn Rayna toward the door. But Rayna doesn't miss Grady's long stare as they wheel her away.

They didn't say anything about Remi being alive.

NOW

IT FEELS LIKE the intake woman at the ER is taking forever to get back to her. She inquired almost twenty minutes ago about a Jane Doe brought in. She even showed the picture of Remi she had with her, hoping to speed up the process, but it apparently did no good.

"Grady," the doctor finally calls from the door. Grady stands quietly and follows him into his office. This can't be good.

He sits down behind his large mahogany desk and leans back in his chair, letting out the breath in his lungs. "I hear you're inquiring about our Jane Doe."

"Yes." Grady sits up straighter. "I believe she's the victim in the missing persons case I'm investigating."

"I understand that. The reason I took so long to get back to you is this Jane Doe you were asking about," he looks down at the paper in his hand, "Remi Casell, just came in a little over an hour ago and..." He sets down the papers on the desk and looks Grady straight in the eyes. "Things don't look good."

She pulls out her iPad, quickly typing in what the doctor just said. "Can you elaborate?" she asks without looking up from her iPad.

"Well, she was brought in unconscious, suffering from extreme hypothermia."

"Who brought her in?" Grady was in her car on the way to the hospital a little over an hour ago and she didn't hear anything on the radio.

"A good Samaritan. He brought her to the hospital in his vehicle."

"And he didn't call an ambulance?" Grady asks. It's odd in this day and age that someone would drive someone they don't know to the hospital. Without waiting for an answer, Grady blurts out her next question. "And can I get his information?"

The doctor shakes his head. "That's what took me so long. I don't know why this guy didn't call the police. He didn't speak to any of our staff, he simply pulled up in a green Subaru." He shuffles the papers in his hand and hands Grady a security camera picture of the vehicle.

"He set her on the ER waiting room floor." He pulls out another picture showing a balding man, probably in his mid forties, wearing a black hoodie, carrying Remi bridal style, wrapped in a quilt into the lobby.

Grady takes the photo from him and studies it intently. The man's features are hard to distinguish in the grainy security camera photo, but she figures her tech team can enhance it.

"—And then he left." The doctor hands her a final picture showing the man climbing back in his vehicle to presumably drive away. Grady takes pictures of all the pictures provided and quickly sends a message over to Brown, with nothing but the words 'found Remi' in the title. She'll call her partner as soon as she's finished.

"Can I see her?" Grady's mind is already running a million miles a minute about how they can trace the license plate, facial recognition the guy, and find the person who kidnapped Remi. But first, she needs to help the poor family waiting in the waiting room upstairs for news of their daughter and sister.

"Yes. But she's not good, like I said. She's unconscious and severely hypothermic. I suspect she spent the entire night outside somewhere. She wasn't wearing any shoes. We are doing everything to raise her body temperature, but it's too soon to tell if it's doing any good." He stands from his desk and crosses the room over to the door.

Grady slides her iPad under her arm and follows suit. He leads her down the hall of the ER, which is surprisingly quiet for this time of the morning.

They stop in front of a room where nurses are crowded around a woman. Grady immediately recognizes her simply from the fact that she looks just like Rayna. The resemblance is completely uncanny.

She's wrapped tightly in hospital blankets, tubes are fed up each of her nostrils, and a small portion of her arm is showing as the nurse switches out the IV.

"We are giving her warmth, keeping her humidified, feeding her oxygen and warmed IV fluids. If things don't improve in," he checks his wrist watch, "less than five minutes we will have to start with peritoneal lavage, which is not easy and has many dangerous side effects of its own."

Grady doesn't know what that is but it definitely doesn't sound good. "What should I tell the family?"

The doctor shakes his head. "Tell them the truth, she might not make it."

She takes that as her cue to leave the room, making note of the room number as she does. She makes her way back upstairs to the waiting room where the family is.

The parents jump up the minute they see her. Rayna observes her apprehensively.

"Is it her?"

"Is she okay?"

"What happened?"

"Who did this?"

The questions come in quick succession from the parents as Rayna continues to sit there quietly. Even though she claims she and Remi don't share a mental connection, it seems to Grady that she already knows.

"I'm pretty sure it's her, but it's not looking good. They aren't exactly sure what happened yet." Grady decides to spare them the gruesome details.

Both parents immediately become very solemn.

"Can we see her?" the mother asks, her eyes once again damp.

"Not at this exact second, they're working to save her life, but I will ask."

"Can I talk to you for a second?" Rayna asks meekly. "Privately," she adds with a glance at her parents.

Grady nods and wheels Rayna down the hall and towards the cafeteria.

"Everything okay?" Grady questions as soon as they're out of the earshot of Rayna's parents.

"Yes, but I want you to take me to see Remi, now." Grady starts to interrupt but Rayna holds up her hand to stop her and continues. "I know they're trying to save her life, I don't need to be in the room. I just need to see her. Just in case."

She doesn't feel right about taking Rayna to the flurry of activity she just left, but figures she'll let the doctor be the bad guy in this situation. "Alright," she replies and turns the wheelchair towards the elevator.

Rayna is quiet on the elevator ride, and Grady knows she's probably feeling guilty, scared, and possibly still in shock. She makes a mental note to recommend a psychiatrist before she leaves the hospital.

They exit the elevator to come face to face with a worried looking Detective Brown. Some of the worry etched on his face fades as he notices Rayna.

"Well look who's good as new," he comments, eyeing the cast. "I've never seen a contraption quite like that."

Rayna tries to shrug and winces. "Yeah it's all the rage these days, you should get one." Sarcasm is evident in her voice. Grady smiles a little bit at the exchange.

Brown shifts his attention to his partner. "Remi?"

Grady shakes her head in dismay. "We are on our way to see her now."

She pushes Rayna up to the counter and asks the nurse to page the doctor she talked with moments before. She does so, and within moments he's pushing open the door.

Just like everyone, he nearly stops in his tracks when he sees Rayna sitting in the wheelchair.

"Twin sister," Grady provides before the guy has a coronary.

He wipes imaginary sweat off his forehead. "The resemblance is uncanny." He looks towards Brown.

"My partner Detective Brown." The two men shake hands. "Now I know you're busy, but Rayna here wanted to just see the room where her sister is. She understands she may not be able to go inside."

The doctor looks between Rayna and Grady. "We just started a blood rewarming procedure, where the blood is removed from her body, warmed, and put back in. Hopefully this works or we will be prepping her for the peritoneal lavage. But you can see her now. Just be careful with all the equipment around." He motions to the wheelchair.

"I can walk," Rayna replies, struggling to stand to follow the doctor. Brown gives her a hand.

Grady smiles to herself as they make their way down the hall. She isn't sure what the department will think of Brown dating a victim in a case, but she can't imagine it will be much of an issue if the case is closed quickly.

The trio makes its way down the hall to Remi's room. The minute she catches sight of her sister, the color drains from Rayna's face.

Brown hesitantly leads her over to the bed, which is surrounded by all sorts of machines. Rayna reaches out a hand and touches her sister's face.

It's crazy. Grady didn't believe Rayna when she said she and her sister were exact replicas of each other, but it's true. They are.

Rayna doesn't say anything. She simply stands there, a hand on Remi's face. Finally, she turns to Grady.

"She'll make it. I know she will."

She doesn't give any explanation, simply turns and leaves the room.

Grady makes eye contact with Brown and shrugs. Maybe they do share a mental connection after all.

RAYNA

Three Weeks Later

"**N**ow lean back so I can wash the shampoo out of your hair," Remi says as she stands on a stool, helping Rayna in the shower. Thanks to the fancy cast that can't get wet, she still needs help with even the most basic tasks.

"Thanks," Rayna says quietly, still a little embarrassed she can't do things on her own.

"That's what sisters are for," Remi replies, equally as quiet.

Things are still a bit strange between them. They've been talking more, but they haven't quite made it back to the camaraderie they had before Rayna moved out months ago.

Remi was discharged from the hospital after a week. Although she made a full physical recovery, her mind still has miles to go. Both girls are currently seeing a recommended psychiatrist who helps women who have been abducted.

Rayna feels a little bad, as she doesn't have near the amount of negative mental implications as her twin. Remi can't stand being in enclosed places, restrained, or in the dark. All repercussions of spending what the police estimate to be four full days locked in the same cellar Rayna was locked in.

Remi quit her job, deciding to take a few weeks off to help Rayna before going back to work as a CPA. She's considering a smaller firm this time, after the mess at Johnson Finance. As it turns out, Jonathon, Remi's boss, was fired for allegedly laundering money from the company through a number of false subsidies. Jared and Lyle both took a plea deal in exchange for testifying against him.

Remi decided to take the high road and dropped the harassment charges against the men for their phone calls and thefts from her apartment. As she told the cops, it wasn't worth the mental stress. Detective Grady agreed.

Katie, who imprisoned both girls in her wine cellar, never made it off the operating table, saving Remi and Rayna from having to testify in court. The police questioned and released Mark after realizing he had nothing to do with his wife's actions. Remi told Grady about the two "henchmen," as she called them, but the police were unable to discover their identities. Whoever they were, they must've gone back to their normal lives, or hired hitman lives, wherever they came from.

Although she says the fact that the two men are still at large doesn't bother her, Rayna knows Remi is just putting on a good façade. Remi changed the locks and had four additional locks put in on the apartment since being released from the hospital. Rayna suggested they move, but Remi said not yet, she really likes this location and wants to wait.

And Rayna knows what she's waiting for. John.

Things between the couple have been rocky at best since the incident. They're still together, and John is filing for a divorce from his estranged wife, but there's a broken trust between them that needs to heal. Remi hopes it will just take time. But she isn't sure if she can honestly ever trust John again. And Rayna knows if Remi calls it quits, they will most likely move somewhere else.

Daisy/Lena finally got the help she needed. Grady referred her to a service specializing in getting women out of abusive and stalker situations. Last Rayna heard, they helped her start a new life. Where, Rayna isn't sure, but she hopes there are no hard feelings about what happened.

Rayna moved back in the day after Remi was discharged from the hospital, effectively kicking Daisy/Lena out, although she was on her way out of town as it was. Remi needs emotional support and Rayna needs help doing basic everyday tasks, so it works well for them to once again live together.

The girls have been talking a lot about why they drifted apart, attributing a lot of it to Rayna's depression, and self isolation as she didn't want to admit she was suffering from the former. It's hard for Remi to deal with what her sister did, but they're working through it, together.

"Okay, lean over so I can squeeze out the water."

Rayna does so and her sister shuts off the water to the shower, helping her step out onto the bathroom rug. She towel dries her hair, than begins brushing it.

"What are you going to wear tonight?" Remi peeks around to look at Rayna's face.

Rayna smiles. "Well, I'm not sure what's going to look good with this cast, but I was thinking maybe that blue blouse that's sort of loose with a black mini skirt?"

"Sounds beautiful to me," Remi responds, still brushing her hair. "Braid?" she asks.

"Sure, French braid please." Rayna can't lie, it's nice to have her sister around to help her with her hair and showering. Otherwise, she doesn't know what she would do.

Tonight is hers and Detective Brown's, Derrick Brown's, first date. They've kept in contact over the past few weeks while he's been closing the case, and found out they have quite a bit in common. Of course, they had to wait until the case actually closed for him to be able to officially ask her on a date, so it feels much overdue. Rayna is excited.

They're going to go to dinner and a movie. Usually she would be more into doing something active, but with her arm, a movie will probably work out better.

"You'll have to tell me all the details." Remi smiles, as if reading her sister's thoughts.

Although they still don't have twin ESP, they have definitely gotten better at reading each other's body language and facial expressions. Something about both of them experiencing a kidnapping has probably helped with that.

"Is John coming over?" Rayna asks, one eyebrow raised.

"Not tonight. I think we are going to go out to dinner and then maybe the arcade."

Rayna smiles at the idea of her sister's date. Even though she and John have been dating for over two years, it sounds like they're truly starting over.

"Are you going to—"

Remi cuts her off. "I don't know yet."

The silence hangs between them. Rayna can't deny that the road ahead of her sister is long.

Rayna certainly doesn't have it easy either. She's decided, while she's unable to do much because of her cast, that she will go back and get her radiologist technician license. Breaking her arm and shoulder showed her a whole new side of medicine. One that she's extremely interested in. She's sure she'll have to wait tables while she finishes the two year degree, but it doesn't seem so bad.

"There, all done."

Rayna turns and looks at the mirror above the sink, her sister's face appearing right next to hers. They still look the same, except for the two inch long slight pink scar on Remi's cheek.

NOW

243

H E KNEW HIS plan would work. *Women are so predictable,* he laughs as he runs a comb through his hair. He picks up his phone from beside the sink and begins to delete all the fake texts he sent himself pretending to be his own girlfriend.

He knew Katie would go crazy over the thought of him cheating. He didn't know how crazy, he was honestly just hoping for her to leave him, but death by cop is acceptable anyway.

And now he's free to start his master plan.

And he won't make any mistakes.

Find out what Mark's plans are in the companion novel *You Can't Run*. Currently available on Amazon.com and Kindle Unlimited!

Adewumi, James. "Twins in West African Culture and Society of the Iron Age." *Artifacts Journal // University of Missouri*, University of Missouri, Apr. 2014, artifactsjournal.missouri.edu/2014/03/twins-in-west-african-culture-and-society-of-the-iron-age/.

DeRuiter, Corinne. "The Embryo Project Encyclopedia." *Conjoined Twins | The Embryo Project Encyclopedia*, Arizona State University, 3 Nov. 2011, embryo.asu.edu/pages/conjoined-twins.

Fierro, Pamela Prindle. "Amazing Facts About Identical Twins." *Verywell Family*, Verywell Family, 10 Aug. 2019, www.verywellfamily.com/identical-twins-2447126.

"Mirror Image Twins." *Twins Research Australia*, National Health and Medical Research Center, www.twins.org.au/twins-and-families/about-twins/171-mirror-image-twins.

Vaziri Flais, Shelly. "The Difference Between Identical and Fraternal Twins." *HealthyChildren.org*, American Academy of Pediatrics, 21 Nov. 2015, www.healthychildren.org/English/family-life/family-dynamics/Pages/The-Difference-Between-Identical-and-Fraternal-Twins.aspx.

If you enjoyed *Before Now*, please take a moment to leave a rating or review, and check out Hope's other mystery novels, *The Fate of Ava Miller* and *Deceptive Perfection*! Available on Amazon.com in both paperback and Kindle!

You can also check out her website at hopeedavis.com.

ABOUT THE
AUTHOR

Before Now is Hope's third novel. When she isn't writing, she is busy traveling the world, trying new foods, or hanging out with friends. A graduate from Metropolitan State University, Hope grew up in Colorado but currently calls The Netherlands her home. To find information about her other or future novels, follow Hope on Instagram: @hopeedavisauthor. She is also on Tik Tok @hopeedavisauthor.